THE VILLAGE INN OF SECRET DREAMS

ALISON SHERLOCK

Boldwood

First published in Great Britain in 2021 by Boldwood Books Ltd.

Copyright © Alison Sherlock, 2021

Cover Design by Alice Moore Design

Cover photography: Shutterstock

A CIP catalogue record for this book is available from the British Library.

Paperback ISBN 978-1-83889-997-4

Large Print ISBN 978-1-83889-996-7

Hardback ISBN 978-1-80280-872-8

Ebook ISBN 978-1-83889-998-1

Kindle ISBN 978-1-83889-999-8

Audio CD ISBN 978-1-83889-991-2

MP3 CD ISBN 978-1-83889-992-9

Digital audio download ISBN 978-1-83889-993-6

Boldwood Books Ltd
23 Bowerdean Street
London SW6 3TN
www.boldwoodbooks.com

1

'Will you marry me?'

Belle Clarke's heart thumped wildly in her chest as the anxiety began to rise deep inside of her.

She glanced across to the front door in the hope of a quick getaway, but her exit was pretty much blocked. Unbelievably, The Black Swan Inn of Cranbridge was actually quite busy that evening, which was a rarity in itself.

Just her luck.

Her gaze flicked over towards the other people in the inn to see if anyone else agreed with her dismay, but everyone was looking at Josh Kennedy who was down on one knee in the middle of the room holding out a diamond ring in front of him.

And, at Amber Green too, who was blushing furiously as she looked down at her boyfriend.

'Yes,' Amber finally replied, breaking into a soft smile. 'Of course I'll marry you.'

A huge cheer went up as Josh stood to take Amber into his arms. Belle could see that her best friend was both equally thrilled and embarrassed at the attention. Amber was naturally shy and would always let anyone else take the limelight away from her. But on that September evening, Amber smiled and laughed as everyone crowded around the happy couple with their congratulations and best wishes.

Of course, everyone knew Josh and Amber, as together they had run The Cranbridge Stores – the popular village shop – for the past year and over the winter their business partnership had become a romantic one as well.

Belle watched as their other best friends, Lucy and Molly, stepped forward to hug Amber and exclaim their delight at the proposal. Belle could hear the excited chatter from where she stood behind the bar, rooted temporarily to the floorboards with shock.

'How wonderful!' she heard Lucy cry. 'I'm so happy for you both.'

'It's just so romantic!' said Molly, near to tears.

Belle knew that she should rush over and join her friends to congratulate Amber. After all, they were a close-knit group. But she was afraid that she would end up blurting out, 'Stop! Wait! Don't do it!' instead.

Even though she loved Amber and Josh very much. Even though she knew how much Josh loved Amber and would never hurt her. Even though they were one of the best suited and happiest couples that she had ever known.

Despite all of that, Belle felt like dragging the glittering diamond solitaire that was now on Amber's finger and throwing it into the river outside.

To trust in love was bad enough with all the heartache that always followed, but marriage ruined everything, didn't they know that? Why couldn't Amber and Josh just stay as happy as they were at the moment?

In her hesitation about how well she could fake her reaction to

Amber's engagement, she was still hovering behind the bar counter when Uncle Mick joined her.

'Isn't it smashing?' said Mick, nodding and smiling along with everyone else. 'Ain't young love grand? And we could all do with a bit of good news these days, eh?'

Uncle Mick didn't notice his niece's frown and was giving everyone his usual amiable smile as he looked around at his customers. With his round, jolly face, he suited the role of congenial landlord very well, having been in the job for over forty years. He was always smiling at anyone, apart from at his own wife.

'Champagne for everyone!' announced Mick to a resounding cheer from the crowd in front of them.

This brought Belle's Aunty Angie rushing along the bar to join them in a fit of barely concealed rage.

'Are you mad?' hissed Angie, her heavily mascaraed eyes almost popping out of their sockets as she glared at her husband. 'We can't afford that.'

'Give it a rest for just one night,' muttered Mick, rolling his eyes. 'Besides, we've got that massive magnum of the stuff in the cellar just sitting there.'

'Which we might be able to sell, rather than you giving it away for free,' carried on Angie, placing one hand on the bar, where her long orange nails tapped in irritation. The other hand went to her red leather skirt.

Whereas Belle always dressed in dark colours, eager not to draw attention to herself, Aunty Angie's view of clothing, hair and make-up was that you needed to be seen from outer space. Preferably without the need of a telescope.

'Nobody ever orders champagne in here anyway,' snapped Mick. 'It'll go to waste otherwise.'

'Humph,' said Angie, shaking her head. 'Well, I suppose you're right, for once. No point keeping it when the inn's going up for sale anyway.'

Belle took a sharp intake of breath at her aunt's words. Despite her own worries about her friend's future marriage, that was nothing compared to Belle's anxiety about the state of the inn. The Black Swan had struggled for so many years, but she knew that it was now teetering on the brink of closure and nothing appeared to be able to save it. Putting it up for sale would be the only solution to their money worries, Uncle Mick had told her. But it made Belle feel ill to even think about it even though she had tried her best not to.

Mick turned around and began to head towards the cellar steps, intent on collecting the champagne, with his wife in hot pursuit. Their heated words could still be heard even as they went downstairs.

Exhibit number one on the disastrous marriage front, thought Belle with a heavy sigh.

She had moved in with her aunt and uncle at the age of twelve and the arguments had grown worse and worse between husband and wife every day since then. She had always been grateful for them giving her a loving home. But although they treated their niece with huge amounts of love and kindness, Mick and Angie's love for each other ran hot and cold, with the emphasis on cold. Almost freezing, in fact.

Very occasionally, and with the help of a large drink, or three, Mick and Angie would share a soft smile and there would be a break in the hostilities, but mostly it was an ongoing war with no hope of a peaceful outcome any time soon.

Most successful inns had a landlord and landlady providing a top-quality service and smiles all round. Despite their best efforts, her aunt and uncle provided neither. Most of the time, any customers actually venturing inside the shabby Black Swan inn were shocked by the continuous arguments that invariably broke out. Coupled with the run-down state of the place, the customers never returned, other than the regulars from the village. Although this was only because there was no other inn within walking distance.

Belle looked back across the inn at the crowd of people. Amber and Josh were still surrounded by well-wishers. She knew that she ought to go and congratulate her friend. She had hesitated too long. The last thing she wanted to do was upset Amber. She cared too much about her.

Amber had only arrived in the village a year ago, but she had quickly become close to both Belle and Molly, who had lived in Cranbridge her whole life. When Lucy arrived in late spring, they had swiftly become a tight-knit group of four. Belle had never had such close friends and was grateful for their friendship and support. Which is why she would support her friend now, even if she didn't think marriage was a good idea.

As Belle headed around the side of the bar, she found Amber coming the other way to see her. Her friend's long blonde hair was all messed up from numerous hugs and she had a bright pink lipstick kiss mark on her face, presumably from Aunty Angie.

'So what do you think?' asked Amber, looking nervous at Belle's expected negative reaction. All of her friends knew Belle's feelings on love and romance.

Belle forced a wide smile onto her face as she stepped forward to hug her friend. 'I think it's brilliant,' she said as she broke away from their embrace. 'Congratulations. I'm so happy for you both.'

'Thank you,' said Amber, breaking into a huge grin once more in relief. 'Did you know?'

Belle shook her head. 'Nope. He kept it very secret.'

'I still can't believe it,' said Amber, giving a little giggle of excitement as her parents headed over to offer their congratulations and sweep her into yet more hugs.

Belle stepped back, with the excuse of bringing out all the glasses that they would need for the champagne.

'You're going to have a long and happy marriage,' she heard Cathy, Josh's mum, say as he too was swept into a hug nearby.

'Thanks, Mum,' said Josh, giving Belle a wink of solidarity over her shoulder as he was almost smothered in his mum's embrace.

Cathy knew all about happy marriages, of course. She and her late husband, Todd, had celebrated their silver wedding anniversary in the inn around five years ago.

Perhaps there was hope after all, Belle tried to remind herself. Perhaps there were long and happy marriages out there and Amber and Josh would be fine. She really, truly hoped so.

But her own experience with marriages didn't bring her much optimism.

If living with Uncle Mick and Aunt Angie had shown her wedded misery, that was nothing compared to her own parents' relationship. They were most definitely Exhibit number two in the case for avoiding marriage.

Growing up, the arguments and tension had been a daily source of wretchedness for Belle. An unwanted only child from day one, she had been the focus and reason for much of the tension. So she had developed a hard outer shell to prevent any more hurt from touching her and rarely trusted anyone with her innermost thoughts.

Her parents had waited until Belle had reached twelve years old and was due to head to secondary school before, to everyone's relief, they had finally brought to an end a most unhappy marriage. With the divorce being spectacularly acrimonious, Belle had been packed off to stay temporarily with her aunt and uncle in Cranbridge. And she had been there ever since.

Belle had fallen in love with Cranbridge, the pretty little village in the heart of the English countryside, by the end of the first day. Best of all, the freedom of being away from her parents had brought her a kind of peace that she had never known until that time. Her aunt and uncle showered her with the love and affection that she had been so desperately starved of in her early years.

But she still kept herself to herself at the local secondary school, always struggling to make new friends after her parents had pretty much destroyed any confidence that she may have had. Her dry wit was misunderstood as aloofness and so Belle retreated further into her own company.

Never having much of a career plan, she had abandoned further education and had become a barmaid instead, eager to stay within the protective walls of the inn. The Black Swan was her safe place, her happy place even with her aunt and uncle's constant bickering. Besides, she enjoyed working in the cosy, historic inn with its small stream of regulars to chat with each evening and the community spirit of the village as a whole.

Meanwhile, once her parents' divorce was finally settled, her mother had headed straight off to the Far East and was currently dating a llama farmer, last time Belle had heard. Her mum was 'living my best life', according to the infrequent texts Belle received.

As for her dad, he had decided to play the field and was currently on wife number four, who was a whole five years younger than Belle. Thankfully they hadn't bothered to invite her to the ceremony.

Uncle Mick reappeared holding the champagne and began to pour out the drinks, trying to ignore his wife, who was still glaring at him.

Finally, when everyone had been given a drink, they all raised a glass.

'To Amber and Josh!' announced Mick.

'To Amber and Josh!' said Belle as they all joined in with the toast.

Josh murmured something in Amber's ear that made her blush and smile.

For a moment, Belle envied the close relationship they had and surprised herself with the idea that perhaps love wasn't something to be avoided. That perhaps she too could be happy, if she ever met the right man.

She sighed and drained her glass in one gulp. As expected, the champagne was not of a stellar vintage, but she hoped it might help make her feel better.

Josh appeared on the other side of the bar to place his own empty glass down on the counter.

'Congratulations,' she told him, heading around the side of the bar to give him a kiss on the cheek.

'Thanks,' he said, with a warm smile.

Despite her misgivings about marriage, she was very fond of Josh. When Belle had first arrived in the village, Josh and his family had played a huge part in welcoming her into the community. The Kennedys owned the corner shop, The Cranbridge Stores, and she had grown close to both Josh and his younger brother, Pete, despite them being a few years older than herself. They had become the surrogate big brothers that she had never had, being an only child herself.

'Can't wait to tell Pete he's got to be my best man!' carried on Josh, laughing. 'That'll shake his jet lag off when he arrives at the airport in the morning.'

'Absolutely!' said Belle, fixing a wide smile on her face.

But as she walked away, her smile quickly faded. Josh's brother, Pete Kennedy, was coming home the following day. She had managed to temporarily forget about Pete for a whole five minutes, but now it was all she could think about.

'We need more crisps,' she heard her Aunt Angie say.

'I'll get them,' said Belle quickly, before turning to head into the small hallway beyond and downstairs into the cellar.

Once she was alone, she sagged against the wall and leaned her head against the cool bricks to try and clear her feverish mind.

There were so many problems in her life right now. But Pete coming home from Singapore was yet another one.

They had always been so close – Belle, Josh and Pete. But where Josh was a little more serious, Pete had been the one to make her laugh with his silly jokes and had brought her out of herself, especially in those early years when she was still reeling from her parents' disastrous marriage.

The brothers had been friendly, flirty and fun, which was entirely what she had needed after the many years of misery hiding inside her bedroom to avoid the rows between her parents.

Josh was the older brother of the two, equally handsome and charming but dependable. Pete was a wild card, always looking for the next adventure. He was a natural flirt, even at the age of thirteen, and all the girls at school had fallen for him, including Belle. She had had a huge crush on Pete growing up, but he had always treated her like a sister and, because of her tomboy ways at that age, sometimes like a brother as well. So she had watched from the sidelines as he had dated and kissed every girl in the village except her. But it didn't bother her. At least, that was what she had tried to tell herself.

As the years passed, Pete had lived all around the world, but he came home frequently, and Pete and Belle had continued their easy, close friendship. He had carried on dating many women and Belle had carried on shrugging off any offers of romance from anyone who showed any interest in her, eager not to replicate the wretched past of her parents' marriage.

But everything had changed three years ago when Pete had

been about to head off to Singapore to work. Pete's father, Todd, had unexpectedly passed away. It had shaken the whole family, but Pete appeared almost numb with shock about losing his dad.

The evening after his funeral, Pete had been in the deepest despair that she had even seen him and had sought out Belle's shoulder to lean on. He had been so sad, so grief-stricken, that Belle had barely known how to console him.

Then, to the surprise of them both, Belle had found herself leaning forward whilst they had been sitting so close and had kissed him on the lips.

It was supposed to have been a kiss of comfort, to try to ease some of his pain and perhaps to also say goodbye as he left for the Far East. But she had been astonished to find him responding to the kiss with passion for a brief, glorious couple of seconds until he had pulled away, staring at her in disbelief.

'I can't,' he had stammered, shaking his head. 'Not with you.'

'It's okay,' Belle had said quickly.

But it hadn't been. Pete had immediately stood up and walked away from her.

And she hadn't seen or heard from him since that day.

She had made a terrible mistake in kissing him and had ruined everything between them, that much she knew. She carried the pain within her, not telling even her closest friends about what she had done. It was too shameful that he had rejected her, so she kept the secret to herself.

And now he was coming back. She didn't know how long he would be staying for, but she hoped that any awkwardness wouldn't last whilst he was living just over the other side of the river above the shop with Josh and Amber.

But the fear of seeing Pete again and facing up to her secret crush was nothing compared to her other worries. The inn was going out of business. And without the inn, she had no home and no job. What would she do? Where would she live? She had no qualifications and no real skills to her name.

Worst of all, she was scared to leave the sanctuary that The Black Swan had provided for so many happy years. She didn't want change. Feared it, in fact.

The inn and Cranbridge had been the only places where she had ever felt at home and at peace. What on earth was she going to do if she had to leave it all behind?

2

Pete Kennedy yawned as the long overnight flight began to take its toll. His body clock was still in Singapore even though he was actually now in England. He had no idea what time it was, let alone what day of the week it might actually be.

'No chance of stopping somewhere to grab another coffee, I suppose?' asked Pete, glancing down at his empty takeaway cup.

His brother, Josh, gave him some side-eye before concentrating on driving his van once more. 'I know you're jet-lagged, but try to remember that you're in the countryside now,' said Josh. 'Not a big fancy city with a Starbucks on every corner.'

Pete nodded in rueful agreement. That much he didn't need reminding of. His life in Singapore was at an end. The economic downturn had abruptly curtailed his career in the finance sector. Without a job, he didn't have a visa. And without a visa, he had nowhere to go but back home.

Home. Was that how he felt about it after being away so long?

He'd missed his family, of course. And the countryside too, he had to admit to himself.

He looked out of the window at the colours that made up the

early-autumn landscape. It was a marked contrast after the tropical urban landscape of Singapore. He'd forgotten how much he loved the changing of the seasons. Outside, the hedgerows were ablaze with sun-ripened flowers and long grasses which were long since faded. As far as the eye could see, the rolling hills were a mix of greens, yellows and soft browns to signal the onset of autumn over the coming weeks.

He had a sudden flashback to their dad lighting a bonfire one autumn day, the sweet smoke of the damp leaves filling his nostrils as they toasted marshmallows near the flames. Happy times. But that was all a very long time ago now.

Besides, everything had changed. Even his big brother, he thought, looking back at Josh. Where Pete had always been dark-haired, Josh was blond, and he appeared to have a couple of new lines around his face. Hardly surprising after the stress of the past few years, thought Pete.

If Josh had followed his younger brother to Singapore, as Pete had encouraged him to do a few years ago, where would his life be now?

But instead Josh had remained behind to take over the running of The Cranbridge Stores, the village corner shop that had been in the family for so many generations. And now it was Josh's turn to be in charge. He had taken over as head of the family after their father had passed away. Josh had been the grown-up one whilst Pete had run away to Singapore from his grief and pain. And his family had let him. Sometimes being the baby of the family was both a blessing and a curse.

All his life, Pete had been laid-back and breezed from year to year, without too many cares in the world. But losing their dad unexpectedly had brought him up short. He had already accepted the job in Singapore, thinking that a few years in the Far East would be fun.

But suddenly he had received a phone call from his brother and life had changed dramatically. Both he and Josh had had to race through the night to the hospital just in time to say their last good-byes. The shock of losing such a powerful, charismatic man as Todd Kennedy had been almost overwhelming for Pete.

After the funeral, Pete had told his mum and Josh that he hadn't wanted to leave. He had tried to convince them that he should stay and help out. But it was all a lie, thanks to the letter that he had found amongst his dad's possessions. It contained a secret that could devastate his family, so he had run away to Singapore to hide from the truth. And he hadn't been back since.

'By the way,' said Josh. 'Be nice to Amber, okay? You haven't seen her for years.'

Amber was the daughter of their mum's best friend and they had all played together as children before her family had moved away when she had become a teenager. She had only to returned to the village a year ago.

'Be nice?' Pete laughed. 'You think I don't know how to speak to a woman?'

Josh glared at his brother. 'If you talk to my fiancée the way you flirt with every other woman, then you'll find yourself flat on your back in the river pretty damn quickly.'

Pete grinned. 'You don't think I could take you these days? I go to the gym, you know.'

'And I'm lifting boxes and stock all day, so bring it on, little bro.' Josh looked at the road ahead once more. 'Look, you remember Amber from when we were small? You know that she's shy. Just be gentle with her, okay? Not your default, flirty self.'

Josh had a point. Pete had chatted to his future sister-in-law online but had not met her face to face for many years. She was extremely pretty but normally had to be cajoled into saying anything more than a few sentences when the family were all together.

'I still can't believe you're getting married,' said Pete.

He watched Josh smile to himself. 'It was one of my better ideas,' he murmured. 'Besides, I was hoping she wouldn't be able to say no with a packed inn watching us. I couldn't have timed it better just after the local village council meeting had finished. Everyone was there.'

Everyone but him, thought Pete, with an unexpectedly dull ache in his heart.

Perhaps his silence spoke volumes as Josh looked across at him once more. 'I'd have waited for you before proposing, but, to be honest, we weren't even sure you were going to make it home until you told us that you were actually boarding the plane. We figured you'd probably go to Fiji or somewhere else far away instead. We know how much of a free spirit you are.'

Pete forced himself to give a nonchalant shrug. 'No worries,' he said, placing a smile on his face. 'You know how I feel about marriage, so I would have probably come out in hives or something if I'd had to witness any proposal.'

Pete thought back to the beautiful apartment in Singapore that he had owned. It had been beautifully decorated, home to some beautiful and expensive furnishings and even more beautiful women whom he had brought back after romantic dates in one of the city's most glamorous restaurants.

Oh yes, Pete knew how to show a lady a good time. They dined at the best restaurants. Ate the best food. Drank the best cocktails. And he always sent them flowers.

It was all wonderful right up to the point where they declared how much they cared for him, or even worse, that they loved him. Then he cut off all ties with an apology and yet more flowers.

It was the fairest thing for him to do. He was never going to fall in love like his brother. Let alone actually propose to anyone. That would be crazy given what he knew about marriage. It was all a lie, wasn't it? At least, that was what he believed these days.

Pete stared out of the window, imagining his brother going down on one knee in the middle of the inn. Had Belle been there? Of course she had, he told himself. Where else would she be? The inn was her home. She would never leave.

He thought back to that evening after his dad's funeral. He had been so upset, so distraught, that he could barely think straight. It was only later, much later, that he regretted the way that he had walked away from Belle after she had kissed him.

But why had she kissed him anyway? That wasn't the kind of relationship they had. Despite dating every other available woman in the area, he had always, and most deliberately, kept their friendship as just that. The evening was a blur of dark, heavy emotion and he supposed that it had all got too much. What other explanation was there?

He hoped there wouldn't be any awkwardness between them. That his silent treatment over the past three years hadn't upset her too much. She was one of his oldest friends and they had been through so much together already. Surely one rash kiss in the heat of the moment could be forgotten? He truly hoped so.

Finally, Josh pulled the van up into Riverside Lane and Pete's long journey was at an end. It was the first time he had been back since that awful time three years ago. Apart from his mum heading out to visit him in Singapore for a holiday the previous year, he hadn't seen his family for such a long time.

Getting out of the car, Pete stretched after having spent the best part of twenty-four hours sitting in airports, airplanes and cars. He took a deep breath and looked around the village, smiling to himself at the familiar view.

Cranbridge was as beautiful as always, with its sandy-coloured brick cottages lining the riverbanks and the green rolling hills surrounding the village peeping through from between each house. Instead of a main street, there was a wide shallow river running down the middle of the village, with three ancient pedestrian stone bridges connecting either side over the clear, bubbling water.

With a contented sigh, he turned to look at the first of the shops along Riverside Lane. The Cranbridge Stores had been in his family for decades, but it had always been a struggle to keep the corner shop going financially.

Josh had casually mentioned that the shop was doing far better than it had ever done before, now that it had been renovated, but Pete had still been braced for the run-down place that he remembered from his last visit.

But it appeared that everything had changed, thankfully for the better.

Whereas before it had been cramped and dark, now it had a brand-new sign and what appeared to be a complete makeover. Josh had mentioned Amber's decorating skills but nothing had prepared him for how pretty the place looked.

The wooden veranda which ran along the length of the shopfront had been refreshed with benches and lanterns. Soft cushions in pale yellows and greens, as well as a couple of matching rugs, hung over the back of two wooden benches. Fresh sunflowers and lavender in galvanised buckets filled the corners either side of the steps, with lanterns filling the remaining space.

Pete was stunned. It looked great.

He slowly became aware of Josh watching him for his reaction.

'You've done well,' said Pete eventually, still staggered at the change since he had last been there. 'It looks incredible.'

'Thanks,' said Josh, nodding proudly in agreement. 'Come on. Let's get inside.'

But before they could even put a foot on the bottom step, the front door to the shop was flung open and there was his mum and Grandma Tilly rushing down the steps towards him.

'You're here at last!' cried his mum, sweeping him into a bear hug.

Pete leant against her for a moment, breathing in her soft, familiar perfume, before stepping back to look at her. She looked even better than she had done when she'd flown out to Singapore to visit him.

After his dad's funeral, his mum had been diagnosed with cancer. Thankfully the treatment had been swift and she had been in remission for over a year, so it was a relief to see her looking so well.

Cathy stepped to one side to let his grandmother come forward to give him a hug. Although, at barely five feet, he could only lean gently on her soft grey hair with his chin whilst she flung her arms around his waist.

'It's good to see you, Peter,' said Grandma Tilly, stepping back to look up at him with her ever-shrewd blue eyes. 'I wouldn't mind one of those suntans myself.'

'Just say the word, Grandma, and we can head off to the Caribbean if you want,' Pete told her with a grin.

Grandma Tilly chuckled. 'Wouldn't say no to one of those cocktails with an umbrella in it.'

'Head off?' Cathy shook her head. 'He's only just arrived.' She reached out to give his arm a squeeze. 'I know you must be upset about losing your job, love, but it's so good that you're home. You must be so happy to be back.'

But as they began to head up the steps into the shop, the words rang hollow to Pete's ears. Happy to be back? He was happy to see his family, of course. Happy to be in Cranbridge which had been the family's home for so many years.

But, despite all of that, the urge to run had never been stronger.

However, it wasn't the thought of being with his family that upset him.

No, it was the thought of his late father that had continued to weigh him down ever since he had found out that his parents' marriage was nothing but a lie.

Because Todd had left behind a huge secret that only Pete was burdened with. And he'd had to hold the secret close to him for the past three years to prevent his family from being hurt any further. The fact was that his parents' happy marriage had been a fraud and yet his mother knew nothing about it. None of the family did.

Only Pete knew the truth. And it was the reason he had been running away from Cranbridge ever since he had found out.

Thankfully he had no plans to remain any longer in Cranbridge than strictly necessary. And that way, the secret could remain hidden. Forever, as far as he was concerned.

3

Belle stood at the bar and looked across the almost empty inn.

Business seemed even worse than usual that night even though it was early. A steady drizzle meant that the pretty garden outside next to the river was out of bounds that evening. Autumn was in a rush to arrive early.

The regulars, Frank and Stanley, were chatting in their usual position in the battered leather wing-backed chairs on either side of the fireplace. Frank and Stanley were two elderly pensioners who had lived in the village all of their lives. Frank was Lucy's uncle and had run the local newspaper, *The Cranbridge Times*. Stanley had been the headmaster of the local school.

Most days, they were to be found on the veranda of the shop, enjoying their takeaway coffee and putting the world to rights. But one evening a week they would treat themselves to a pint in the inn. Belle didn't mind that they made their drinks last for the whole evening. They were two amiable gentlemen and their company was both friendly and much-needed.

The inn had various regulars but they barely numbered double figures. And who could blame them, she wondered, as she looked across the main lounge.

It was quite a generous space with oak beams and a couple of lovely fireplaces, but the overall feeling was of shabbiness. She'd tried to fix the peeling wallpaper and polish the floorboards, but it mostly felt as if it were a losing battle. The furniture was all ancient, and not in a stately manor kind of way. A couple of leather chairs by the fireplace were saggy and uncomfortable, having long since collapsed under the weight of use.

Belle had tried to get her aunt and uncle to change the interior décor of the inn, but there was never any urge to change anything, as far as they were concerned.

'The inn's failing,' Aunty Angie had told her. 'A splash of paint isn't going to change that.'

'Besides, it's a grade II listed building, innit?' Uncle Mick had added. 'It'll cost us an arm and a leg to do anything.'

But in spite of all of that, it was a sixteenth-century village inn of historic local value. Surely that would be enough to keep it from being sold?

There was the sound of crashing from the cellar on the ground floor below. Uncle Mick was sorting out the last few barrels of beer. He hadn't bought any more to replace the low stock. His heart wasn't in it, he had confided in her, especially since agreeing to put the place up for sale.

Mick had been an inn landlord for almost forty years and he had declared more than once over the years that it was his perfect job. She wondered what on earth he and Aunty Angie would do with themselves if the inn was ever sold.

She looked up at the unexpected sound of the front door opening.

Dodgy Del walked in, nodding and saying 'Good evening' to Frank and Stanley as he walked cross to the bar.

Del, or Dodgy Del as everyone referred to him, was the local coach driver. He was around the same age as Josh and was always dreaming up ways to help the village and himself become more profitable, despite the somewhat dubious methods involved. But everyone knew he had a good heart, if you knew where to look.

'Good evening, Del,' Belle said, with a smile when he arrived in front of the bar.

'Evening,' replied Del, settling down on the stool on the other side of the bar. 'Not finding much good in it today though, to be honest.'

'Pint?' she asked.

He nodded. 'Please.'

Del was normally an upbeat guy, but he seemed particularly morose that evening.

'What's up?' she asked, as she moved across to grab a pint glass from the shelf underneath the bar.

'My bloomin' family,' said Del, with a heavy sigh.

'All of them or just certain members?' said Belle, pulling the handle on the beer pump to fill up the glass.

Del had a vast and extended family, of which there were first, second and third cousins who always seemed to be at war, normally because of some remark over the buffet at a wedding or a dispute over some silverware that had gone missing many years ago. But for all their arguments, Del's family continued to meet at every holiday and event. Presumably for the only reason that there could be a new argument to keep the feuds going over the years still to come.

'It's my nephew, Brad. My sister's eldest boy,' said Del, making a face. 'Just out of college and the kid's not got any job or any prospects.'

Belle made a sympathetic face as she placed the pint of beer on the counter between them. 'It's pretty tough out there job-wise at the moment,' she told him.

'Yeah. I mean, the lad's got talent and deserved that catering diploma or whatever you call it,' carried on Del. 'I've tasted his burgers at the family barbeque and they were epic. Trouble is, nobody's hiring. I just worry that he's going to go down the wrong path with frustration or boredom, if you know what I mean.'

'Has he tried the restaurants in Aldwych town? Or the cafés?' suggested Belle.

Aldwych was ten miles away. It was a bustling market town which took a lot of Cranbridge's custom.

Del nodded. 'Tried them all. They're not taking anyone else on.' He sighed heavily. 'Don't suppose your Aunty Angie's going to retire any time soon and let a real cook come in here?'

Belle smiled even though her heart was heavy. 'I'm afraid not,' she told him.

'Shame,' muttered Del, with a grimace.

Angie's cooking was legendary and, unfortunately, not in a good way. Her food was almost always revolting and was normally soggy, dry or inedible. Sometimes all three at once.

Occasionally, an oblivious family would head into the inn and order a meal. But nobody made that mistake twice and the only repeat customers were the locals, who only ordered chips and pizza, with a follow-up order of indigestion tablets.

There was no point offering to help, as Belle had tried many times before. Aunty Angie had always assumed that everyone was happy with the food and nobody had ever been brave enough to tell her otherwise.

'Anyway, as the inn's likely to be going up for sale some time soon, maybe he'll have a better chance of a catering job with whoever buys the place,' said Belle.

Del looked up at her, eyes wide in shock. 'Up for sale?' he spluttered. 'The Mucky Duck?'

It was the villagers' nickname for the inn and suited it far more than the elegant Black Swan moniker.

'We're not exactly packed out in here every night, Del,' Belle told him, gesturing with her hand around the almost empty room.

'Yeah, I know, but you can't sell,' said Del, frowning. 'Where would we all go in the evenings? I don't want to have to get in my car to go anywhere so I can enjoy a proper drink and not worry about taxis and all that fuss. Besides, some of those fancy places in Aldwych charge an arm and a leg for a pint of beer.'

Belle shrugged her shoulders. 'Yeah, I know,' she said, with a heavy sigh. 'But we're just not making any profit.'

Del frowned, hard in thought. 'What about one of them inns that the whole village owns? We could all pitch in.' He broke into a grin. 'I like the idea of pulling a pint for the punters.'

Belle shook her head. 'I don't think the village can afford to take on all of our debts,' she said. 'But you're always welcome to help out behind the bar. Anyway, let's change the subject. It's too depressing to even think about.'

'Where will you go?' asked Del, suddenly looking across the bar at Belle with concern etched in his face.

'I honestly don't know,' Belle told him, her heart aching at the thought of leaving.

Uncle Mick and Aunt Angie had tentatively talked about heading out to Spain to buy a far cheaper property and how they would buy a big enough place for the three of them.

Even so, Belle couldn't imagine leaving Cranbridge, let alone the country. Her friends were here and they were part of her family.

Yes, she had learnt to be feisty and independent. She'd had to, otherwise she would have been drowned out by all the shouting, first from her parents and then from her aunt and uncle. But she needed her friends around her.

Del gave her a wink. 'You know, my bed is a king size. Plenty of room for us both if you find yourself out on the streets.'

Belle laughed. 'Thanks, but I'm not sure how your girlfriend would feel about that.'

She knew Del was joking, but it highlighted just how empty her life was without the inn. Especially that evening when business seemed even quieter as their normal infrequent customers had all been in the previous night to see Josh's proposal to Amber.

'Well, thank you for another lovely evening,' said Frank, coming to place the two empty pint glasses on the bar as Stanley shrugged on his raincoat.

'I did nothing but pull a pint for each of you,' Belle told him. 'But, as always, you've been good company.'

'Have you heard?' said Del, turning to look at the elderly gentlemen. 'The Mucky Duck's going up for sale!'

Frank's grey eyebrows shot up. 'Really?' He looked at Belle in astonishment. 'Well, I'm very sorry to hear that, my dear. Times are certainly tough out there at the moment.'

'Such a shame,' said Stanley, coming to stand next to the counter alongside his friend. 'This inn has given us such lovely memories over the years.'

She knew that the gossip about the inn being up for sale would spread like wildfire amongst the villagers, especially now that Dodgy Del knew about it. He couldn't keep a secret if he tried.

She knew that her friends wouldn't be surprised, but they would be as upset as she was.

But Belle couldn't conjure up money from thin air. She'd tried to make good on the meagre money that they made to keep the place clean and tidy, but it needed a new roof, floorboards and a whole lot more.

She had tried other means such as lottery tickets, special events such as a gin evening, but nothing had helped.

She felt both helpless and hopeless.

After all, who was going to buy a run-down inn in the middle of nowhere?

4

Pete sank down onto the sofa, clutching the beer that Josh had just handed him. His brother sat down on a nearby armchair with a grateful sigh.

'What a day,' said Josh, leaning his head against the back of the sofa and closing his eyes.

'Busy one?' asked Pete, feeling guilty that he had spent most of the day asleep thanks to a sleepless night on his overnight flight.

Now it was evening time and Cathy and Amber were preparing a special welcome home dinner in the kitchen opposite them, with Grandma Tilly supervising from the seat next to Pete.

The apartment over the shop had been the family home for many years, but now it was just Josh and Amber living there. Amber's pretty decorative touches were in evidence once more. The oak beams and furniture were mostly the same, but there were modern pictures on the walls, fairy lights across the beams and tea lights everywhere. Just like the shop, it was modern but cosy.

There had been quite a few changes in his absence, thought Pete. His grandmother now lived in a tiny bungalow at the end of the village. His mum had also moved out and was now living in a self-contained annex in the grounds of her best friend Deidre's house. Deidre just happened to be Amber's mum. They had grown up together in the village.

'Fridays are normally our busiest day of the week until the weekend hits,' said Josh, suppressing a yawn. 'But it's all good for the bank account anyway.'

If Pete had been stunned by the change to the outside of The Cranbridge Stores, that was nothing compared to his amazement as he had stared around the inside of the place.

When he had last seen it, it had been cramped, dark and unappealing. Now it was light and airy, modern and yet chic country-style.

'I still can't believe how incredible it looks downstairs,' said Pete. 'It doesn't even look like the same place.'

'They've both worked so hard,' said Cathy, as she placed the salt and pepper pots on the table.

'We all worked hard, including you and Grandma Tilly,' said Amber, giving them both a soft smile.

'I made all the difference,' said Pete's formidable grandmother with a giggle as she gave him a nudge in the ribs.

Apart from being a few years older, Grandma Tilly hadn't changed at all. She was still a pocket rocket of good humour and strength.

'Dinner's ready,' called out Cathy.

They all gathered around the oak table ready to eat. But once everyone was seated, Cathy wanted a toast first to welcome home Pete.

She picked up her glass and then appeared to falter. 'I don't know what to say,' she said, looking at Josh for help.

Josh was the head of the household in some ways, despite both Cathy and Grandma Tilly being active members of the family. He had taken over the role from their late father with very little fuss. Pete both envied him and felt sorry for his brother too.

'Okay,' said Josh, rolling his eyes before giving his brother a grin. 'Welcome home, little brother. Let's eat.'

'Is that it?' said Cathy, sounding exasperated.

'I hope your wedding speech will be a bit more entertaining,' said Grandma Tilly, giving Amber a wink before taking a sip of her glass of wine.

'My dinner's getting cold and it's only Pete,' said Josh, picking up his knife and fork. 'Besides, he'll be off to another job before too long.'

'What do you mean?' said Cathy, looking at Pete with worried eyes. 'You're staying home for a while yet, aren't you?'

'Mum,' groaned Pete. 'I only landed in the country this morning.'

'He didn't answer the question,' murmured Grandma Tilly, also looking concerned.

'I'm here for at least a week, okay?' said Pete. 'I've got a Zoom interview set up in the city later this week. So after that, who knows?'

Cathy said nothing but, to Pete's dismay, immediately began to blink rapidly, as if she were going to cry. The last thing Pete ever wanted to do was cause his mum any more grief as he had obviously done spending so long away from home.

Amber reached over and squeezed Cathy's hand before saying, 'The roast looks amazing as usual, Cathy.'

'It's my recipe for the roast potatoes that makes it,' said Grandma Tilly with a wink.

'Of course it is,' said Amber, smiling at her.

But Cathy was still looking concerned at her youngest son. 'You're really leaving again?' she asked, this time her voice a little tremulous.

Pete sighed. 'There are no jobs for me around here, Mum,' he replied. 'It's not exactly a thriving financial market, is it?'

'And we can't afford to hire him in the shop, can we?' said Josh. 'Not that he's exactly qualified for the role anyway.'

'You know, I deal with customers all the time,' said Pete, in a pointed tone despite not really wanting to hang around and work in the shop.

'Yeah, it must be tough for all those millionaires deciding which luxury yacht to buy with all their shares,' said Josh, with a grin.

But his fiancée was giving him a stern look across the table.

'He started it,' said Josh, with a shrug.

'When?' asked Amber, raising an eyebrow.

'When he was born,' said Josh, with a wink.

Amber smiled as she shook her head at Josh. Pete liked her. She was quite quiet but warm and kind. And attractive, of course. He could certainly see why his brother had fallen in love with her.

The conversation flowed over dinner, with Pete mostly listening and trying to catch up with all the goings-on in the village. He found out about the community hub that had been set up by the local newspaper in the building next door. And he found out about the new vicar, Glenda, who apparently was already pencilled in for Josh and Amber's wedding next summer.

'It's such a pretty church,' said Amber, smiling.

'And a lucky one too,' said Grandma Tilly, taking her hand and squeezing it. 'After all, it's where I got married and later on Todd and Cathy as well.'

'Hopefully you'll have better weather than we both did,' said Cathy, with a grimace. 'It actually hailed in July, would you believe?'

'Good job we're thinking of late August then,' said Josh, finishing his dinner and putting his arm along the back of Amber's chair.

'That's almost a year away,' said Cathy, looking dismayed. 'Such a long time to wait.'

Josh shrugged his shoulders. 'We're in no rush, are we?' he said, looking at his fiancée.

Amber shook her head. 'Not at all,' she replied.

'As long as you don't change your mind in the meantime,' he said, with a soft smile.

'No chance,' she replied.

'Your father and I got married a month after getting engaged,' said Cathy, turning the diamond ring around and around on her finger.

'Well, Dad was always impatient for everything,' said Josh.

Pete's eyes drifted to a nearby bookcase where there was a photograph of his dad on the veranda of the shop, playing his guitar as he did so often on a Sunday afternoon.

Todd had never wanted to be a shopkeeper. A lead guitarist for a few rock bands, his musical antics were still all over YouTube. He had been a huge magnetic force of personality, instantly drawing people to his side as soon as he entered a place. But the rock and roll lifestyle had taken its toll and once Pete's grandfather had passed away, his dad had persuaded the family to move to Cranbridge for a much-needed quieter life.

Pete's breathing caught at the memory that he had tried to bury deep inside of him. His dad was famous for being a rock guitarist, but Pete's sweetest memories were of the simple, acoustic guitar that his dad had preferred in later years. Of his soft voice as he crooned along to various songs whilst out on the veranda with an adoring Pete sat at his feet watching him. In later years, Pete had played alongside him.

Unlike Josh, Pete had inherited his dad's musical skills and so their mum had insisted that the guitar be handed down to Pete after their father had passed away. He may have inherited the guitar, but Pete had been unable to even look at it since the day their mum had handed it to him and so it stayed hidden away out of sight in its case.

'We could always have a singalong with the guitar later,' said Cathy, breaking into his reverie.

Pete tried not to blanch in reaction so that his mother would notice.

'With my brother's singing? That's enough to put me right off my food,' said Josh with a grin.

Pete put down his knife and fork with a clatter on his empty plate. 'Well, dinner was great, thanks,' he said, pushing his chair away from the table and getting up. 'I'll start on the washing-up.'

'We have a dishwasher now,' said Josh, looking up at him.

But if Pete didn't do something soon to keep busy he was going to explode. The talk of happy marriages was making him feel ill.

He started to load the dishwasher until Grandma Tilly came to stand next to him.

'If you carry on like that, there'll be no crockery left to eat on in the future,' she said, taking a plate out of his hands and placing it more gently into the rack.

After they had finished, Cathy picked up her jacket and umbrella. 'Well, I'm a bit weary having had that early start at the farmer's market. I shall take Grandma Tilly home and then head off myself.'

'Do you want us to walk with you?' asked Amber.

Cathy smiled and shook her head as she gave Amber's arm a squeeze. 'We'll be fine, thanks, dear.'

'Yes, it won't be like at Easter when I had a funny turn,' said Grandma Tilly. 'That was down to the roast lamb, I'm sure.'

'That was down to the amount of sherry you consumed,' drawled Josh with a grin.

They all joined in the soft laughter in memory whilst Pete stood and watched them, feeling totally adrift. All the memories he had missed by being away. It was almost as if he didn't know his own family any more. Perhaps it would be good to catch up with them all over the next week and become closer to them again.

Once they had said their goodnights, Josh and Amber collapsed onto the sofa.

'Netflix?' said Amber, looking up at Pete, who was still standing in the middle of the room. 'What's your favourite show?'

'You know what?' said Pete. 'I think I'll head out for a bit of fresh air.'

Josh's eyebrows rose up. 'And go where?'

Pete shrugged. 'I don't know,' he replied. 'Just out for a bit. I fancy a walk to clear my head after all that airplane air.'

'Okay,' said Josh, putting his arm around Amber and drawing her closer to him. 'We probably won't wait up.'

But Amber was looking up at Pete. 'Do you want some company?' she asked, giving Josh a nudge with her elbow.

'No, I'm good, thanks,' said Pete.

'Excellent answer,' murmured Josh, leaning in to give Amber a soft kiss on her neck, who gave a soft squeak in reply in embarrassment.

Pete headed into his tiny old bedroom and picked up his coat, determined not to be a gooseberry for a moment longer as he headed out into the night air.

5

Belle was standing behind the bar polishing a glass that didn't need polishing. There really wasn't much more to do. Her aunt and uncle had gone upstairs to watch some police drama on the television, but it wasn't as if there was going to be a rush to the bar any moment.

Dodgy Del, Frank and Stanley had left an hour ago and the only customers left were a small group of local mums who had come in to celebrate something and were sharing gossip and laughter over some drinks. They didn't order any food so had obviously eaten in The Black Swan before and experienced Aunty Angie's awful food.

And that was it. No other customers were likely to come in at all that evening.

Her fear over the inn being sold was equal to it being shut down anyway due to lack of profit.

She looked around the lounge, trying to envisage what any newcomer would see. Being built in the sixteenth century, she had always thought that it was full of charm and history. But screwing her eyes up, she looked beyond her rose-tinted glasses and knew that it needed serious money and renovation.

The oak beams certainly gave the large lounge some charm, but the ancient maroon patterned wallpaper was peeling off the walls and the fringed lamps dotted about didn't help the feeling of darkness, and the oak floor needed a proper polish.

Yet, despite the overall dark and gloomy façade, there was still an attractive nature to the place. Although that was probably due to the fireplaces. The largest was on the outside wall and was enormous, complete with inglenook and large mantelpiece. The smaller one was on the inside wall to her right, next to the additional lounge. That probably made it feel much darker than it could be inside, she thought. However, she also knew that the second lounge, which had been boarded up years ago due to lack of customers, was in equally a bad state as the main one.

It wasn't any wonder that nobody wanted to come in here, she thought, blowing out a sigh.

So when the front door suddenly opened, Belle looked up in surprise.

To her amazement, it was Pete Kennedy standing in the doorway. And even more surprising, he appeared to be alone and not with his family.

As he walked towards the bar, Belle noticed the group of mums glance over and sit up a little straighter in their seats at the sight a handsome stranger. He flashed them a nod and a wide smile, which caused a wave of giggles to cascade around the group.

The smile grew wider as he came up to stand on the other side of the bar. 'Hi,' he said.

Belle smiled back. 'Welcome home, stranger,' she said.

Despite her fears about the embarrassment of facing him again after their kiss, she really was pleased to see him. His skin was golden from the warmth of the Far East and his short dark hair had flecks of a lighter colour from the sun. He was as good-looking as ever.

'Thanks,' he told her, sliding onto one of the bar stools. 'It's good to be back.'

'Liar,' she said quickly. She knew that he had always hated the fuss that erupted whenever he came back to see his family.

He laughed. 'You know me so well.'

'They're just pleased to see you,' she told him.

'Yeah,' he said, his smile quickly fading. 'So what about a drink?'

'Well, you're in the right place,' she replied.

Pete laughed once more, a throaty deep laugh which caused the group of women to glance over once more at him.

His teeth gleamed white against his suntan. Belle felt like a vampire, such was the white of her skin. She had tried sunbathing, but her skin always went from bright white to scarlet in a matter of hours, so she tended to stay in the shade instead.

'So what would you like to drink?' she asked.

'I'll have a pint of beer, please,' said Pete. 'It's been ages since I've enjoyed a decent one of those.'

'Nearly three years,' said Belle, before immediately regretting her words. She hadn't even realised that she'd been counting all this time that he'd been away.

He raised an eyebrow at her. 'Quite right. Three years next month, in fact.'

'I only noticed because it's been so much easier to get intelligent conversation since you left,' she said, turning away to pour his beer and hoping he couldn't see the blush she felt on her cheeks.

'I see,' she heard him murmur, with a chuckle.

'So how was life in Singapore?' she asked, keeping an eye on the beer and away from Pete.

'Wonderful,' he said. 'Right up until a month ago when I lost my job.'

'Such a shame,' said Belle, placing a pint of beer on the counter in front of him. 'But business is tough everywhere at the moment.'

Pete looked up at her, his green eyes bright against his golden skin. 'Here too?' he asked.

She shrugged her shoulders. 'Has it ever been anything else?' she told him.

He nodded thoughtfully before taking a sip of his beer. 'Mmm, that's good.'

At that moment, one of the group of women came up to order a round of drinks. She shot Pete a look with a flirty smile to go with it.

'I'll bring them over,' said Belle, her tone a tad rougher than she had hoped for.

'Thanks,' said the woman.

She and Pete exchanged one more long glance of unspoken questions before she walked, or rather sashayed, away.

Pete turned to look at Belle with a smile on his face.

'Don't even think about it,' Belle told him. 'She's married to a guy who's a gym fanatic. He'd knock you into the river if you tried anything with his wife.'

Pete held up a hand in defence. 'I'm just here for the drink, not to make any trouble.'

'That would be a first,' said Belle, before turning to pour the drinks.

So that wasn't so bad, she thought as she measured out a gin and tonic. She was still able to talk to Pete and make light conversation, even after all this time.

Maybe, just maybe, their long-lasting friendship would be enough to survive something as insignificant as one mistaken kiss.

* * *

It felt as if he had never left, thought Pete.

The inn hadn't changed, of course. It was as run-down and

dismal as always. But, in a way, he found that familiarity comforting.

And then there was Belle. Had she changed? Her smart wit was still evident, as was the gleam in her dark brown eyes. Despite her normal dark clothes, her pretty face was still the highlight of the inn.

'By the way, you're back just in time for Uncle Mick's birthday party,' she told him. pointing to a nearby poster in bright lettering.

Pete grinned. 'Well, your aunt and uncle did always throw a good party,' he said, laughing.

She rolled her eyes. 'Good and loud normally,' she replied. 'And it's fancy dress, just so you're forewarned.'

'That's a shame,' he told her. 'I threw away my Batman cape before I moved back here.'

'I thought your mum had banned you wearing that when you tried to jump from the bridge into the river that time,' she said.

He grinned at her. 'I wasn't jumping, I was learning to fly, if you remember.'

'I only remember the bruises from your busted ankle when you crashed,' she said.

He nodded at the memory and smiled to himself.

When he looked up, he found Belle watching him. She seemed almost embarrassed about having been caught.

She appeared to hesitate before saying, 'It's good to see you, city boy.'

He smiled. 'You too. But, you know, there's still some country left in me,' he told her.

She raised an eyebrow at him before placing the drinks on a tray. 'Not in those fancy trainers. Don't think they'd survive the mud around here.'

As she walked away, he was reminded what an attractive woman she had grown into. It was such a marked difference to the twelve-

year-old girl who had arrived in Cranbridge all those years ago.
Belle had appeared almost broken in those days, such was the
unhappiness of her life up until that point. It had taken many
weeks of cajoling and shy teasing by both Pete and Josh to get her to
smile and open up to them.

But now she was a confident woman. He watched as she chatted
to the group of women who she obviously knew. Her long dark hair
swung around her shoulders as she made them all laugh with some
funny tale. Her skin remained pale, with only a few freckles here
and there to indicate that it was the end of a long, hot summer.

Perhaps it was the dark clothes that she always wore that made
her seem paler, he thought. But even they didn't disguise the curve
of her body, nor her long legs, despite her flat ballerina pumps.

She was actually a very pretty woman, who would easily tempt
men to want to kiss her, he found himself thinking. And yet, the
only kiss he and Belle had ever shared had shocked him to his very
core.

Emotional after his dad's funeral, he had taken himself off for a
walk to think over the day alone. He had bumped into Belle and
they had sat together on one of the benches next to the river for a
long time. They were so used to each other, so close, that the silence
as he stared out at the river deep in thought had been comfortable.

And then he had finally let the tears come. He had held off all
day for his family but, as always, with Belle he could be himself.
She had put her arms around him and held him close whilst he
sobbed. Finally, when there were no more tears to shed, she had
brushed the hair away from his forehead before looking up at him
with a soft smile.

But neither of them had broken the look and, in that moment, it
felt as if there could be something so much more between them. So
when she had leaned forward to kiss him gently, he had found
himself responding before finally coming to his senses.

After all, this was Belle! The woman he had always thought of as his little sister was suddenly in his arms and feeling so right. But he couldn't think of her that way. Wouldn't allow himself to. It wasn't fair on her.

Because didn't she realise what he was like after all those women he had dated over the years? He took after his father, that much he had discovered.

And he wouldn't hurt her when she had already been through so much.

But despite keeping away for the past few years, he felt better for seeing her that evening. Their back-and-forth banter felt natural and he was relieved that everything felt like normal since the last time they had spoken.

It was all his fault, of course. He should have contacted her somehow before, but he never knew what to say. Which was ridiculous because it was Belle. His oldest friend.

But perhaps they would be okay after all.

He glanced over as she walked back to the bar, smiling at him, and he automatically found himself wondering what it would be like to kiss her again.

He shook his head out of his reverie with a shudder that ran through his whole body. The jet lag was obviously far worse than he had thought.

Belle would be staying put in Cranbridge, having always stated a desire never to leave the village. He, on the other hand, was most definitely leaving as soon as he could.

And that would be the end of it. Whatever it was that he was feeling, he told himself.

Because he had to move on despite Cranbridge being his home.

When the family had moved there, he had been ten years old. Back then, it had been a child's dream with a river to play in, trees to climb and fields to explore. It had felt like a wonderland after his early years in urban London.

Even the shop had felt exciting, with its till to play with and a whole backroom of stock to rummage through.

In later years, it had been a place of comfort to catch up with his family and spend time with his dad.

But just before the funeral, he had found the letter amongst his father's possessions as they had begun to clear away some of his things. Then everything had changed. And all he had wanted to do was to get away. To run away.

Because the truth was that nothing had been real, after all. The whole happy family, happy life was all lies.

And it was the lies, the deceit that he couldn't bear. That was why he had kept away. And why he had never wanted to return.

Because, one day, the truth was all going to come tumbling out and then where would it leave his family?

6

Belle stood outside the front door of The Black Swan and gave a satisfied smile to herself as she looked around her home village.

The previous day's drizzle had disappeared and left behind a glorious September day. Everything had that faded look about it as the summer came to an end.

She looked back at the inn and sighed, her happiness dissolving a little. The Black Swan was also faded, but not in a good way.

Uncle Mick still hadn't bothered to order the missing letters of The B ack S an, which had long since fallen off from the sign. The white paint on the outside wall was now a mottled grey and brown and the black paint on the window frames was flaking off. The whole place had an air of collapse about it and looked every inch of its four hundred years old. No wonder they couldn't tempt any new customers through the front door.

She had tried unsuccessfully to persuade her uncle and aunt to spend a bit of money on the outside, to spruce it up a bit. Especially now that The Cranbridge Stores was doing so well.

She glanced over to the shop, the first in the parade of four shops along Riverside Lane that ended at the old watermill.

At least the first two shops had now been transformed. Both shopfronts were so pretty, with their window boxes and decorations. Of course, the corner shop won the beauty prize, but the community hub/local newspaper office next door was no slouch now either. And both places were busy, with people heading in and out most of the day.

The corner shop had been transformed over the past year and was now a prime target for local people looking for food or anything else from local producers. Next door, the community hub was a thriving meeting place for villagers looking for advice or just company. There were also a number of small clubs held there such as the Mother and Toddler group and a new art club, which had just started up on a Tuesday afternoon.

However, the other two vacant shops were as equally run-down as The Black Swan. Even the watermill had never been in use, from what she could recall. There had once been a hairdresser's and some kind of ironmongers there when she had first arrived many years ago. But slowly people had moved out of the village and into the bigger towns and cities to find jobs.

However, life was beginning to return to Cranbridge and a small community spirit had begun to emerge once more in the past year. It was part of the reason that she didn't want to leave. That feeling of being in it together. As well as having her best friends live right on her doorstep.

Having never had any proper, close friends growing up, apart from Josh and Pete, it was still a shock to her to be a part of such a close-knit group of women.

Molly had always lived in the village, but it had taken many years for her sweet nature to overcome Belle's natural distrust of anyone and for them to become close. Their friendship had grown deeper when Amber had arrived in Cranbridge only a year ago. All of a similar age, give or take a couple of years, they had immediately bonded as Amber had helped Josh transform the shop.

Then Lucy had arrived at the beginning of the summer and their group had become a quartet. Lucy's natural knack of getting the best out of people's talents had resulted in the creation of the community hub. In addition, she had managed to encourage Molly to break out of her dull receptionist role and become the social media manager for both the hub and the newspaper which had given Molly some much needed self-belief.

Belle looked across the river once more. It felt as if everything was coming together for Amber, Lucy and Molly and yet, for Belle, her own life was on hold. Even going backwards as the inn continued to fail financially.

She frowned to herself. She was happy being in Cranbridge. What more dreams did she need to have?

Spotting Amber heading out onto the veranda of the shop, Belle wandered over the narrow pedestrian bridge across the river towards The Cranbridge Stores.

Amber was weaving some fake autumn leaves over the veranda in anticipation of the coming season.

'Good morning,' said Amber, straightening up with a smile when she saw Belle.

'Is it autumn already?' said Lucy, coming out of the hub next door with her dog, Keith, alongside her.

The grey shaggy dog immediately went up to Belle wagging his tail.

As Belle bent down to give him a stroke on the head, Molly headed around the corner with her hands full of decorated cupcakes.

'Morning,' said Molly, holding the cupcakes high out of the way of Keith's longing face. 'Sorry, Keith. They're for the community hub, not for you.'

'Spoilsport,' said Lucy, before turning to look at Belle. 'I was talking to Uncle Frank this morning. Is it true that the inn's going up for sale?'

Amber and Molly both turned to look at Belle with horrified faces.

'No!' exclaimed Molly.

'It can't be,' moaned Amber in dismay.

Belle gave them all a small shrug. 'It's no surprise, is it? But it doesn't mean to say that it's actually going to be sold,' she said, trying to suppress the sick feeling in her stomach. 'Who's going to buy it in that state?'

'This is awful,' said Molly, looking tearful.

'These things can take years,' said Belle. 'So don't let's dwell on it for now.'

If they talked about the inn closing, then it would make it all the more real. Besides, despite trusting her friends, she still had trouble opening up to them about her innermost fears.

The silence stretched out until Molly finally spoke. 'Okay. Well, let's change the subject onto happier things. So when are you going to get married?' she asked Amber.

Molly was the youngest of their group and was the polar opposite of Belle with her views on romance, despite having broken up with the most ghastly boyfriend over the summer. At that moment, her blue eyes were shiny with romantic excitement over the upcoming wedding.

'Steady on,' said Amber, laughing. 'He only proposed a couple of days ago.'

'I know, but I love weddings,' said Molly with a happy sigh. 'And Tom will definitely propose to Lucy at some point and then it's just me and Belle left on the singles front.'

'Don't say that to Tom!' laughed Lucy, shaking her long dark hair frantically. 'He'll run a mile!'

'Of course he won't,' said Amber, smiling. 'He's crazy about you.'

Belle nodded in agreement. Lucy had arrived in Cranbridge only the previous summer but had fallen in love with the editor of the local newspaper, Tom, and they too seemed blissfully happy.

'So what do you think, Belle?' asked Lucy, with a gleam in her eye. 'Once we've found someone for Molly, it'll be time to set you up with your very own Beast!'

Belle rolled her eyes. 'A Beauty and the Beast joke? Really?' she said. 'And I thought we were friends.'

Her mother's choice of name for her daughter was a source of constant irritation for Belle. Growing up had been a nightmare with the teasing from her classmates at school.

'Sorry,' said Lucy, putting her arm around Belle and giving her a squeeze. 'Blame all this glorious fresh air. It won't happen again, I promise.'

Lucy certainly had a point about the day. The air was still and the sky was a vivid blue, which brought out the yellowing leaves on the trees nearby even more so.

'Besides, that wasn't love, if you remember,' Belle told them. 'The Beast was a multimillionaire with a castle and a huge library, so Belle was just making a sensible life choice.'

Her friends shook their heads and sighed, but they were used to her cynical attitude towards romance.

'You do realise that we haven't met up for a proper catch-up for at least a fortnight,' said Molly. 'We need to sort that out.'

As they all nodded their heads in agreement, Belle thought that it was funny how quickly life changed. When Amber had first arrived a year ago, there had been no problem in meeting up every Friday night for girls' night. But by the time Lucy had moved to Cranbridge in the spring, things had already begun to change. Amber had fallen in love with Josh and, as well as working late, was beginning to spend more time with him in the evenings. Then Lucy had started going out with Tom and, with Molly working hard on the social media for the paper, they had hardly had a night in for weeks.

'She's right,' said Lucy, with a firm nod. 'We need to get something in the diaries before we all get booked up again. How about next Friday?'

'What's wrong with this Friday?' asked Amber.

'It's Uncle Mick's birthday party, remember?' said Belle.

'Oooh yes,' said Molly. 'A fancy-dress party!'

'Maybe you can come as a bride,' said Belle, giving Amber a wink.

Amber looked down at the ring on her finger. 'I still can't believe it,' she said. 'Isn't it funny how life can change so rapidly? One minute I'm in New York, lonely and miserable. The next, I'm living in Cranbridge and getting married to the man I love.'

'Well, it would be a pretty awful thing to be getting married to someone you didn't love,' drawled Belle.

'I thought you said you were never falling in love,' said Lucy, raising an eyebrow at her.

'And I stand by that statement,' said Belle. 'I'll leave all that to you three.'

Molly shook her head. 'Don't include me in that,' she said. 'I've had enough of men for the time being.'

'Gary was an idiot and you're so much better off without him,' said Lucy.

'I know,' said Molly. 'But I do miss dating someone, especially with the cold months coming up. You know, someone to snuggle up with in front of a warm fireplace.'

'Gary would have to be pretty careful around me near a fireplace,' said Belle with a grimace. 'I'd be very tempted to roast his chestnuts on an open fire.'

They all laughed. Molly's ex-boyfriend had been truly hideous.

'So you've not made any tentative plans yet?' said Lucy, turning to look at Amber.

'Not much so far,' said Amber. 'It's definitely going to be next summer. This winter is too busy and I like the idea of an outside wedding reception. Beyond that, we really don't mind. Except we want to get married in St Barnabus's, of course.'

St Barnabus was the tiny church at the other end of Cranbridge.

'But there was one thing I wanted to ask,' said Amber, looking nervous but excited. 'As you know, I don't have any sisters, so I was wondering whether the three of you would mind being my bridesmaids?'

'Mind?' said Lucy, grinning. 'Why would we mind?'

'We'd love to!' said Molly, laughing in delight, as she reached forward to give Amber a hug.

Amber looked across her shoulder at Belle. 'Are you sure?' she mouthed.

Belle nodded. 'Absolutely,' she told her, despite her reservations at what would no doubt be a colourful, long bridesmaid's dress and totally out of her comfort zone of dark clothing.

But as the excited chatter continued about all things wedding related, Belle was left wondering whether she would even be living in the village at that point if the inn was sold. A fact she didn't bring up as she didn't want to ruin the happy mood.

She should try to be optimistic, she supposed. But despite her name, she knew that her very own happy ever after was never going to happen. After all, true love was for fairy tales, not for real life.

7

After she had finished chatting with her friends, Belle bought a loaf of bread from the shop and was just about to head back to the inn when she heard someone calling out her name.

She turned to find Grandma Tilly rushing out of the community hub towards her.

'Good morning,' said Belle. 'How are you?'

'Fine, fine,' said Grandma Tilly, looking a little distracted. She took Belle's arm and led her off towards one of the three bridges that crossed the river.

'Is everything okay?' asked Belle.

Grandma Tilly glanced behind her once more, but Riverside Lane was temporarily quiet, with no one to be seen.

She gave a nod to herself and then turned to find Belle studying her with a worried look.

'Oh, everything's fine,' said Grandma Tilly quickly. 'I just need a favour from you.'

'Of course,' said Belle, still a little concerned about the pensioner's secretive behaviour. 'How can I help?'

'Do you still have your grandmother's old sewing machine?' asked Grandma Tilly, in a low voice.

Belle nodded. 'Oh yes, I could never get rid of it,' she said, with a smile.

Her grandmother had been a source of great comfort when Belle had moved to Cranbridge. A kind-hearted, gentle woman, she was in stark contrast to Angie, her brightly coloured, loud and brash daughter and Belle's own mother. Her grandmother's peace and calm had been just what Belle had craved for so many years and it turned out that they had a shared interest in sewing. Starved of close friendship in those days, Belle had always enjoyed dressing up her dolls in various pieces of material which she had then sewn to fit.

Her grandmother had taught Belle how to use her 1930s Singer sewing machine to make clothes and quilts. They had spent many happy hours sewing together, matching pieces of leftover materials to make quilts for all their beds.

Grandma Tilly sighed. 'Oh yes, I remember how close you and your grandmother were.'

Belle nodded. 'I do miss her.'

'Me too, dear,' said Grandma Tilly, squeezing Belle's arm.

Grandma Tilly had been close friends with Belle's grandmother as they had grown up in the village together.

When her grandmother had passed away a few years after Belle had arrived, she had inherited both the sewing machine and left-over rolls of materials. But Belle had never had the heart to do anything with them. It wasn't as much fun as when she had been spending time with her grandmother.

'So what do you need the sewing machine for?' asked Belle.

Grandma Tilly checked over her shoulder once more to make sure nobody was nearby.

'I stupidly said that I would make some quilts for one of the stalls for the Christmas fete,' she said.

Grandma Tilly had always been good with sewing and knitting.

Belle nodded. 'Well, that's a few months away yet. Plenty of time.'

'Yes, but I'm not as quick as I was,' said Grandma Tilly with a grimace. 'So I wondered if I could borrow the machine. Just for a short while to move things along a bit.'

'Of course,' said Belle.

'Can we keep this just between us for now,' said Grandma Tilly. 'It's probably only a touch of arthritis and the family will all fuss otherwise.'

Belle nodded. 'I understand. Look, Mondays are my night off. Shall I come over then?' She smiled at Grandma Tilly. 'Unless you're on a hot date, that is.'

'I'll just have to cancel him, dear, won't I?' said Grandma Tilly with a chuckle. 'Anyway, I'm worth the wait. Besides,' she said, giving Belle a mock stern look, 'aren't you the one who should be on the hot dates?'

Belle shook her head as the pensioner laughed softly.

'Life's too short, my dear,' said Grandma Tilly with a wink. She squeezed Belle's arm once more and then walked away.

Belle headed back to the inn deep in thought. Registering that her aunt and uncle were embroiled in their latest row, she bypassed the kitchen where they were shouting and headed upstairs to the family's living quarters.

The apartment was surprisingly spacious, with its own kitchen and lounge, both of which were hardly used apart from at breakfast time. The family's lives were more or less lived downstairs, apart from sleeping, but the apartment did at least feel homely, albeit a bit draughty as the boiler was extremely temperamental and the heating pretty much non-existent.

Down the short corridor, there were three bedrooms and a bathroom. The first, the biggest of the double bedrooms, was her aunt and uncle's. The next, Belle's bedroom, was smaller but was still large enough for a double bed and a few pieces of furniture.

But it was the third bedroom, the smallest, which had been her beloved grandmother's bedroom and always brought a smile to Belle's face. Even now as she pushed open the door, she could imagine that she could still smell her grandmother's rose perfume in the air.

She went over to the small, rickety desk under the window and ran her hand over the smooth metal of the sewing machine, which she ensured was regularly dusted. It was her most prized possession. It was lovely and simple, unlike everything else in her life up until that point. It had no fancy gizmos, just a bobbin, a tension dial and a needle. Once she placed her foot on the pedal on the floor, all her cares and worries instantly drifted away. She found the sound of the machine purring into life very comforting.

Not that she did much sewing these days, she had to admit. She had made a few half-hearted efforts once her grandmother had passed away, but her heart wasn't really in it.

As well as the sewing machine, Belle had also inherited her grandmother's clothes. She had been something of a clothes horse and had made all her own clothes. There were styles from every decade and most of them were beautiful and timeless. Even now, hidden away in moth-proof bags, Belle could see the kaleidoscope of colours. It was in marked contrast to her own dark clothes that she always wore.

Occasionally she had given in to her grandmother's urging and tried on a couple of pieces. But then she would go back to her own dark clothes.

'You're so pretty,' her grandmother had told her. 'Why don't you wear a bit of colour now and then? Brighten yourself up a bit, girl.'

But Belle had just shaken her head in response. Having lived on eggshells throughout her childhood, waiting for the next argument between her parents to erupt, she preferred to blend into the background.

Besides, Aunty Angie's clothes were already so bright that you needed sunglasses to look at her and that was more than enough colour for one family.

There was never any need to wear any of the clothes that she had spent so much time admiring. It was enough for her to just look at the pretty materials and sigh longingly.

There was one dress in particular that was her favourite. It was red and draped down to the floor in soft waves. Her grandmother had made Belle promise to one day 'show yourself off' by wearing it. But when would Belle ever have the chance to wear it anywhere? Maybe Amber's forthcoming wedding, she mused. But she knew she wouldn't be brave enough.

But even the sight of the sewing machine and all the materials couldn't bring Belle comfort for too long. The inn was going to be sold and then where would she end up?

She looked around the tiny box room. Wherever she went, she would be taking her rolls of material, grandmother's vintage clothes and beloved sewing machine with her, of course.

But she still found a lump appearing at the back of her throat as she fought back the tears. Despite the worn-out furniture, the dodgy roof which leaked every time it rained and the temperamental heating in the apartment upstairs, it was home.

She just wasn't sure for how much longer.

8

The last thing Belle wanted to do that evening was host a birthday party at the inn for Uncle Mick. Her heart was heavy and every time she stepped outside The Black Swan, there was a brand new For Sale sign, which made her feel even worse.

Aunty Angie, however, loved a good party. 'Come on,' she said, checking her lipstick in the mirror at the bottom of the stairs out the back. 'Cheer up. We're supposed to be celebrating.'

Belle made a face. 'I'm wearing an outfit, aren't I?' she said.

To Belle's horror, Uncle Mick had insisted that it be a fancy-dress party, which meant a change from the safety of her normal, nondescript clothes.

Aunt Angie rolled her eyes. 'You've got a cheap plastic witch's hat on, black jeans and a black jumper. It's hardly a big change for you, is it?'

'Well, I didn't want to upstage you,' said Belle with a forced smile.

It would have been pretty hard, anyway, she added silently to herself. Her aunt had really outdone herself this time. She was wearing a bright blue shiny jumpsuit which ended in huge flares of material at her wrists and ankles. Angie had added a pair of silver platforms and a silver wig.

She flicked a silver lock of hair behind her and nodded at her reflection appreciatively. 'Can't believe I can still fit into it,' she said, with a smug smile. 'That Abba appreciation weekend was years ago.'

Uncle Mick appeared at the top of the cellar stairs with a puff. He was wearing some kind of 1920s suit, which was entirely suitable for bootlegging, given the dodgy bottles of liqueur he was holding.

'You look like a right Super Trouper,' said Uncle Mick, giving his wife's bottom a pinch as he walked past.

Aunty Angie giggled and Belle was left wondering whether her uncle had been drinking his own home-made punch.

The punch was legendary in its alcoholic levels. Only one year ago, it had almost caused a riot in the inn. Belle could barely remember the evening, only that she, Amber and Molly had been extremely drunk. And that the power of speech had been hard to hold on to. It was something that, once tried, was definitely to be avoided a second time.

But at least her aunt and uncle appeared happier than they had done for a while. Their financial woes had been a constant worry for the past few years, so it was nice to see them relax a bit to celebrate the birthday that evening.

Belle walked out into the bar just as her friends arrived, where she found herself smiling for the first time since the inn had gone up for sale.

Amber was dressed as a Pink Lady from *Grease*, Lucy as a hippie from the 1970s and Molly was some kind of Disney princess.

'You all look great,' she said, as they laughed at each other.

'I still think we should have made you up as a flapper girl,' said Lucy to Belle, giving her black costume a once-over. 'You could have totally pulled off that green fringed dress of mine.'

Belle shook her head. 'No way. Besides, this way I can still cast a spell over any of you if you make any trouble,' she said.

'And disappear into the background as normal,' added Amber.

Belle blushed and made busy pouring out everyone's drinks to avoid any more questions. She knew she should make more of an effort, but sometimes it was just easier to avoid any attention.

Soon the dodgy punch was flowing, accompanied by some raucous laughter. Mainly from Aunty Angie, who was in great spirits. Belle was just hoping that she didn't take over the karaoke and break into a medley of Abba hits. She could still remember the horror from two years ago when her aunt had decided that Celine Dion was worthy of a go.

At least everyone appeared to be having a good time. She could just about see Pete and his family over the other side of the crowded room. Pete had found a Dracula outfit from somewhere, although his suntan was still a bit too glowing for the Count's normal pale skin. Josh appeared to be dressed as a pirate and Belle wasn't surprised to see that Grandma Tilly had arrived, as promised, dressed as punk rocker, the large spiky wig adding at least another foot to her tiny stature.

As she listened to the sound of laughter fill the air, Belle suddenly realised that this might be one of the last parties that they would hold at the inn with their friends and fellow villagers. That everything was coming to an end, including her life at The Black Swan.

She had spent the previous evening chatting with her aunt and uncle about their possible futures when the inn had been sold. They still seemed determined to travel to another country and perhaps settle somewhere cheaper like Spain to make the best of their limited funds.

Belle had tried to nod along enthusiastically when they explained what kind of work the three of them could find out there, but her heart was breaking at the thought of leaving Cranbridge. She still couldn't believe it.

She ignored her previous experience and poured herself a glass of Uncle Mick's punch before taking a large gulp. But, if anything, it heightened her emotions rather than smothering them, as had been her intention.

Beginning to blink back the unexpected tears that threatened to spill down her cheeks, she murmured some kind of excuse to her uncle and headed towards the ladies' toilet. But she kept walking past the cloakrooms and pushed open the door to the inn garden. She looked around, almost expecting somebody to be out there, but thankfully there was nobody in the darkness. She shivered in the cool air but made no effort to turn around and head back into the warmth. It was too painful to be around her friends and family. The Black Swan had been her sanctuary for so long and now, well, now she didn't know where she was going to end up.

She raised her eyes up to the golden harvest moon which was just above the tree line and found herself sending up a silent wish. *Please let me stay in Cranbridge*, she pleaded.

It was a ridiculous thing to do, she thought. Besides, dreams never came true, did they? That much she had learned.

9

Pete had enjoyed the birthday party in the inn so far. He'd reused his Dracula outfit from a Halloween party he had attended years ago and it had been quite fun laughing with the family about their various costumes. Grandma Tilly in particular looked spectacular that evening, although his mum dressed up as a cowgirl was a close second.

Unfortunately, the main topic of conversation amongst the villagers was the inn going up for sale. Everyone had seen the For Sale sign outside as they had headed inside.

He frowned to himself. Belle hadn't said anything about the inn being up for sale when he had seen her a couple of nights ago. But then again, he hadn't asked. But this was the last thing he had been expecting. The Black Swan, for all its many faults, had been part of the village for as long as he could remember. His dad had frequented the place almost every night, from what he could remember.

Surely if the shop was doing so well profit-wise, the inn would benefit? But looking around the place now, it was as run-down as always.

He wondered how upset Belle really was by the inn going up for sale, but there was no way of talking to her privately when the place was so crowded.

Her aunt and uncle appeared to be taking it in their stride. Mick was serving everyone's drinks asking, 'Anything else? Peanuts? Crisps? I've got a nice cheap inn for sale!'

A few people were talking about a 'save our inn' campaign, but that would take serious money and nobody in the village had that.

Except Pete, of course. He actually had quite a substantial amount of savings built up over the years, in addition to the sale of his apartment in Singapore. He was planning to put his money into some kind of flat in London.

But later in the evening, the questions had begun. How long was he staying in Cranbridge? What was he going to do next? Was he going to help out in the shop?

He had tried his best to come up with some witty answers, but in the end he had had to excuse himself away from his mum's sad expression. He had had a Zoom interview the previous day for a job in the financial heart of London which had gone really well. But he knew that his family were unhappy that he would be leaving again so soon. At least he was likely to remain in the same country this time.

Thankfully Mick's home-made punch was deadening most of the pain. Pete had no idea what was in the stuff, but it was lethal and he was sure he would pay the price in the morning.

Heading out for some fresh air, he went past the bar and out into the back garden, where, to his relief, it was empty.

There were some well-worn wooden picnic benches and tables nearby, and to make sure he wasn't seen from inside, he went and stood in the darkest corner. Thankfully, his Dracula costume would give him added protection from any more questioning.

Even in the semi-darkness, the garden was much larger than he remembered. It was as wide as the inn and then narrowed to a point at the far end. It was mainly lawn, with a white picket fence running alongside, beyond which he could hear the river trickling past.

He stood and looked at the night stars twinkling high above him and he realised that he had missed seeing the familiar constellations the past few years. It was only when he drew his head back and it swayed alarmingly that he realised how strong Mick's punch really was.

The sound of the back door opening startled him and he backed even further into the corner by the brick shed, desperate to avoid any further questions from anyone.

He realised it was Belle and hesitated. For a moment he considered joining her, but then again, perhaps she just wanted some peace and quiet as well. Heaven knows she wouldn't get much with her aunt and uncle in full party mode.

So he watched her for a while. She had lost her witch's hat early on and now her long dark hair lay against her shoulders as she stood with her arms hugged around her. He couldn't see her face and yet he knew she was distressed about something. Her shoulders were tense and even across the dark garden he instantly knew that she was upset.

He was just about to step out into the light to comfort her when the back door opened again. The brief shaft of light from inside showed that it was Amber who had followed her outside.

'Hey,' he heard Amber say. 'I saw you sneak out here. Is everything okay?'

Expecting Belle to brush off any show of weakness as per usual, Pete was shocked when he saw her stricken face in the light as she turned to look at her friend.

Amber too was shocked. 'Oh my goodness,' she said, rushing up to stand in front of her friend. 'What is it?'

But Belle was having trouble speaking, Pete realised. And he could only watch as Amber took her friend into her arms. He saw Belle's shoulder's heaving and realised that she was actually crying. It shocked him to his core. This was Belle. He had never seen her so upset since they had first met all those years ago.

Amber lay her head on top of her friend's for a moment. 'It's the sale of the inn, isn't it?' said Amber, softly. 'Of course it is. How could it be anything else?'

Belle sniffed and finally stepped back from her friend's embrace. 'What am I going to do?' she said, her voice breaking. 'Where am I going to go?'

Amber reached out to squeeze her shoulder. 'I don't know,' she said. 'But you know that we have a spare room. Once this place is sold, you can stay with us for as long as you want.'

'I thought Pete was using the spare bedroom,' said Belle, with a sniff.

Amber shook her head. 'He's looking for a new job and then he won't be around much longer,' she said.

Pete nodded in agreement with Amber's wise words as he stood nearby in the darkness.

'But then what?' asked Belle, with what sounded like a sob. 'This is my home.'

'I know,' said Amber. 'But you can stay with us until you figure out what you want to do, if you don't want to go with Mick and Angie.'

'I'm happy here,' said Belle.

'I know that too.' Amber reached out and put an arm around her friend. 'Come back inside. It's freezing out here. Come and have some of your uncle's punch. That'll numb your feelings.'

'And my tongue,' said Belle, with a small smile.

Pete watched as she brushed what he supposed were tears from her face before straightening up and pulling the door open.

He stood in the darkness for a while longer, his head fuzzy with both the dodgy punch and emotions that he didn't recognise. As always, Belle's pain was his pain. But how could he possibly help?

His head still reeling, he finally went back inside.

As it happened, the first person he came across was Mick.

'All right, mate?' said the landlord, giving him a cheery smile as they stood in the narrow hallway. 'You want another glass of punch?'

'No, thanks,' said Pete quickly, hearing his words slur slightly.

'Awww, that's a shame,' said Mick. 'It's my best recipe. Don't suppose you've got 350 grand on you either, eh?'

As Mick turned away, laughing at his own joke, Pete suddenly had a brilliant idea.

'Actually I do,' Pete found himself saying. 'How about I buy the inn?'

Mick laughed over his shoulder. 'Yeah, good one, mate,' he replied.

Pete shook his head to try and cure the muzziness that his brain felt. 'Actually, I'm serious, Mick,' he said.

Mick's laughter faded as he turned around to stare at Pete in shock. 'You are?' he asked, his eyes wide.

Pete nodded. 'Absolutely.'

Mick's face suddenly lit up. 'Oh my God, this is amazing!' he cried. 'Angie! Angie! You gotta come here, love!'

The couple were overjoyed and Pete found that he was swept into Angie's considerable bosom as she hugged him and sobbed out her grateful thanks.

Meanwhile, Pete tried to make sense of what had just happened. What had he done? And why?

But as the news spread like wildfire throughout the bar, he realised that he couldn't take it back now.

It appeared that he had just bought The Black Swan inn.

10

Pete woke up with the dull sensation that he had done something really stupid.

That and an enormous hangover, which could only be contributed to the disgusting punch that Mick had been serving the previous evening.

Pete then immediately sat up as the realisation hit. He had offered to buy The Black Swan inn!

He groaned out loud at the two-way tie between a raging headache and his own utter stupidity.

What on earth had he been thinking? Except he hadn't been thinking. Well, certainly not thinking straight after all that punch. After all, what on earth did he know about running a country inn?

He flopped back against the pillows with a sigh, rubbing his aching head before turning over to check the time. It was just after 10 a.m. The inn normally opened at midday. Perhaps there was still time to apologise and retract his offer. He just hoped Mick and Angie would be willing to listen and understand.

He quickly got dressed, trying to ignore his thumping head all the while. What had been in that punch? He had heard people talk about it beforehand, but it was only now that he understood the full horrible effects of that wicked drink.

He wondered what he was going to say to his family as well. They hadn't had much chance to talk whilst he had still been surrounded by well-wishers. In fact, they had left him to it at some point in the celebrations, but had definitely looked thrilled about the news.

He groaned to himself. What a mess that he had got himself into.

But he knew that he would have to face the family first so he headed downstairs into the shop after grabbing some toast and coffee.

'Morning,' he said, walking onto the shop floor. There were a couple of customers inside the shop browsing the shelves, but there was no sign of Amber. Just his brother.

'Almost afternoon, I reckon,' said Josh, glancing at his watch.

'Food poisoning,' lied Pete. Although having tasted Angie's pizza slices, he couldn't be certain that it wasn't that.

'More like a roaring hangover, I should think, based on the amount of punch you consumed last night.' Josh looked up as Amber came inside, holding punnets of strawberries in her arms. 'If you're not too weary, can you give me a hand shifting some boxes out the back?'

'Sure,' said Pete, despite needing to head over to the inn as soon as possible to start retracting his offer.

But as soon as they had reached the packed stockroom, Josh spun around to face his brother.

'So, that was an interesting evening last night,' he began. 'You didn't think to, oh, I don't know, tell the family your plans to buy the inn before you told the whole village instead? If only so that I don't have to lie to my friends about knowing all about it.'

Pete ran a hand through his dark hair. 'Yeah, sorry. It was a spur-of-the-moment thing.'

'Mick's punch can do that,' said Josh, looking worried. 'Listen, do you even have that kind of money?'

Pete nodded. 'As it happens, I do,' he replied. 'As well as my apartment, I part-owned a fancy restaurant in Singapore with a work colleague.'

'Wow,' said Josh, looking impressed. 'I didn't know that.'

'It worked out really well,' Pete told him. 'Right up until the moment when the whole block was sold off for redevelopment.'

But it had been a gold mine while it had been open. He grabbed his phone and flicked through the photos to show Josh. It had been modernistic, even stark, but that had appealed to the young, urban crowd that it had attracted. They had hired the best chef, the trendiest waiting staff and it had been a big success.

But nobody could replicate that in quiet Cranbridge, could they?

'So, that's your investment idea?' said Josh.

'Yeah, about that...' Pete began. But his voice trailed off under the scrutiny of his brother's gaze. How could he possibly tell him that it had all been a huge, drunken mistake? That he didn't actually want to own the inn after all.

'I'm still struggling to understand something,' said Josh. 'You managed to form a couple of coherent sentences last night. Something about flipping the inn for a profit.'

'I did?' Pete blinked at him and then quickly nodded. 'That's right. I did.'

It wasn't a bad idea, he thought. Perhaps he could save face after all. Renovate the inn, make it look and work a whole lot better and then sell it on, preferably for a large profit.

'So you're not planning on staying in Cranbridge after you've done up the inn and then resold it?' asked Josh.

Pete shook his head. 'Probably not.'

Josh sighed and looked dismayed. 'Then you'd better have a word with Mum and Grandma Tilly because they're both thrilled and thinking that you're doing up the inn to stay here for good.'

Pete frowned. 'I never said that.'

The truth was that he couldn't even remember what he had said the previous evening.

'It doesn't matter what you did or didn't say, little bro,' said Josh. 'They're desperate to see more of you and think that it's an amazing idea.'

Pete sank onto a box of tinned food. 'And you don't?' he asked.

'I just figured it was some kind of drunken mistake thanks to Mick's dodgy punch.'

Pete gulped, trying not to give away how close to the truth his brother really was.

'If it was a mistake then you need to start telling everyone and fast,' he heard his brother say.

Something flared inside of Pete. A desire to prove his brother wrong. To prove that his actions didn't always make everything worse.

'It wasn't a mistake,' he said, quickly standing up before immediately regretting his action as his head pounded once more.

'Good,' said Josh, breaking into a grin. 'For the record, I'm really pleased, both for the inn and for the village. We need to keep the inn open. And it'll be good to have you around for a while longer.'

Pete smiled back at his brother, his anger disappearing as quickly as it had arrived. 'I figure you can't take all the glory around here,' he said. 'Well, I'd better go and see Mick and Angie.'

'And Belle,' added Josh in a pointed tone. 'She seemed pretty pleased last night.'

'She was?' Pete felt a slight lightening of his heart at the thought that he had somehow stopped Belle from crying any more. The memory of her being so upset the previous night was too awful to think of.

Which was the reason why he was in this mess, he had to admit to himself. It had been the only solution that he had thought of to stop her being upset. To give her the security that she had always craved so much. To keep her home and livelihood intact.

However, he obviously hadn't been thinking straight, he realised. Buying The Black Swan was a crazy idea. But perhaps he could get something out of his mistake and be out of Cranbridge by the end of winter. And maybe even his bank account could profit as well.

After all, he had been thinking of investing his savings in some kind of business. Of course, he had planned that it would be some trendy bar in Soho. But perhaps the inn would be a prudent investment, however much his gut instinct was that it was a terrible error of judgement.

He sighed to himself. It turned out that he hadn't needed his Dracula outfit for the previous night's party to become the scariest night of them all.

He could joke all he liked to his brother, but the joke really was on him. Because staying in Cranbridge would mean that he would have to work even harder to keep the family safe from the secret that threatened all of their happiness.

11

Belle woke up feeling unbelievably happy that morning. She had a feeling of calm that she hadn't felt for a very long time. Since first arriving in Cranbridge all those years ago, in fact.

Well, that and an enormous hangover, as the celebrations that the inn was going to be kept open by a local family had meant that the party had gone on into the early hours.

She was still having to pinch herself after all the many nights of sleepless worry. The inn was saved! She was still a bit hazy on the details, but at some point the previous evening, Pete had approached Uncle Mick and offered to buy the inn!

She still couldn't quite take in the incredible news. After all, it was a strange decision that Pete had made, not that she wasn't truly and utterly grateful. Pete was no inn landlord and all of his jobs so far had entailed working in the financial markets. She couldn't see what on earth had tempted him to offer to buy the place.

But she was pleased that he seemed to have finally come around to the idea of staying in Cranbridge. And maybe he might even need a barmaid to help out too, she wondered, finding that she was smiling to herself in expectation. After all, they were old friends, weren't they?

Of course, there was still the question of what on earth her aunt and uncle would do now, but without the threat of foreclosure hanging over them all, it did feel as if a lot of the stress of the last few years had faded away. Surely they could walk away with enough profit to have some savings to their name, at least.

She hadn't been able to speak to Pete the previous evening. As soon as Uncle Mick had made the announcement, Pete had been surrounded by well-wishers eager to congratulate him.

So when he knocked on the front door of the inn late in the morning, she couldn't stop herself from rushing forward to give him a huge hug.

'Thank you so much,' she said, hating how gushing she sounded but for once ignoring it. It was too important now for any kind of pride on her part. 'This means the absolute world to me, I mean, to us,' she carried on, hearing the tremulous sound in her voice which was filled with emotion. She was just so relieved that all the worrying was over. 'Buying the inn is such a huge thing that you've done. For all the family, I mean.'

Pete looked embarrassed, dragging a hand through his hair as he shuffled from foot to foot.

'Belle—' he began.

'How about a drink?' she said, talking over him. He was being modest and obviously uncomfortable at all the attention he was getting. Which was strange because this was Pete, after all.

'Not sure I've got the stomach for anything after your uncle's punch, to be honest,' he replied with a small smile.

'I know what you mean,' she told him. 'But I do pour a mean non-alcoholic cocktail, if I do say so myself. After all, I've got so many years' experience as a barmaid.'

She was still smiling at him expectantly when her aunt and uncle appeared from upstairs.

'Pete!' cried Mick, heading straight over to the door to shake his hand vigorously. 'Oh, mate, you don't know the weight you've taken off my mind. I've had the first decent night sleep in years. Years, I tell you!'

'That's great,' said Pete. 'But...'

He didn't have time to finish his sentence as Angie was giving him a huge hug. 'Oh, you lovely man!' she cried. 'You've no idea how much this means to us. We've got a real future planned at last. No more debts. No more worry. I still can't believe it.'

Belle was looking at her family and beaming a smile at their happiness. She was still a little stunned by the quick succession of events. Only twelve hours earlier she had been crying in Amber's arms at the thought of having to move out of the inn forever. Now, suddenly, there was real hope that The Black Swan would stay open and perhaps there was a job in it for her as well.

'Isn't it amazing?' said her aunt, turning to look at her with a wide smile. Her heavy eye make-up was streaked down her face somewhat, due to what Belle expected was relieved tears of joy.

'Incredible,' replied Belle.

'We've spent all morning planning our cruise,' carried on her aunt. 'Your uncle wants to go to Europe, but I told him, let's go for it. How often am I going to see the Caribbean, eh?'

Belle was confused. 'Cruise?' she stammered, looking from her aunt to her uncle and back again.

'You know,' said Angie, rolling her eyes. 'We've been hanging on to our savings to try to see us through the future, but that doesn't matter now. Pete's buying the place and once that money goes through, then the world's our oyster. So we may as well spend a little upfront now.'

'Right,' said Belle, trying to keep up. 'Well, I'm sure that will be a nice break for you both in the new year.'

'Oh, we're going sooner than that,' said Angie, beaming.

'Too right,' said Mick, nodding in agreement. 'Chances are that the sale will be done in a month or so, is that right, Pete?'

Pete nodded, still looking a little stunned himself.

Belle was beginning to feel worried. A month didn't give her very long to start planning her own future if that was all the time they had left living in The Black Swan. And they still needed to organise where they were all going to live afterwards.

'Well, I can see that Pete would want to get going on becoming the new landlord as soon as possible,' said Belle finally.

'Briefly anyway,' said Mick, with a smile.

Belle looked at her uncle before looking at Pete. 'What do you mean?' she asked.

'Well, he's not going to stay on for too long, is he?' said Mick.

'I don't understand,' said Belle. 'He's only just bought the place. Why would he be leaving again?'

To her surprise, Angie shook her head. 'No, love. You've got it all wrong. Pete told your uncle that he wants to buy the place outright, do it up and then sell it on for a profit. And who can blame him? Running an inn's hard work.'

Belle almost staggered where she stood. 'Sell on?' she repeated, in shock.

'What did you call it, Pete?' asked Angie. 'That funny phrase you kept saying last night.'

'He's going to flip it,' said Mick, with a knowing nod.

Belle found herself speechless, her mind racing to understand what she was being told. She noted that Pete had remained conspicuously quiet during the recent revelations.

'So we thought we'd put a cruise on our credit card,' carried on Angie. 'Now that we don't have to worry about all those debts, we thought it was time to treat ourselves. I don't know the last time we had a holiday.'

'Where's those holiday details, Angie?' asked Mick.

'It's on my iPad,' she replied. 'Come on upstairs, both of you,' she added. 'We'll show you where we're thinking of going over a cup of coffee.'

'We'll be up in a minute,' said Belle, finally finding her voice. 'I just need a moment with Pete.'

Her aunt and uncle disappeared upstairs, chatting excitedly.

Meanwhile, the reality had finally sunk in. So she wasn't saved after all. The inn would still be sold in the near future, not once but twice. Pete was just doing it to line his own pockets.

Belle was embarrassed that she had hugged and thanked him. She had trusted him! Suddenly incensed, she placed her hands on her hips and glared at him.

'So you're what, using the inn to make a profit on the side?' she asked. 'With no thought about what happens to the place afterwards?'

'Listen,' he began to say, but she was too upset to hear what he had to say.

'No, you listen, Pete Kennedy. I can't believe you've done this!' she said, just about managing not to shout at him.

'What have I done? I was trying to help,' he told her.

'How is this helping?' she wailed. 'You've just delayed the inevitable. The inn's still going to be sold. I'm still going to lose my home.'

'Not necessarily,' he told her. 'I'm going to renovate the place. It's an investment.'

'Yes, that much I understood,' she replied, lacing her voice with sarcasm.

'But what I mean is that maybe the new owners will want some decent staff when they buy it from me,' he told her.

'And maybe they won't.' Her voice caught. 'And it won't be the same. Ever again. Not if my aunt and uncle aren't here.'

'Look, someone's going to need to run the place in the meantime,' he said. 'I'll need your help, so you don't have to move out. You can stay on here for a while longer yet.'

It was a lifeline, but it was still all moving too fast for her and suddenly the tears were pricking her eyes.

'Don't cry,' he said, taking a step towards her. 'I hate it when you cry.'

But Belle instantly shied away from him.

'Well, you haven't helped at all,' she told him. 'You've made everything ten times worse.'

'How have I done that?' he snapped. 'I'm putting *my* money into this place. This rotten, run-down, grotty inn is going to make a profit and become a good thing for the village.'

But she was too upset to listen to him. She gulped back the tears. 'Well, I hope all the profit you make will keep you warm at night, Peter Kennedy.'

'Don't you worry about what keeps me warm at night, Belle,' he said, with a cheeky grin, obviously trying to lighten the tense atmosphere. 'I do just fine.'

She rolled her eyes. 'So I've heard,' she snapped.

She went to say something else, but she was so upset that the words wouldn't come. So she settled for marching away from him before he saw the tears streaming down her face.

It wasn't happy ever after. It was still the end of her life in the inn as she knew it.

12

Pete stood on his own in the inn after Belle had walked away from him, or rather stormed off.

Mick and Angie's reaction had been bad enough to the news that he was buying the inn. One word and they were booking an expensive cruise! But Belle's was even worse. She had never been that upset with him before.

And now it appeared that he was definitely stuck with an inn that he didn't want.

He turned slowly and stared at the dark lounge. The wallpaper was peeling off the walls. It was dark and dingy. It was going to need a massive injection of money to tempt someone else to buy it.

Why couldn't he have bought a glamorous restaurant instead? Those he knew all about and were certainly devoid of creaky floorboards, dark oak beams and fireplaces. The one thing those restaurants did have though were customers and plenty of them.

Perhaps that was an idea, he thought, looking around once more. If he turned The Black Swan into something more modern, then perhaps the customers would flood in and so would the business.

And that was the point of it all, he thought. Why couldn't Belle see that? It was just business.

And yet, it was also a lie. He had lied to Belle about his initial idea for buying the inn and he had no idea why. Well, perhaps not complete lies but there was an underlying reason for him putting up the funds for the inn and he didn't want to look too closely as to what they were.

Because if there was one thing he had learned, it was that if he began to look at his motives he would only end up being more disappointed in himself.

'You all right, mate?' said Mick, suddenly appearing back in the bar. 'I heard my niece shouting.'

Pete sighed. 'I think she's a bit upset that I'm not planning on making it a permanent move, to be honest.'

Mick nodded. 'Yeah, she does hate change. But you know that, you've known her for long enough.' He laughed. 'I remember her pushing you in the river many a time in those early years.'

Pete smiled to himself. 'Me too.'

'Listen, she'll come round,' said Mick. 'It's just a bit of a shock, that's all.'

'I know the feeling,' muttered Pete, looking around the lounge once more. 'It needs serious work.'

'Well, I have some good news where that's concerned,' said Mick. 'Obviously a place this old is Grade II listed. You wouldn't believe the hassle involved, I tell you. Anyway, I got permission to update the décor and all that two years ago. But then money got tight and we didn't have the funds to do it.' He held out some paper-work for Pete to take. 'The great news is that you've still got six months before the permission lapses, so at least you can do the upgrades without the council wanting more money.'

Pete nodded. 'That's good news indeed,' he said.

In actual fact, that was a small break and heaven knows he needed one.

'Well, I'll get the solicitors started on everything,' said Pete.

'Great,' said Mick, holding out his hand for Pete to shake. 'Once again, thanks for this, mate. It's taken a huge weight off our minds.'

'You're welcome,' said Pete, realising that the heavy weight had now transferred to his own shoulders.

He wandered outside, grateful for the fresh morning air, to try to clear the headache that he couldn't seem to get rid of. There was a distinct chill in the air as if autumn was ready to get going.

As he headed back over the pedestrian bridge, he looked around for Belle but couldn't see her anywhere. He desperately needed to talk to her, but it seemed that everyone else was wanting to talk to him that day.

First, Stanley and Frank came up to shake his hand.

'Well done, sir,' said Stanley, grasping his hand and shaking it up and down. 'We heard the great news. What a marvellous thing for the village to have The Black Swan saved.'

'It certainly is,' added Frank, once he had the opportunity to shake Pete's hand as well. 'Something for us all to celebrate.'

'Isn't it wonderful?' said Cathy beaming, as she headed down the steps of the shop with Grandma Tilly.

'It is,' said Stanley. 'It can do only good for the local economy and jobs to have the inn brought up to scratch at last.'

'Family discount on a sherry, I hope?' said Grandma Tilly, with a grin.

'Of course,' said Pete quickly.

'Best of all, it means we get to enjoy you for a bit longer,' said Cathy, stepping forward to give her son a huge hug. 'First the shop and then the inn!'

Pete smiled at his mum as she stepped back. 'Well, here's hoping that some of that Kennedy luck will rub onto me too.'

'I'm sure it will,' she told him.

'So what are your big plans for the inn?' asked Frank.

'It's a good size,' said Pete, trying to think like a property developer. 'Run properly and with some decent decoration, I reckon I could turn it into a decent gastro restaurant.'

'Gastro restaurant?' Stanley's grey eyebrows shot up in surprise. 'Is there much call for that around here?'

'There should be,' said Pete. 'I mean, think of it. It could be a real opportunity for change.'

'Folks around here are a bit twitchy about change,' said Grandma Tilly with a frown.

'I know what I'm doing,' lied Pete, trying to sound more confident than he actually was. 'I have experience in owning a decent restaurant.'

Cathy thought for a moment before nodding. 'Okay, I can see it could be really good for the village if it's a success.'

'Which it will be, of course,' said Grandma Tilly. 'Right, who's for a coffee. I need to head back in. Wind's turned to the east today.'

Pete hesitated before he followed them back into the shop, turning around to look at The Black Swan Inn once more. Maybe he could do this after all. It would mean staying on in Cranbridge for a while longer whilst he turned the business around, but as long as he kept his nerve and didn't blurt out the secret he was keeping from his family then perhaps it would turn out all right in the end.

13

After bawling him out that morning, Belle was finally ready to face Pete as they sat around one of the tables in the inn lounge with Mick and Angie to discuss the future later that day.

She knew that she had no choice in the matter. That they all had to move on. But she was still shocked about how very unsettled her life had become so quickly.

A small part of her was anxious to hear Pete's plans, especially as they appeared to involve her.

'So I thought we could get a few things straight so that the sale goes smoothly,' said Pete, with a smile.

He was all easy charm, thought Belle. The same charm that had won over so many women in the past. But it wasn't going to be quite so easy winning her over when her future depended on it.

'Because the inn is freehold and therefore not tied to a lease with any brewery, my solicitor assures me that the sale should go through within the next six weeks or so,' said Pete.

'That quick?' said Mick, looking pleased.

'It's a straightforward purchase,' replied Pete.

Belle sat and wondered whether purchasing commercial properties worth at least £350,000 was an everyday occurrence for Pete. She knew that his various jobs around the world had been in finance so perhaps he was used to dealing with those kinds of large sums of money.

Belle looked at her aunt and uncle, but they seemed quite relaxed about the fact that they had to find somewhere else to live in the next six weeks.

'Six weeks doesn't give us long,' she said in a pointed tone.

But sitting next to her, Aunt Angie was all smiles. 'I don't think that'll be a problem. In fact, that will tie in with our plan,' she said.

'What plan?' asked Belle, with a frown.

'Well, you know we were thinking about a cruise,' began Uncle Mick.

Aunt Angie giggled. 'We've decided to upgrade a bit,' she said.

To Belle's amazement, her aunt and uncle were actually smiling and laughing with each other. It was as if they were a completely different couple.

'Now that the sale is definitely going through, we've decided to use up all of our savings. So the cruise we've chosen sets sail in a fortnight's time, in fact,' said Aunt Angie, turning to look at Belle.

'In two weeks? Isn't that a bit soon?' asked Belle, looking across to her uncle. 'That doesn't leave much time to pack up when you get back.'

'Well, that's the thing,' said her aunt, grinning. 'We'll be gone for three months, so we'll have to do all our packing before we leave.'

Belle looked at her aunt in amazement. 'Three months?' she spluttered.

'Actually it's 109 nights,' said Mick, with a grin.

'With an extra night in Southampton before we set sail,' added her aunt.

'I assumed you were just going around the Mediterranean,' said Belle, stunned.

'No, love. We're going around the world!' said Mick, laughing.

'The whole world?' murmured Belle.

'We've always wanted to,' said Angie, her eyes gleaming. 'We were keeping the money to pay off some debts, but it doesn't matter now, does it? Thanks to lovely Pete here, we'll still have a small nest egg when the sale of the inn goes through.'

'But when you come back you'll have nowhere to live,' said Belle. 'And I'll be homeless before that.'

'Actually I wanted to talk to you about that,' said Pete quickly. 'I don't know much, or anything really, about running a country inn. I don't even know how to change a barrel of beer.'

'I can show you,' said Mick.

'Thanks,' said Pete. 'But when you're halfway across the word, I'm going to need an experienced pair of hands.' He turned to look back at Belle. 'So I was hoping that you could stay on as a live-in manager.'

Was it really too good to be true? That she didn't have to move?

'For how long?' asked Belle, with a gulp.

Pete shrugged his shoulders. 'At least until I sell the inn,' he told her.

That brought Belle down to earth with a bit of a bump, but at least it was some kind of respite.

'In fact,' said Pete, turning to look at Mick and Angie across the table. 'You can both stay here when you come back. That would be fine with me.'

'That's very kind,' said Angie, reaching out to give his hand a squeeze. 'I mean, I can't tell you how relieved we are that the inn is in local hands. And that Belle here will be looked after.'

'For the time being,' added Belle. Was she the only one to remember that he was going to sell on the inn?

'It helps this transitional time anyway,' said Angie, giving Belle a fierce glance.

Pete cleared his throat. 'So, with that in mind, and because there's so much to do around here, I was wondering how you felt if I started the renovations in the next few weeks. Before the sale of the inn goes through officially, I mean. I've already been in contact with a local builder. But I don't want to step on anyone's toes.'

'But legally it won't be yours yet,' said Belle, turning to Pete with a worried look.

'That doesn't matter,' said Mick, waving away his concern with his hand. 'I've given Pete all the paperwork already regarding the original ideas that we had for doing the place up.'

Belle blew out a sigh. She hadn't planned on everything changing so quickly and was beginning to panic.

'And I'll be keeping you company in the meantime because I'll be moving in as well,' said Pete.

'You?' Belle gave a start. 'Why do you need to move in here when you're staying in the apartment over the shop?'

'I hate to be a gooseberry when Josh and Amber clearly need some time to themselves,' he told her with a grin. 'Besides, as I'm buying this place, it might as well become my temporary home.'

Belle ground her teeth. 'Well, I don't know,' she began.

But her aunt interrupted her. 'Oh, it doesn't matter, does it?' she said. 'After all, the place will be Pete's pretty soon. And your uncle and I will be away for three months anyway so you'd be rattling around the place on your own.'

'We got a cracking last-minute deal,' added Uncle Mick. 'Couldn't stop ourselves hitting the confirm booking button, could we, Angie?'

Belle had a sudden vision of her aunt and uncle being trapped on a long sea crossing, arguing and snapping at each other. Man the lifeboats indeed, she thought. Her aunt and uncle in an enclosed space with no exits other than emergency ones didn't bear thinking about.

'I'm going to have to go clothes shopping for some new things,' said Aunt Angie. 'I've not got a thing that's suitable.'

Belle wondered whether the world was ready for her aunt's super bright fashion.

But none of that was the biggest problem. That was the fact that Pete appeared to be moving into the apartment, which they would then be sharing. And they'd never even discussed the kiss that happened three years ago.

'Go and get my iPad, would you?' asked Angie. 'It's on the kitchen table, I think. Then I can show you where we're going.'

Belle nodded dumbly in reply, still trying to take all the new information in.

'I'll come with you,' said Pete, quickly getting up. 'Just so I can get a feel of the place, if that's okay.'

'Well, it'll be your home soon enough,' said Mick, with a smile.

Belle stood up and headed through to behind the bar and then up the stairs in the hallway. She showed him into the small kitchenette first. It was just big enough to cook a meal in. There was a small table as well. It was pretty outdated, but it all worked. Next door was the lounge area which also had a fireplace. Nothing like the scale of the ones downstairs, but it made it cosy on the odd day that they used it. But as the family were normally downstairs working, it wasn't used that much.

'Reasonable size,' murmured Pete.

Belle nodded. 'We all fit in here with no problems,' she said sharply.

'So I guess you and I will be just fine,' he said.

She spun round and found him unexpectedly close, his eyes studying her as he stared down at her.

'So how upset are you on a scale of one to ten about me buying the place?' he asked, leaning against the door frame to stop her leaving the lounge. 'I mean, compared to this morning.'

She shrugged her shoulders. 'I was just surprised, that was all,' she said. 'I mean, I know the place was up for sale, but I thought we had a while longer here.'

'You do,' he said softly. 'We both do, in fact. Maybe we can both work out what to do next with our lives whilst we do the place up together.'

Belle frowned. 'What do you mean "we"?'

'You don't expect me to do all the work myself, do you?' he said, with a grin. 'Besides, I was thinking that with you as temporary landlady, I would be more of a silent partner.'

She sighed as he turned and walked down the corridor. Perhaps it might work, she thought.

She looked at his wide shoulders and back which tapered down to some very tight-fitting jeans before quickly looking away.

And perhaps not, she told herself.

Because she still had no idea how she felt about Pete himself and living with him would throw up a whole more load of questions that she had no answers for.

14

Everyone in the village was still talking about Pete buying the inn a few days later.

'Isn't it marvellous?' said Grandma Tilly when she opened the door to Belle on Monday evening. 'Maybe we should change the name to Kennedy Bridge instead of Cranbridge as my family appear to be taking over the whole village.'

'It's an idea,' said Belle, trying to sound enthusiastic.

But, in reality, she was confused about all of it. She was grateful to Pete for giving the inn some respite so she could stay on for a few more months. But she was also cross that he was treating the whole thing as some kind of investment plan.

'Here we are,' said Grandma Tilly, leading Belle into the lounge of the small bungalow.

Belle smiled at the glasses of sherry and biscuits that were already laid out on the table. She placed the heavy sewing machine onto the floor next to her as she sat down on the sofa.

'It's so kind of you to let me borrow this,' said Grandma Tilly, before looking worried. 'Nobody saw you walk this way, did they?'

Belle shook her head, still somewhat mystified at all the secrecy.

Surely it was just quilting?

'So are these all your pieces?' asked Belle, looking at the different squares of cloth that were piled up at the other end of the sofa. 'Lovely colours.'

'That's what I thought,' said Grandma Tilly, with a smile.

'I'm sure they'll be sold out within minutes at the Christmas fete,' said Belle.

Grandma Tilly's smile dropped a little. 'If I can get them all done in time,' she said. Then she appeared to shake her head a little and beamed at Belle once more. 'Now, let's have a sherry first and you can tell me all about this cruise that your aunt and uncle are going on. Are they really away for three months?'

'Oh yes,' said Belle, half-heartedly.

'Let's hope the other passengers have their earplugs with them,' said Grandma Tilly. 'Never known a couple to argue like them two.'

Belle nodded in agreement, but she knew that she would miss them terribly, especially over Christmas. That had been the biggest shock, that they would be away until after the new year.

Aunt Angie had sighed heavily when Belle had pointed this out to her only that morning.

'I know,' she had said, drawing her niece close to her and putting an arm around her shoulders. 'And if we didn't think you'd have offers from all of your friends and wouldn't be alone, then we wouldn't have booked it. You know that, don't you?' Then her aunt had smiled. 'But you don't want another Christmas day of arguments anyway, do you? You can have a nice peaceful one with your friends, just this one time. And then next year we'll be rowing over who has the last piece of the Christmas pudding just like every other year, okay?'

Belle had smiled and told her aunt that it didn't matter. But it did. It felt as if she were on a runaway train and everything was out of control.

'They'll be back before you even know it,' said Grandma Tilly gently, breaking into Belle's thoughts.

'And they're going to FaceTime every chance they get,' Belle told her.

'An argument for every continent, how wonderful,' said Grandma Tilly with a grin.

Belle laughed. 'Now, what about this sewing machine? Do you want me to show you how it works?'

'Yes, please,' said Grandma Tilly.

So Belle showed her how to thread a needle and how the bobbin worked. She even sewed a couple of squares of material together to show how neat the stitches were.

'Looks great,' said Grandma Tilly, nodding enthusiastically.

But Belle could tell that she was straining her eyes to look at the material up close.

'Maybe I've had too much sherry to focus properly,' said Grandma Tilly.

'Not to worry,' said Belle. 'I can sew and chat at the same time if you need me to lend a hand tonight.'

'Excellent,' said Grandma Tilly, looking far more cheerful.

Belle hesitated before speaking once more. 'Have you had your eyes tested recently?' she asked.

'Oh, they're fine,' said Grandma Tilly quickly. 'Besides, I don't need to see these wrinkles in focus first thing in the morning, do I?'

The subject was quickly changed so Belle carried on sewing the pieces of material together whilst they caught up on the latest village gossip.

But even so, she was worried enough to wonder whether she should mention her concerns to Josh or Amber. Or perhaps even Pete?

But Grandma Tilly had assured her that all was okay, so Belle just had to trust that it was.

They spent a pleasant evening chatting and putting the world to rights whilst Belle sewed. Grandma Tilly was thrilled that Belle managed to complete one quilt over the course of the evening.

'How fast you are,' she said. 'Just like your grandmother.'

Belle shrugged off the compliment. 'It's nothing.'

But the evening had given her a sense of comfort, she found. She had missed sewing and it gave her the same feeling of contentment as when she had been sat with her grandmother all those years ago. For a while, at least, all her other worries had faded away.

'On the contrary, it's been a huge help,' replied Grandma Tilly. 'I don't suppose you want to come over on your next Monday night off, do you?'

'I'd love to,' said Belle.

'Just between us,' added Grandma Tilly quickly.

'Of course,' said Belle, giving her a nod of assurance.

So she left the sewing machine tucked away in a cupboard in Grandma Tilly's bungalow. After all, Belle knew that she wouldn't be using it any time in the future.

With a hug and a wave, she left the bungalow and headed the short distance back along the river to the inn, relishing the peace and quiet of the darkness. The stars were out and twinkling in the dark sky above as The Black Swan came into view.

For a second, she paused and looked at the inn, all lit up in the darkness. It looked cosy and comforting. Home. Familiar. But, of course, everything was changing. Aunt Angie and Uncle Mick would be leaving soon, Pete would be moving in and then there were his ideas for the renovation of the inn.

Nothing was staying the same and all Belle wanted to do was press the pause button and hang on to that moment for ever.

But, with a soft sigh, she began to walk once more towards her uncertain future.

15

Pete was clutching a much-needed coffee as he showed Mr Reynolds, a local builder, around the inn for an estimate as to the work required. The builder had been very quiet as they had moved around the property and Pete was guessing that the renovation was going to be pretty costly.

The inn certainly appeared to have been run on a shoestring for a very long time. Even when Pete had discussed the stock inventory with Mick, the landlord had confessed, 'I always buy the cheapest booze, crisps, everything, really.'

This hadn't been a huge surprise, but Pete had plans to up their game and the quality of everything served, both food and drinks.

But, first of all, the inn needed updating and fast. Pete just hoped that the savings he had left over after buying the inn outright would cover the cost.

Thankfully, the living quarters in the apartment upstairs appeared to be in reasonable shape, so Pete was happy to concentrate the building work on the downstairs and outside of the property, which would have the most benefit in luring potential customers, and hopefully a new buyer, over the threshold.

'So what do you think?' asked Pete once he and Mr Reynolds were stood outside in front of the inn after a full inspection.

It was definitely cooler now that October had nearly arrived. The river had been shrouded in an autumnal mist that morning and all the leaves on the trees had changed colour already. Pete sincerely hoped that the fireplaces were up to scratch as he had felt permanently cold since landing back in England after the heat of Singapore.

Mr Reynolds looked up at the outside of the inn with a serious look on his face before scribbling once more onto his notepad.

Pete peered over and was worried enough to see how long the list was. Not that he didn't trust Mr Reynolds. His credentials were brilliant. He had even renovated Willow Tree Hall, the stately home which was a couple of miles away. And if he could renovate a large mansion like that, he was good enough for The Black Swan.

'I'll start at the top, shall I?' said Mr Reynolds, with a warm smile as he turned back to face Pete. 'Part of the roof needs replacing, I'm afraid. You can see where some of the tiles are either broken or have long since fallen off. Also both chimneys need repointing.'

Pete nodded. Perhaps it wouldn't be as bad as he had feared. This sounded hopeful. But his hopes were soon dashed as Mr Reynolds carried on with his list of jobs.

'Then there's the exterior,' carried on Mr Reynolds. 'The plaster is cracked in places and will need patching up before painting. Thankfully the woodwork is sound, by some miracle, and so that will just need sanding down before repainting. And a new sign, of course, as well as updating the external lighting. So you're going to need scaffolding up whilst that work is completed over the next month.'

'And what about inside?' asked Pete nervously, unsure he'd have anything left in the bank at all.

'You've asked me to leave the living quarters, but you'll need a brand-new boiler up there as the current one should be condemned, to be frank.'

Pete nodded in agreement. The chilly feel of the place appeared to be down to the non-existent heating.

'And what about downstairs?' asked Pete, fearing the worst.

'Thankfully, the walls and ceilings are in good condition so you're probably just looking at new customer toilets and a new kitchen, as well as redecoration. However, the electricity box is years out of date, so we'll need to do some rewiring to get it up to health and safety standards. The same with the other lounge, I guess.'

Pete looked across to the other side of the front door where there was a single-storey extension with an apex roof. It was the one bonus in the whole debacle of buying into the place. He had had no idea, but there was an entirely unused second lounge area which had been hidden behind a closed door. Belle had told him that she couldn't remember it ever being used except possibly for parties many years ago. It would be a perfect space for the restaurant that he had planned.

Mr Reynolds gave Pete a small smile. 'It's all going to add up, I'm afraid.'

Pete blew out a long sigh. 'I expected it would, to be honest.'

'But you do at least have the Grade II permission to upgrade and that's still in date,' said Mr Reynolds. 'That's a huge bonus and means we can get started next week, otherwise it could take months and months. We can replace it all, like for like. I've dealt with the council before with listed buildings so I know what they're looking for.' Mr Reynolds looked at the inn once more. 'The place has got real charm, though. I've popped in for a pint many a time on the way home.'

'Give it a month or so and you'll be able to add a decent meal to that journey as well,' said Pete with a smile.

But, in the meantime, serious money was going to have to be spent on doing up the inn. And the figures that Mr Reynolds had quoted him were eye-watering. It would mean using up almost all of his savings. He just hoped it was worth it.

Once more, he wondered how much a split-second decision thanks to Mick's dodgy punch was going to cost him.

Only that morning, the day before they were due to leave for their cruise, Mick had handed Pete the keys to the inn.

'Now you take good care of my home,' Mick had said, with a smile. 'Because she's taken good care of my family over the past forty years.'

'I will,' Pete had replied, suddenly feeling the weight of responsibility of owning The Black Swan. There was no going back now.

Mick had even provisionally signed the sales deed as he trusted Pete so much. And it was a huge act of faith in Pete. After all, it was not only Belle's place but Mick and Angie's too. He'd known them all for a very long time. And he knew nothing about running an inn.

But he would just have to make it work, he told himself, as he checked his phone. He felt a dull ache as he read the email in his inbox. He had been offered the finance job in the City of London after his interview. The world of financial transactions and the vibrant capital seemed a very long way away from Cranbridge in that moment.

Thanks to his drunken error of buying the inn, Pete had to reply and reluctantly turn down the job. By some mean feat, he had managed to trap himself in Cranbridge. He just hoped the price, both professionally and personally, wouldn't be too high.

16

Time, thought Belle, passed very quickly when you least wanted it to.

The fortnight had rushed past and suddenly it was the night before her aunt and uncle were due to leave for their three-month cruise.

Most of the village had turned out for their last night as landlord and landlady at the inn and the place was as crowded as Belle could remember it being for a long time.

'You okay?' asked Josh, as he ordered drinks for his family.

She nodded. 'I'm good, thanks.'

It was a lie, of course, and she was pretty certain Josh knew it as well.

'If Pete becomes a pain in the neck whilst he's living here, just let me know,' said Josh in an undertone. 'I'll sort him out for you.'

She smiled at Josh. He had clicked into big brother mode since Pete had returned. It made her wistful that she'd never had any siblings to look out for her like that. In a funny way, that was exactly what the brothers had been like. But since Pete had left, she had grown closer to Josh, whereas Pete felt more and more like a stranger. She was actually quite nervous of him moving in and working alongside her as she had no idea what they even had to say to each other any more.

'I can sort him out for myself,' Belle told Josh. 'But thanks anyway. I'm sure you'll be glad to get some space back in the apartment.'

Josh nodded. 'Too right,' he said, flicking a look over to Amber with a soft smile.

Belle turned away, also smiling to herself. How nice it would be if someday somebody could look like that at her. As if they could never get enough of her, wishing the world away from them so they could be alone.

Which was a ridiculous thought because she had always been alone and been absolutely fine, she reminded herself.

She turned back to place the gin and tonic on the counter when Dodgy Del appeared through the crush.

'Not sure I like this,' said Del, sitting down at one of the few vacant stools.

'What, a packed inn?' said Belle. 'No, you're right, Del. It should stay empty and riddled with debt just like all businesses.'

'All right, all right,' said Del, holding up a hand in defence. 'You know I didn't mean it like that. I just wasn't in the mood for a party tonight.'

'But you came anyway,' said Josh, in a pointed tone.

Del shrugged his shoulders. 'It's Mick and Angie, innit? They're the life and soul of the place. Won't be the same without them.'

'Gee, thanks,' drawled Belle.

'No, no, no,' began Del, looking upset. 'I didn't mean it like that, Belle.'

'I know,' she told him. 'I was only teasing you. Pint?'

Del nodded. 'Please.'

She poured out his beer into a pint glass before handing it over to him. 'So, what's up with you tonight?'

'My nephew again,' said Del. 'Getting into trouble because he's bored with no work, no hope, nothing.'

'Oh dear,' said Belle. 'Can't you find him something to do on the coach?'

Del shook his head. 'Tried that, but he says it's boring. Anyway, you don't want to hear about all this. I'm sure you're already upset that your aunt and uncle are leaving.'

'It's not forever,' said Belle, forcing the cheerful tone in her voice.

But as she said the words, she still wasn't sure. What if they enjoyed a country so much that they decided to emigrate? What if they didn't want to even live in the area any more and needed a change? And where would that leave her?

Everything was up in the air and she wasn't quite sure where she fitted in any more.

She glanced over at Angie, who was hooting with laughter at something. Mick meanwhile was surrounded by a group of well-wishers, eager to find out details of their cruise.

Del was right. She was upset, truly upset. But she just didn't show it, as usual.

Even the haven of her grandmother's old bedroom had to be cleared of all the handmade clothes so that Mick and Angie could pile up all their personal possessions in there. Belle had moved the clothes and spare materials into her own bedroom to make space.

She had half expected her aunt and uncle to be upset about all the changes, but they just seemed excited. But she couldn't join them in feeling the same way.

It was supposed to feel like a new beginning but to Belle it felt as if everything was ending.

* * *

The following morning, Belle found herself blinking away the tears pricking her eyes as Mick and Angie completed their last-minute packing. The taxi was going to pick them up at noon.

'Have I got everything?' asked Angie, for the fiftieth time that morning, looking down at her bulging suitcases.

'There's no room left in your third suitcase,' Mick told her. 'Or mine, come to think of it as you've nicked some of that space as well.'

'But what if I've forgotten something?' said Angie, still frowning.

'They have a shop on the ship, don't they?' asked Belle, who had been sitting on the end of the bed and watching the mayhem.

'Several,' her uncle said. 'Plus, you know, we're going around the world. Surely there'll be something to buy in America, Australia, the Far East...' His voice trailed off as he grinned at Belle. 'Still can't believe we're going.'

'Me neither,' said Belle with a smile. She couldn't begrudge them their dream trip when they had worked hard for so many years. She looked over at her aunt. 'Perhaps you could arrange to see Mum whilst you're in the Indian Ocean,' she said, tentatively as a sort of joke.

Unsurprisingly, her aunt shook her head. 'She doesn't want to see me,' she said, looking downcast for a brief moment. Her aunt suddenly stepped forward to lean down to give Belle a huge bear hug. 'You know how much you mean to me and your uncle, don't you?' she muttered into Belle's hair. 'We'll miss you terribly. You're still our family. Always will be.'

Belle nodded, still smothered against a bright blue mohair jumper as the tears once more threatened to fall.

'Now, have I definitely got my hair straighteners?' said Angie, straightening up and moving over to her suitcase.

'You'll be all right, you know,' said Mick, coming to sit on the edge of the bed next to Belle and putting an arm around her. 'Pete's a good lad. He'll see the place right. After all, he's a Kennedy. They're Cranbridge through and through, aren't they?'

Belle smiled and nodded but didn't relay her internal fears to her uncle. They were taking a well-earned break and didn't need to worry. After all, the inn wouldn't be their responsibility after that day.

It would be hers, she reminded herself. She had to keep the legacy of the place intact. Keep the customers happy. And, with a bit of luck, keep the home that she had made for herself as well.

Later on, as she watched the taxi whisk her aunt and uncle away to the coach station before heading to the port, she realised that life as she had known it had changed. She just wasn't sure it would feel right ever again.

But a tiny part of her actually felt empowered. Perhaps it might do her some good to finally stand on her own two feet. She just hoped she didn't step on Pete's toes as she did so.

17

That afternoon, Pete found himself packing up his suitcases again. But this time he was only heading across the river to stay in The Black Swan.

He was still very nervous about how his so-called brief stay in the village had turned out, thanks to Mick's magic punch, but he just hoped it would be a prudent investment that would pay off pretty quickly.

Not that there were any suitable properties for him here even if he wanted to stay, he thought, as he dragged one of his wheeled suitcases across the tiny pedestrian bridge towards the inn. The village, whilst admittedly pretty with it's chocolate-box cottages, was light years away from the modern places that he had bought so far in his adulthood. He liked things without character, he had decided. Modern, pristine and blank. Nothing with history or reminders of happier times.

Not, he thought with a grimace, as he looked up at the cracked paint on the façade of the inn, this kind of place at all.

However, the place wouldn't remain in that state for too long. He had already hired a team of contractors to start the following week on upgrading everything downstairs, from the kitchen to the bar and the furniture. It all had to go. It would make quite a dent in his savings, but it would be worth it to attract the right buyer and make the biggest profit.

Not wanting to drag his suitcases through the inn lounge, he made his way around the side entrance to where the back door was.

Belle had, reluctantly, handed over a spare key for the back door and he found himself almost surprised when it actually worked and turned the lock.

He couldn't blame her animosity, he supposed. She had already accused him of only renovating the inn for the money, which was entirely true, of course. He just couldn't understand why she was being so impossible about it all. Wasn't he trying to help keep The Black Swan open?

He had tried to describe his vision to Belle a few days ago of how he wanted the inn to look once the renovations were finished.

She had actually looked horrified!

'You're kidding, right?' she had finally said. 'Tell me this is a joke.'

Pete was nonplussed. 'What are you talking about? Of course it's not a joke,' he had told her.

Belle had looked down at the list of ideas that he had had about decoration once more.

'So you mean to paint everything grey, put some sofas in a corner and make it some bland business-lounge-type place?' she had said, her voice laced with disdain. 'This is an inn. You need to understand the charm of the place. You're being too arrogant.'

'And you're being impossible,' he had replied. 'The whole place is too dark, too gloomy. And then there's the food...' His voice had trailed off. He had to be careful not to insult her aunt, but on the other hand, she had to realise how awful the food was.

'Well, Aunt Angie's not going to be around, so what are you going to do about the food?' she had asked.

'I'm going to hire a top chef,' Pete had told her. 'I'm already putting out feelers. I want to make this place top-notch. Preferably with a Michelin star or two.'

Belle had looked at him with wide brown eyes. 'A Michelin star?' she had stammered.

'Well, perhaps that's pushing it a bit far, but some kind of amazing menu anyway,' Pete had said. 'I've dined in plenty of places like that. Incredible restaurants around the world. Trust me, this certainly isn't one of them.'

'No, it's not,' she had replied hotly. 'Because it's a village inn.'

'Inns can be modern too,' he had told her.

'Michelin star food?' she had repeated, rolling her eyes. 'Are you mad? Can you see Dodgy Del hunched over a single prawn and some caviar any time soon?'

'Well, perhaps he can find somewhere else to eat!' Pete had snapped.

'So you want to alienate all our current customers, is that it?' Belle had replied. 'The ones that have kept us going all these years. Now you want to chuck them out and what, get your banker friends in here to look down their noses at us all?'

'That wasn't what I meant,' Pete had said, realising that he had to try to defuse the tense atmosphere.

But Belle was too cross to listen to him and had carried on. 'I mean, perhaps Grandma Tilly will want some sourdough bread for her chip butty? Or what about some chickpeas instead of apple crumble for your mum?'

'Listen,' Pete had said, almost shouting so that he could stop her from carrying on. 'This is how it's going to be. So if you don't like it...?'

'What? You think I'll just walk out? Not a chance.' She had put her hands on her hips and leaned forward. 'I'm going to be here every step of the way to make sure that you don't completely destroy everything that I love about this place.'

With that, she had spun around and marched out of the inn lounge, leaving Pete sitting on his own and wondering how they were ever going to work and live together when they were so far apart in every other respect.

As Pete dragged his suitcases through the upstairs apartment, it felt as if he was heading back into the lion's den. He and Belle had actively avoided each other during the past few days but that was no longer an option now that they would be living and working together.

He just hoped that the changes would make all the difference to The Black Swan's business. And that he and Belle would still be friends at the end of it too.

But at that moment, he wasn't certain about either.

18

Later that day, at six o'clock precisely, Belle watched as Pete went across to unlock the front door to the inn.

She had actively stayed out of his way that afternoon whilst he had been unpacking his belongings in the apartment upstairs.

'Ta-dah,' said Pete, looking almost pleased at the prospect of being a landlord.

As he walked back towards the bar, Belle told him, 'You need to turn the Closed sign over.'

'Oh. Well. Never mind,' said Pete, with a shrug. 'Our regulars will know that we're open and until I get this place sorted, we won't have any other sort of customer anyway.'

Belle continued to polish the glasses as he stepped behind the bar to stand next to her.

'So what's next?' he asked.

'Everything's sorted, thanks to Uncle Mick,' she told him. 'The beer is all connected in the cellar, everything's topped up here in the bar. Aunt Angie even left some of her delicious cuisine in the freezer in case anyone's hungry.'

Pete shuddered. 'Not a chance,' he muttered. 'That lot's being thrown out as soon as the first skip arrives.'

They both looked up as the front door was cautiously pushed open a little.

Dodgy Del peered around the corner. 'You open?' he called.

Belle nodded. 'Of course,' she told him. 'Come in.'

'Only the sign still says Closed,' said Del, with a frown.

Belle shot Pete a knowing smile. 'I'll fix it,' she told him, crossing the floor to turn over the little sign.

When was Pete going to learn that she had quite a lot that she could teach him? There might actually be some hope for the future of the inn if only he wasn't so determined to do everything his way, she thought.

She looked out of the window. It was dark already now that October had arrived and the nights were beginning to draw in. As the days shortened and everyone slowly segued from outside to in, with a drizzle falling onto the river, it was unlikely they'd be busy on a cold and damp night.

She went back across the room and had just reached the bar when she heard Del say, 'I'm not sure I can drink that, mate.'

She looked to where Pete had poured out a pint of beer into a glass for Del. Except there was more froth than beer.

Del looked at Belle with a grimace. 'Any chance of anything more than a half pint?'

'I'll pour it out,' she said, brushing past Pete to stand in front of the lever. 'It needs a bit of a wiggle,' she told him. 'And you need to hold the glass at an angle right up against the glass to ensure it's beer and not froth that ends up in the glass.'

'Right,' he said, frowning. 'Okay. Well, I'll learn.'

But Pete was positively blushing when Josh came in a short time later and Del told him about his brother's efforts.

'How can anyone not know how to pour a pint of beer?' said Josh, laughing.

Pete cleared his throat. 'The bars I'm used to are more cosmopolitan than countryside,' he told them in a lofty tone.

But it didn't stop Josh and Del from carrying on laughing.

Belle thought later on that she really hoped he was going to learn how to be a landlord a lot faster than he had that evening. Despite only a handful of customers coming in, Pete had managed to overcharge nearly all of them, had got the till stuck, had caused the contactless payment machine to need rebooting and had given out vodka instead of gin.

All in all, he wasn't a natural, she decided. But she still found she was smiling, despite the customers' grumbles. In a way, it was nice to see him outside of his comfort zone. For a while, Pete had lost that arrogance that had suddenly appeared and had even given her a sheepish grin when he had made yet another mistake. Perhaps some of the old Pete remained after all, she decided.

He looked shattered when Belle locked the door later that evening after everyone had left.

They walked past the lounge and kitchen and into the short corridor where the bathroom and bedrooms were. It had been decided that Pete would take the master bedroom and that Belle would remain in her own.

But when she glanced inside her aunt and uncle's old bedroom, she was surprised.

'You've rearranged the furniture,' she said.

Pete had had a brand-new bed and bedding delivered, but whereas the old bed had always been underneath the window, the new one was now in the centre of the room.

'It makes more sense like that,' he told her. 'And I like to sleep in the middle of the room, not up against a wall.'

'I see,' said Belle, who found herself smiling to herself as she bid him goodnight.

Hearing the rain becoming much heavier outside, suddenly she was in surprisingly good humour as she went to bed.

* * *

Belle's reaction to him moving the bed to the middle of the room had confused Pete. Her smile had almost made him think that there was some kind of private joke that he wasn't party to.

It didn't matter, he told himself, as he settled down in the bed. There was a draught howling into the room from somewhere and he huddled further under the duvet. The place seemed to be permanently cold.

He found it very odd to be lying in the bedroom with Belle next door. He was still aware of her soft perfume lingering in the air.

He shook his head and tried to force himself to go to sleep. But his mind was racing and it took some time before he finally began to drift off to the sound of the rain hammering down outside.

But a short time later, he came to with a start and switched on the bedside light, looking around him in a daze.

As another splash of water dripped onto his cheek, he looked directly upwards into the eaves of the roof where the rain had begun to leak into the middle of the room.

It was then that he finally got Belle's private joke about him moving the bed.

Back in her own bedroom, Belle smiled to herself as she heard Pete drag the bed back across the room to put it under the window before she turned over and went back to sleep.

19

Belle was staring into space, waiting for the kettle to boil the following morning, when Pete came into the kitchen.

'So I now have proof that the roof leaks,' he announced, sounding pretty grumpy.

'And a good morning to you too,' she replied.

She did feel a little mean about not warning him about the leaking roof in the master bedroom, but he seemed so determined to ride roughshod over everything in the inn, including her, that a tiny bit of playful revenge had made her feel slightly better.

To be fair, he did look positively dishevelled. Normally so well turned out and immaculate, that morning he had bags under his eyes and even his dark hair was messed up.

'I hope there's a mug of coffee somewhere in this kitchen that you're going to make me to apologise for not telling me about the leaky roof,' he said, yawning.

Belle looked at him with an arched eyebrow. 'Yes, but first off there needs to be a "please" in that sentence,' she told him. 'And second, if we're going to be sharing this apartment for the foreseeable future, we need to set some house rules.'

'Do we have to do this now?' he groaned. 'I've had barely any sleep. I'm frozen in my bones and pretty soggy around the edges too.'

'Yes, we do,' she said. 'For the record, I won't be doing any of your laundry, cooking or any other housewifely type duties.'

She was surprised to see a smile played on the corner of his lips.

'What?' she asked, wondering what on earth he had found funny.

'Just trying to imagine you wearing a frilly apron,' he told her.

She made a face at him. 'Funny, but I can imagine you wearing one very easily.'

He gave a short grunt of humour before moving over to the nearby breakfast bar. He had already drawn out one of the stools before Belle even had a chance to shout, 'Wait!'

All too late, she watched as Pete sank onto the rickety stool which instantly broke underneath him, plummeting him to the floor.

He swore and leapt up to glance around at Belle in utter disbelief. 'Does nothing around here work?' he exclaimed. 'I spent half the night being dripped on through the leaky roof, then the other half huddled under the covers in the coldest room known to man.' He looked down at the broken stool. 'Is the whole place riddled with woodworm or is it just some kind of giant cosmic joke that the universe has decided to play on me?'

'That stool has been dodgy for some time,' she told him smoothly, going to pick up the pieces from the floor. 'And I did suggest that the bed was better off under the window.'

'You failed to mention the leaking roof,' he added.

'Yes, I did, didn't I?' said Belle, smiling as she straightened up to place the broken stool next to the kitchen bin.

Pete sighed heavily. 'Can we just start again?' he asked. 'I can't fight you this early in the morning.'

'It's half past eight,' she told him in a pointed tone. 'But listen, I agreed to carry on living and working here because you said that you'd be a silent partner in this place with me being in charge.'

'And?' he asked, hesitating before leaning against the breakfast bar with his full body weight and crossing his arms in front of him.

'And I haven't seen much of the silent bit so far, to be honest,' she told him.

'I lied,' he replied, with a grin.

Belle rolled her eyes. 'Great. Anyway, I *will* make you a coffee just this once,' she said, turning her eyes to grab another mug. 'Seeing as you've just fallen on the floor. But you're going to have to wise up that this was *your* idea to invest in the inn, which most certainly isn't perfect, I agree. So can you please just try to enjoy being here for however long we're stuck together?'

'I know you're not happy about all of this,' he said. 'But with a successful restaurant and a decent chef, I think this will make an attractive proposition for one of the large inn chains, I'm sure.'

Belle made a face. 'We like being independent,' she told him.

'And I like having money in the bank,' he replied.

'Couldn't we just do bar food?' she asked. 'Surely we don't need to have a restaurant when it's never mattered before. How do you know if anyone will even come?'

'They'll come if there's a decent chef here,' he said. 'We want modern, beautifully presented food that will attract punters from miles around.'

Belle made a face. 'Modern food?' she said.

He shook his head. 'I understand that the inn needs to be the heart of the community,' he said. 'Can't you see that I'm trying to save it for you? I mean, for everyone?'

'A fancy restaurant?' she murmured, still trying to take it in.

'It's not open for discussion,' he told her. 'I'm going to make this a successful business even if it kills me.'

'Not unless I get there first,' she said, before walking away.

She was so annoyed with Pete's attitude.

It hurt because they had always been so close. When she had first arrived, she had thought the Kennedy boys would be too sophisticated and cool to play with her as they were a couple of years older. But they were always messing around in the village and the countryside beyond so she had joined in, ever the tomboy at that age.

The anger went out of her as quickly as it had arrived, replaced almost immediately by sadness. Because it seemed as if their friendship really was buried in the past.

20

Monday and Friday nights were Belle's normal nights off from the inn for as long as she could remember. But she was unsure as to how that would fit in with Pete. However, Grandma Tilly had caught her in the lane that morning and asked if Belle had remembered to pop in again that evening to help with more quilts. Normally it wouldn't have been an issue, but with nobody else other than Pete to help behind the bar, it was a problem.

In addition, Grandma Tilly once more wanted their get-together to be kept secret from the family which Belle still didn't understand but reluctantly agreed to.

So Belle was going to have to lie to Pete about meeting his own grandmother for an hour or so.

Not that she wasn't grateful to take a break from the inn that evening. She had endured a day of clattering and clanging whilst the scaffolding had been put up around the inn. The Black Swan was now completely surrounded by a shroud of metalwork and was almost unrecognisable underneath.

Customers were still able to head between the poles to get to the front door, which was essential as they needed to stay open despite the mess. But at least everything remained the same on the inside, for now. Because Pete had opened up the door through to the second lounge downstairs to try to imagine what was going to be the new restaurant area.

That evening, once more, Belle found him standing in the dark space looking across the large room.

In truth, she had almost forgotten about the second lounge as the doorway through to it had been blocked for so very long. She could barely remember it ever being used and that had to have been at least fifteen years ago. She was surprised that it was such a large space. It had a fireplace that mirrored the one on the other side of the chimney breast in the main bar area. But apart from some very old and tatty-looking chairs, it was devoid of anything else.

Pete, however, was very pleased with the space. 'It's going to be great,' he said, nodding at the darkness beyond. 'We can get loads of tables in here.'

Belle still wasn't so sure. If there were hardly any customers in the normal bar on a daily basis, what was the point in making the place even bigger with a fancy restaurant? But it was his money, she supposed.

She looked back at the main bar where only one customer sat by the fireplace. Ned Shearing had lived in the village for many years, but his brusque, somewhat abrupt manner meant that he didn't appear willing or able to socialise at any of the events. Lucy had told Belle that she never saw him in the community hub, which was a shame as that was a good meeting point for the villagers these days. Ned lived alone in his cottage a few roads away and came into the inn on a Monday night where he would sit alone for exactly an hour before leaving.

'I'm just heading out for an hour or two,' Belle told Pete.

He spun round to look at her in surprise. 'You are?'

'It's my night off,' she told him. 'I did remind you of that earlier.'

'I know. So, what are you up to?' he asked.

'Oh, er, I'm just meeting someone,' she stammered.

He raised his eyebrows in surprise at her lack of information. 'Who?'

'Just someone,' she told him, zipping up her winter coat. 'I'm sure you can handle the rush in the meantime.'

She rushed out before he could interrogate her any more, anxious not to break her promise to Grandma Tilly.

* * *

Pete frowned as he watched Belle close the door behind her, disappearing into the inky black night beyond. Who on earth could she be meeting on a Monday night?

Not that it was any of his business, of course.

But still, her secretive manner had concerned him. Was she in trouble? Was she upset? Apart from being hacked off with him, he wasn't sure.

Of course, Belle had always been a closed book in regard to her emotions. But he had always been the one to cajole her into talking, especially in those early days when she had still been so scarred from her parents' disastrous marriage.

More often than not, she would disappear for hours on end, with Mick and Angie tearing their hair out with worry as to where she had gone. It was Pete who had discovered her that first time when looking for her in the countryside, following the river as it split off into smaller tributaries along the way. One stream wound its way through a nearby wood where there were many ancient trees in various stages of decay. The largest one was almost hollow inside and Josh and Pete had been messing around in there all summer, hiding inside the huge empty trunk and jumping out to give each other a fright.

In a rare moment of openness, Belle had declared the hollow tree trunk a magical place. And that was where Pete had guessed he would find her. And he had been right, to his relief. She was curled up in a corner, arms wrapped around her skinny knees, her brown eyes sparkling with tears. Apparently she had made contact with her dad to ask about their future plans. He had told her in no uncertain terms that her life with them was at an end and that she was staying put in Cranbridge.

'Good,' she had muttered, when she had finished telling Pete about the phone call. 'I never want to leave here anyway.'

Pete remembered how much she had loved the peace of Cranbridge after her tumultuous early years. And why she had been so defensive of the inn in recent weeks.

He sighed heavily to himself. In trying to help, it felt as if he had only made matters worse.

He looked up to find Ned, the only customer in the inn, watching him.

Pete gave him a nod. 'Can I get you another drink?' he asked. 'On the house. I'm going to pour myself one.'

Ned shook his head. 'You won't make a profit that way, son. Not that you Kennedys ever worried about things like that.'

Pete looked at him questioningly. 'I'm sorry, but have we met?' he asked.

'Not since you were a mere lad.' The elderly man stood up slowly, shrugging on his coat and slipping on his flat cap. 'I'll be off now.'

Pete noticed he had a hole in the sleeve of his coat.

He watched Ned leave and continued to stare at the door after it closed behind him. He made a mental note to ask Josh about Ned.

His face rang a very vague bell but Pete couldn't recall where he recognised the elderly man from.

Pete continued to stare at the door for a while longer before glancing at his watch, once more questioning where Belle had gone to. He had a sudden thought that she might have even gone out on a date? And then wondered why on earth it mattered so much to him. He was just looking out for her, as he had always done. That was all. Wasn't it?

21

'So, what do you think?' asked Pete.

Belle stared down at his phone and read the advert on the screen once more.

'Top-class chef needed for brand new restaurant,' she read out loud. 'Michelin star quality a bonus. Will be able to design creative menus for discerning customers.' She looked back up at Pete. 'Discerning customers?' she said, before looking around the inn, which was completely empty that Wednesday evening apart from Frank and Stanley.

It was ironic, she thought, that the inn was so empty in the evenings when you couldn't move in the place during the day without tripping over somebody working on the inn. All day, there had been hammering on the roof as the tiles were secured, as well as the general chatter among the plasterers as they patched up the outside wall and the builders singing along to the radio as they repointed the chimneys.

It didn't help that the scaffolding made it even darker inside, added to the fact that the lights were flickering on and off as the rewiring of the electricity still needed to be done.

'The customers will soon arrive just as soon as the good reviews start coming in,' said Pete in a confident tone as he took back the phone from her proffered hand.

'Don't you think that the builders need to finish the downstairs kitchen first before you start hiring anyone?' she asked.

Only that morning, yet another skip had arrived and the whole kitchen had been dismantled, leaving an empty shell in its place.

Pete shook his head. 'No time. We need to get this place up and running in order to maximise our profits over the coming months. Especially the Christmas trade. Think how much we could take in pre-bookings alone if we get the right chef.'

Belle nodded but was still concerned about Pete's plans as she headed over to put another log on the fire. She just wasn't sure where all these new customers were going to come from. But perhaps he would be right. Perhaps the new, more upmarket clientele would be flooding in from the surrounding area.

Then again, she thought, as the front door opened and Dodgy Del came in, perhaps not.

'Good evening,' said Del to Frank and Stanley, who replied in kind.

'Hello,' said Belle. 'You're early today.'

It was only just past six o'clock and Del didn't normally come in for his pint until later on in the evening.

'Coach tour got cancelled,' said Del, coming to stand next to her by the fireplace. 'So I thought I'd come in here and drown my sorrows instead.'

'What's up?' asked Belle. 'Still got family troubles?'

Del nodded. 'My nephew got himself into trouble over the weekend,' he whispered to Belle. 'Messing about with his friends out on the streets. Police came along. Only gave them a caution, but I just know it's going to lead to something worse.' He sighed heavily. 'Trouble is, there's just no jobs out there at the moment.'

'This one's the chef, isn't he?' she asked.

Del nodded. 'Got his certificates from college and all that. But he's only managed to get a job in McDonald's over in Aldwych so far and he only lasted a month there. It was pretty grim, apparently.'

Belle thought back to the conversation she had just been having with Pete.

'You know, Pete's looking out for a new chef for this place,' said Belle in a loud voice.

Del's mood immediately brightened up. 'Is he? That'd be great,' he said, looking over to where Pete stood.

'Hold on,' said Pete, shooting Belle a glance. 'Unfortunately we're looking for a Michelin-starred chef.'

'A what?' said Del.

'It's a fancy chef,' explained Belle, as they walked towards the bar. 'But if business is going to take off like Pete's expecting it to, then this chef will need some help in the kitchen.'

She and Del both looked at Pete with expectant faces.

Pete shifted from foot to foot, looking as if he was caught between a rock and a hard place. 'I'm not sure—' he began.

'Listen, the lad's desperate,' said Del, leaning forward on the bar. 'He's all right. I'll make sure he doesn't cause any trouble around here.'

'Trouble?' Pete looked startled.

'It doesn't matter,' said Belle quickly, shooting Del a warning look to keep quiet about his nephew's recent brush with the law.

Del nodded. 'He's a very hard worker.'

'Which we'll need for the Christmas rush,' added Belle, coming to stand next to Pete behind the bar. 'Who else is going to help the chef? I'll be too busy serving all the drinks to the many new customers.'

They both continued to look at Pete, who finally nodded his

head. 'Okay,' he said. 'I'll meet with him, all right? But I'm not making any promises.'

'You won't regret it,' said Del, breaking into a winning smile. 'I'll give Brad a call to tell him the good news.'

As he wandered away to make his call, Pete turned to look at Belle.

'Why do I think that you just engineered that whole thing?' he asked, raising his eyebrows at her.

Belle smiled. 'I don't know what you're talking about,' she told him.

To her surprise, and pleasure, Pete laughed. 'Yeah, right.'

'But surely we'll need some help in the kitchen,' she reminded him.

'I'm not sure what kind of help anyone from Del's family would be giving us,' said Pete, with a grimace.

'His heart's in the right place,' said Belle.

'Now you're pushing it,' said Pete, with a wink.

She smiled to herself as he walked away, but her good mood did begin to falter as she considered what a fancy chef would do to a place like The Black Swan. How grand a dining experience was Pete talking about?

It worried her that he was taking the gastronomic dining to a whole new level and leaving Cranbridge, and Belle, far behind.

22

It was Friday night and the four best friends had finally sorted out their calendars and found a free night to meet up.

Belle drained the last dregs of the Prosecco in her glass and reached for the bottle on the coffee table in front of her to pour another drink.

'I was going to ask how your week's gone, but you've just answered my question already,' said Lucy, who was sitting next to her on the sofa.

They had arranged to meet in Amber's apartment above The Cranbridge Stores. It was beautifully furnished, with a light airy feel, helped by the oak beams which rose to an apex in the roof. Amber's flair for decoration which had begun in the shop had also been put to use in the apartment. It was modern but cosy country chic and Belle had often wistfully thought how nice it would be to live in a place like that. It was certainly in stark comparison to the damp, dark inn.

'It's all such a mess at home,' said Belle, handing the bottle to Lucy, who placed it back on the table. She hadn't even finished her first glass yet. 'The scaffolding's up but they've already ripped out both the kitchens and left everything covered in dust. Plus the electricity keeps going on and off so all the chiller cabinets for the wine and soft drinks keep switching off too.'

'I think it's a good thing,' said Molly, who tended to see the positive in everything. 'The inn's going to look great when it's finished.'

'It is,' said Amber, smiling at them all in contentment as she sat down to join them. 'You know, it's been way too long since we did this.'

'I know,' said Lucy. 'It's been so crazy busy recently, this is the first time I've had to draw breath.'

'So where's Tom tonight?' asked Molly.

'He's gone to the inn with Josh,' Amber told her.

'So we're an entirely man-free zone,' said Lucy, with a smile.

'Cheers,' they all said, clinking their glasses together.

As usual, the conversation was non-stop as they all caught up properly after weeks of only bumping into each other in the shop or on the lane.

'Who's in charge of the inn tonight if you're over here?' asked Molly, with a frown.

'Pete,' said Belle in a grim tone.

She had no idea what kind of state she would find it in when she returned. He had only just learnt how to pull a pint properly.

'Josh will keep an eye on things and make sure that it's okay,' said Amber, with a soft smile.

'I hope so,' muttered Belle.

'Look, I know you're not happy but at least the inn will stay locally owned, just as it's always been,' added Amber, who was pouring out some crisps into a bowl.

'But it doesn't necessarily follow that I'll be here to see all that success,' said Belle, biting her lip in worry. 'Pete's planning on selling the inn as soon as it's up and running and there's no guarantee that I'll be able to stay on after that.'

Amber looked across the oak coffee table at her friend. 'Pete will make sure that you're okay. Josh says that they've both always looked out for you and I'm sure that hasn't changed.'

'I'm not so sure,' said Belle with a heavy sigh.

'Well, perhaps we can try and persuade him otherwise at Cathy's birthday party next week,' said Molly, with a nod.

Cathy was celebrating her birthday at the inn the following Monday.

'Is he really going to try to turn it into a fancy restaurant?' asked Lucy, with a grimace. 'I don't understand why he thinks that there would be much call for that around here.'

'Because he's turned into a snob,' Belle told her. 'It's like everything has to be the biggest and the best. I mean, who does he think he is?'

'The son of a famous rock guitarist?' ventured Lucy, with a sly smile.

'One who looks mighty fine in those jeans,' added Molly in wistful tone.

'Ewww!' said Amber, screwing up her face. 'He's going to be my brother-in-law!'

'I'm just saying he's very handsome,' said Molly.

'And he knows it,' snapped Belle. 'Any larger and his head wouldn't be able to fit through the door.' She sighed once more and placed her empty wine glass on the table. 'Don't let me drink any more,' she told her friends. 'I've got yet more builders starting early in the morning and I won't be able to handle all that noise if I'm hung-over.'

She was really quite worried about the builders. Not the level of the work, but perhaps the inn would lose something in the renovations. Perhaps it wouldn't even feel like home any more. It was already strange without her aunt and uncle there. And what with bumping into Pete every five minutes, it all felt awkward and unfamiliar.

Having been deep in thought for a while, she looked up to find Lucy studying her.

'What?' asked Belle.

'I was just trying to decide if you two are going to fall in love or kill each other,' said Lucy, leaning her head on one side whilst she studied her friend.

'Love?' spluttered Belle. 'I think you'd better just settle for a nice clean murder.'

After all, whatever had happened in the past, there was no way she was ever going to fall in love with Pete Kennedy. No way at all.

23

Monday evenings were normally the quietest night of the week but Pete's family had decided to celebrate Cathy's birthday in The Black Swan and had invited all their friends to join them.

Thankfully Angie's awful food had been thrown out along with the rest of the kitchen so Pete and Josh had organised for a substantial buffet to be brought in by an outside caterer instead.

'You could have picked somewhere that wasn't a building site, mum,' said Josh, glancing around the room as he ordered their round of drinks.

'It doesn't matter what it looks like,' said Cathy. 'It's a family business.'

Pete smiled in thanks at his mum but inside he was feeling a little embarrassed about the state of the place. Half the walls were shrouded in plastic sheeting and the dust could be seen hovering in the air in front of the lights. Pete almost found himself hoping for yet another power cut from the dodgy circuit board which had yet to be replaced. At least then nobody would be able to see the mess.

It was the last place he would have chosen to celebrate his

mum's birthday but she had insisted. Despite the disarray, he was grateful for his family's support.

Cathy and Josh headed away to join the large group of people that had turned up to join in the celebrations.

Pete looked across at Belle who had just finished pouring out some more drinks.

'Thanks again for giving up your night off,' he said quietly, as she came closer to use the till.

'It's fine,' she told him. 'It's a nice atmosphere when it's busy like this, isn't it?'

Pete nodded in agreement. There was a warmth about the place when it was full of conversation and laughter. He was beginning to see why it meant so much to the villagers to keep the place open, even during the building work.

The shop and community hub were great places to meet during the day but it was at night that the villagers needed somewhere to go and there was nothing else open.

Spotting some empty glasses, he walked across the lounge to pick them up. Along the way, he was greeted by quite a few people. He was beginning to learn people's names and he found he was starting to enjoy the role of landlord. Only temporarily, of course, he quickly reminded himself.

However, not everyone was enjoying the convivial atmosphere that evening. Ned Shearing was in his normal position next one of the fireplaces and sitting by himself.

'A bit more lively in here than your usual Monday night,' said Pete, with a smile as he picked up the empty pint glass.

As usual, the smile wasn't returned.

'I'll say,' said Ned, with a grimace. 'Can't hear myself think.'

'Would another beer help drown out the noise?' asked Pete.

Ned shook his head and slowly rose from his seat. 'Just the one is enough for me these days,' he said, shrugging on his coat. Pete noticed again that it was threadbare and very worn.

'Are you off, Ned?' asked Cathy, coming to stand next to Pete.

'Can't stay,' said Ned. 'But I'll give you my best wishes for the next year.'

'Thank you,' Cathy told him with a soft smile.

Then, before anyone else could speak, Ned had shuffled away to the front door and left.

Pete turned to look at his mum. 'I can't make him out,' he said. 'He comes in every Monday, hardly says two words and then leaves again after exactly one hour.'

Cathy sighed. 'I know,' she said. 'But he's always been a touchy so and so. Your dad was the only one who could bring him out of himself.'

'Well, dad was a charmer,' said Pete.

Cathy laughed. 'He certainly was. And, of course, he'd known Ned since they played together in a band.'

Pete was startled. 'Ned was in a band with Dad?' he said.

Cathy looked at him, surprised. 'Didn't you know? In those days he was known as Noddy. The drummer that your dad played with for many years.'

Pete couldn't believe it. He couldn't reconcile Ned the grumpy old man with the vibrant, almost manic drummer called Noddy whom he had watched so many times on YouTube playing with his dad in the early days of his career.

'I can't believe it's the same man,' said Pete, shaking his head.

Cathy shrugged. 'We all get older, love,' she said, with a sad smile. 'And I think life's been pretty hard for Ned especially since we lost your dad. Your dad could always slip him a fiver and get away with it. But he won't accept anything from anyone else. Not that we haven't all tried, anyway.'

'Maybe I can try and talk to him,' said Pete, wondering how he could help.

Cathy's eyes filled up. 'You're so like your dad,' she said softly.

Pete found he couldn't hold her gaze for too long. The thought of his dad still pained him, especially with the secret that burned deep inside.

'I'm so thankful to have my whole family around me today,' carried on Cathy, her voice a little tremulous. 'It's made for one of the best birthdays I can remember.'

'Mum...' began Pete.

'I know, I know,' she replied quickly. 'You're not here for long. But that doesn't mean that I can't enjoy being with you in the meantime.'

Suddenly someone called out her name so Cathy gave Pete's arm a quick squeeze before fixing on a bright smile as she wandered away.

* * *

Belle hadn't minded too much about giving up her night off to help out behind the bar especially as it was a happy celebration of Cathy's birthday. Besides, she wasn't sure that Pete would have been able to cope with such a large crowd by himself.

She felt a little guilty about having to forgo her meeting with Grandma Tilly to complete some more quilts but in a way it was somewhat of a relief as the secrecy didn't sit well with her. She was still concerned about Grandma Tilly's health but was pleased to see her that evening in fine form, telling a group of people nearby about her recent trip out to Willow Tree Hall.

As she went across to the fireplace, Belle pulled out her phone and made sure the volume was turned up so she could hear it above the noise of the crowded bar. She was expecting a call from her aunt and uncle now that they had settled into daily life on the cruise ship.

She had just added another log on the fire when Dodgy Del rushed in.

'It's pouring down out there,' he said, quickly removing his soaking wet coat and hanging it on the chair that Ned had just vacated. 'Must be the start of that storm they're talking about for later this week.'

'You're a bit late tonight,' she said as Del collapsed onto a chair.

'Had to make an important purchase,' said Del, giving her a wink as he pulled out a somewhat sodden box from underneath his jumper.

Belle raised her eyes. 'I hope that's not a box of soggy chocolates for me,' she said.

Del laughed. 'You don't wanna eat this lot,' he told her. 'They're indoor fireworks.'

Belle was immediately alarmed. 'Del...' she began in a warning tone.

'What's going on?' asked Tom and Lucy, coming to join her.

'Del's got indoor fireworks,' Belle told them in a pointed tone.

The couple looked equally worried and immediately took a step backwards.

'No, no, they're all right,' said Del. 'They've got hardly any gunpowder in them at all these days thanks to bloomin' health and safety.'

Lucy rolled her eyes. 'I'd like to believe you but seeing as I almost lost my eyebrows thanks to your flammable gin last summer, I'm going to sit well out of the way over here with Keith.'

Amber and Molly followed Lucy and the dog to the safety of a far corner of the lounge.

However, Tom remained and had been joined by Josh. They

were both now staring down looking somewhat alarmed by the contents of the box.

'Isn't a bit early for fireworks?' asked Josh.

'I want to test them out tonight to see if I can sell a few before bonfire night,' said Del, who was always looking to make a quick profit where he could.

Grandma Tilly also joined the small group. 'I remember these from years ago,' she said. 'They were always pretty pathetic.'

Josh nodded in agreement but as Del opened up the box, he still took a step sidewards so that his grandmother was behind him.

'Oy!' cried out Grandma Tilly. 'I can't see all the excitement.'

'That was the point,' muttered Josh, as they all watched Del light the first firework.

As it turned out, Josh had nothing to fear regarding his grandmother or anyone else being hurt.

Belle looked down at the barely glowing lump on the table. 'Is that it?' she asked, laughing with relief.

Del frowned. 'The bloke said they were top notch,' he said.

'Try another one,' said Tom, taking another small step away from the table.

But again, the next firework was yet another disappointment. In fact, it didn't even glow this time.

'I'll get you a pint,' said Belle, relieved that her concerns had all been for nothing.

'If you can bear to tear yourself away from all the excitement,' said Tom, laughing.

However Del could find no humour in the situation and looked most upset that he had wasted his money.

'What's going on?' asked Pete, when Belle headed back behind the bar to pour Del's pint.

'Dodgy Del has bought the worst indoor fireworks ever,' she told him, laughing.

Pete glanced over to where the small group were still gathered next to the fireplace. 'Shouldn't he be testing them out on a non-flammable surface?' he said with a frown. 'And further away from the fire?'

'Don't worry,' said Belle. 'They're pretty unexceptional. You'll get more flare from a single match.'

She took Del's pint over to where there were now four lumps of leftover sludge on the table.

'I hope you're going to clear that up,' said Belle, as she placed his pint of beer on the table. 'The new furniture doesn't arrive for a few weeks yet.'

'This is awful, Del,' said Josh, shaking his head. 'It's not exactly a great spectacle is it?'

Pete came over to stand next to her, obviously still worried until he saw the extent of the fireworks. 'Maybe you should be paying us for the privilege of watching this disaster,' he said, joining in the laughter.

Even Keith, the dog, had wandered back to see what was going on and had settled down underneath the table so that he could warm himself next to the fire.

'I still don't believe I was mugged like this,' said Del, lighting the next one to watch it go out almost immediately.

'One born every minute,' said Grandma Tilly, giving him a sympathetic pat on the shoulder.

'Good job you're not organising the village bonfire night fireworks this year,' said Tom.

With a heavy sigh, Del brought out the last firework which was a different shape to all others. It looked like a small, fat tube which he stood upright on the surface.

'Oh well,' he said, holding out his lighter to the firework. 'Let's hope I've saved the best until last.'

Once lit, the tube immediately started to glow brightly. The air was then filled simultaneously with both dark smoke and a large bang which made everyone jump. Suddenly there were huge flares of bright sparks going in all directions and everyone was ducking for cover.

Keith, the dog, immediately shot out from underneath the table in alarm, cannoning Pete into Belle's arms as he ran away.

Such was the force of Keith's doggy muscle, Pete fell over and Belle found herself lying on the floor underneath Pete. She quickly glanced over his shoulder to see that Josh had dragged Grandma Tilly out of the way in time and nobody appeared to be hurt.

She looked up at Pete and blushed, suddenly realising that they were touching from shoulder to feet, every muscle of his blended with hers. His face was inches away and they stared into each other's eyes for a moment.

'You okay?' he asked.

She nodded, feeling somewhat breathless.

He looked at her for a moment longer before lifting his body away from hers. Belle sat up to join him in looking around the lounge. Everyone appeared to be all right, thankfully. Keith, the dog, was hiding underneath Lucy's legs but some crisps were helping keep the shock at bay.

Only Del looked somewhat worse for wear as his face was black from the smoke. In front of him, the small wooden table had completely disintegrated.

There was a stunned silence as everyone stared at Del who finally broke into a wide smile, his teeth white against his blackened face.

'Good job I didn't buy the Catherine wheel instead, eh?' he said, with a grin.

At which point everyone burst into laughter and the birthday party carried on until Pete called for last orders later in the evening.

24

Pete stood at the doorway and peered out through the driving wind and rain that was hammering against the front door that evening. He could hear the tarpaulin on the roof flapping away in the gusts of wind. At least his bedroom was now finally leakproof thanks to some new tiles.

'I don't think anyone else is going to venture out in this tonight,' he said, turning around to look at Belle, who was wiping down a nearby table of yet more dust. 'Shall we call it a night?'

She frowned. 'It's only half past nine,' she told him, glancing up at the clock.

'Yeah, but this weather is going to keep away any customers, I reckon,' he said, hopeful of an early night.

He closed the front door behind him, grateful to shut out the heavy wind and rain that evening.

It had been a full-on couple of days since the builders had begun work. Thankfully they had already completed the majority of the work on the roof so hopefully it would withstand the autumn storm raging outside.

The builders were both competent and friendly. Perhaps too

friendly, he had decided. He didn't like the way a couple of them had been leering at Belle and making her laugh with their dirty jokes. They were supposed to be professionals, after all. He would have a word with Mr Reynolds.

But the real battle was with Belle herself. She questioned every idea that he had, every choice he had made, when all he was trying to do was make the inn a better place to live and work in.

But even that argument didn't seem to settle her down. She was desperate to keep the interior of the inn lounge cosy whilst he wanted to make it more modern and brighter.

She seemed determined to disagree with everything that he was trying to do with the place. And, to be honest, the constant arguing was getting him down. Sometimes, he found himself wishing that he had never got involved.

Which begged the question, why had he?

The answer was something that he had yet to figure out.

Hearing the rain lash against the windows, he glanced outside once more. It was hard to see in the darkness, but in the soft light of the street lamps, he could see the large willow trees that were dotted along the riverbank swaying in the high wind.

'I'm locking the front door,' he announced.

He turned the key in the lock before sliding the top and bottom bolts shut.

As he turned around, he found Belle frowning at him.

'You don't really think that anyone's going to come out tonight, do you?' he asked.

She shrugged her shoulder in response. 'They might,' she replied.

Pete laughed. 'We could shut for a week and I don't think anyone would notice.'

'That's because you don't understand what it means to people around here,' she told him. She sighed. 'Coming in here for an evening or two each week reduces the loneliness for some people. People like Frank and Stanley. And Ned too. Not that I'd expect you to understand about that.'

'About loneliness? What makes you think that I haven't been lonely?' he asked, suddenly keen for her answer.

'I understood that you worked every day and then were out in some fancy restaurant or bar each evening,' she told him. 'At least, that's what you've been telling me. Not much chance of being lonely then, is there?'

'Then you've obviously never been lonely in a crowd,' he blurted out.

Belle gave a start as she looked at him with those big brown eyes of hers. To his surprise, a blush filled her creamy cheeks.

'Have you?' she asked, softly.

He nodded.

'Me too.'

The words were so soft that he almost didn't hear them above the noise of the storm outside.

The front door rattled on its hinges with another gust of wind, breaking the moment and their eye contact.

Belle shivered and turned around to head over to the fireplace to put on another couple of logs. He watched her as she stared down into the flames for a moment.

'You go upstairs, if you're tired,' he heard her say. 'I'll stay down here for a bit. Just in case anybody needs us.'

'Why would they need us?' he asked, bemused.

She looked up at him in surprise. 'Of course,' she murmured, almost to herself. 'You weren't here last year during the storm when the village flooded.'

Pete had heard all about it from his mum, of course. The shop and inn had become beacons of light for the villagers who had been flooded out. Everyone had banded together. His brother had been some kind of hero, helping out stranded elderly villagers in particular.

Pete still felt shame that he had never done anything so heroic in his life. He had been safe and warm in Singapore. As always. Until that moment, he had never felt as if he had been missing out on village life. Then he thought about everyone helping each other in times of need and realised that perhaps something was absent in his life after all.

Sensing that Belle was watching him, he merely nodded and said, 'But I understood that some new flood defences have been built further upstream.'

'Hopefully they'll hold,' she said, nodding. 'But that wind is liable to cause some damage.'

'What happened to the inn in the storm last year?' he said, suddenly feeling vulnerable and glancing at the front door.

'The cellar flooded, but that was all,' she told him.

'I see.' The overhead lights suddenly flickered and he looked at Belle, who was smiling at his reaction.

'Don't worry,' she said. 'It's the same every time the wind gets up. You never know when it will...'

The electricity suddenly cut out completely and the inn was plunged into darkness.

'... Go out,' said Belle.

25

Plunged momentarily into darkness, it took a few moments for Belle's eyes to adjust.

Thankfully, the glow from the fire took the edge of the inky black and she was able to see Pete's horrified face.

'And this happens a lot?' he said, glancing around him in dismay.

'Most of the time when it gets really windy,' she told him. 'The trouble with living in a rural area is that all the electricity comes from overhead lines and they often get ripped up in high winds. You don't remember this from when you were younger?'

Pete shook his head. 'I guess not. What if we had had a restaurant full of customers this evening?' he said, running a hand through his hair.

Belle shrugged her shoulders as she headed over to the high mantelpiece above the fire and picked up a couple of candles which weren't only there for show.

'They'll have to eat a sandwich instead,' she told him, before bending down to light the wicks on the candles from the fire.

'Well, that won't do,' she heard Pete say. 'We need an emergency generator of some sort as backup.'

'It's a fact of countryside life,' she said, as she straightened up. 'There are torches under the counter of the bar, by the way. And more candles too.'

But Pete wasn't listening. 'I'm going to talk to Mr Reynolds first thing,' he said, bringing out his phone to make a note. 'We can't lose business just because of bad weather.'

Belle watched him for a moment. He was so tightly wound up these days. What had happened to the relaxed Pete of old, joking and laughing as he and Josh tried to push each other into the river.

'Well, I'm going to text the girls and then pour myself a drink,' she told him. 'What can I get you?'

He looked up from his phone, somewhat startled. 'Oh, yeah, thanks,' he said. 'A glass of red wine would be nice.'

'You wouldn't say that if you'd already tried the wine,' Belle told him but headed over to the bar anyway. Uncle Mick had never been too fussy about the quality of the wine that he had bought.

She felt around in the dim light under the bar for a torch, which, thankfully, she had checked the batteries of only the previous week. Then she poured out two rather large glasses of red wine and brought them over, along with the torch to the fireside.

Pete had already sat down so she sank into the soft chair opposite and placed the wine glasses on the table between them.

'Thanks,' he said with a sigh. 'What a night!'

'You get used to it,' she told him, thinking that he just wasn't used to rural life any more. She supposed that living in a major city was a stark contrast to life in sleepy Cranbridge.

He took a sip of the wine before making a face. 'Remind me to source some new wine suppliers,' he said, with a grimace.

She brought out her phone from her jeans pocket and checked the WhatsApp group she used with the girls. Amber and Lucy had

already posted that they and their families were okay. Molly was at
her mum's, so Belle knew that she would be all right there.

'Lucy says it's the whole area that's out, according to Tom,' she
said out loud. 'Power's out for at least five miles.'

She watched as Pete was about to place his wine glass on the
table. 'I suppose I should check on the family,' he said, almost to
himself rather than Belle.

'No need,' she told him. 'Amber says that Josh has done that
already.'

'Oh. I see.' Pete frowned before taking a large gulp of wine to fill
the silence.

'I guess Josh has always been local so he's used to it,' said Belle
softly.

Pete stayed quiet, watching the flames in the fire next to them.

If Belle had to guess, she'd have put money that he was actually
feeling guilty about the burden of the family falling onto his older
brother.

'Josh had to get on with it,' she carried on, keen to ease Pete's
pain a little. 'There was no choice when he took over the shop.'

'But I had a choice,' said Pete suddenly. 'And I ran away instead.'

Belle was startled. 'Ran away?' she asked. 'From what?'

He kept staring into the fire as it crackled next to them. 'From
Dad,' he finally said.

Belle opened her mouth to say something and then closed it.
She picked up her glass of wine instead and took a sip, waiting for
him to speak. Eventually he did.

'He was such a force of nature,' began Pete, looking up at Belle
finally.

She nodded and smiled softly. 'He truly was.'

'And when he died so suddenly, it was like I couldn't breathe.
Like my oxygen had been turned off.' He sagged back in his chair
and looked at the flames again. 'I was already regretting taking the

job. I don't know. I just had a bad feeling about it. But after the funeral, Mum and Josh insisted that I still go.'

'They just wanted you to be happy,' said Belle.

He nodded. 'I know. And maybe I was.' He suddenly looked so stricken that Belle had the urge to rush over and give him a hug. 'The trouble was that I was so grateful for the job, I didn't have to think. To worry or even to grieve.' He sighed. 'I'd promised to come back for Christmas, but I couldn't face being in the shop without him there. So I made some kind of excuse.' He gave a grim laugh to himself. 'I had the worst, most miserable Christmas ever. Not that I ever told them that. And then I carried on.'

'Is that why you never came back until now?' asked Belle, surprised that he was being so open all of a sudden.

'Sort of.'

Belle studied him for a moment and knew that he was holding back something. Some secret pain on top of the grief he had spoken about.

'Maybe being here will give you the time you need to grieve,' Belle told him.

'Perhaps.' He smiled to himself. 'I'm jealous of Josh, you know.'

'Why?' she asked.

'Because he's got it all,' said Pete. 'The successful shop, the happy life, the girl. He's living the dream.'

'I don't think he'd say that some mornings when he's opening up the shop at 7 a.m.,' said Belle.

She was grateful to see Pete smile at her small joke.

'Yeah, I have to say, I'm more of a night owl than an early bird,' he said.

'I'd never have guessed,' she said, picking up her glass once more.

She nodded thoughtfully to herself before taking a sip of wine. Despite her sadness at the pain that he had just revealed to her, she was grateful that Pete still trusted her with his innermost thoughts. She also understood why he had stayed away for so long and it had nothing to do with their kiss.

Belle suddenly felt hopeful that they were beginning to find their way back to the friendship that she had missed so much.

26

Pete picked up his glass and drained his red wine in one gulp.

What had just happened?

They were sitting in the soft firelight, which was, admittedly, very comforting and cosy, and suddenly he had revealed his inner-most thoughts, his very soul, to Belle of all people.

He looked across the small table to where she sat. Her pretty face was softly lit by the flames. The sharp retorts, the constant warring, were all gone that evening. In the firelight, she too had become softer around the edges.

She looked up and he was almost embarrassed that she had found him watching her.

She appeared to hesitate before speaking. 'I actually think that Todd would be proud of you for taking on a mess like this,' she said.

'You do?' he asked, stunned.

She nodded before giving him a sly smile. 'Not sure he'd have wanted a fancy restaurant though.'

Pete laughed. 'We might have to agree to disagree about that.' Then he looked at her. 'About this lounge,' he began.

She sighed, but he interrupted her before she could begin to speak.

'Look, why don't you take on the renovation of the lounge,' he said, thinking quickly. 'Decorate it however you'd like. And let me deal with the restaurant side of things.'

Belle was shocked. 'Really?'

'I trust you,' he said.

She looked pleased. 'Thanks. That would mean a lot to me. I've got a few ideas. Maybe even some live music once in a while.'

'That's an idea,' he said, nodding his approval.

They were quiet for a while with just the crackle of the logs on the fire to listen to above the odd gust of wind outside.

Pete looked up at Belle once more. He knew he could trust her. But could he trust her with the biggest secret of all?

In that moment, he knew the answer. She was still his best friend, whatever their differences regarding the inn. She would keep his secret because she cared for him as much as he cared for her. And he so desperately needed someone to talk to about it.

So he pulled out his wallet to where the letter was tucked in the very back. He paused before finally holding it out for her to take.

'What's this?' she asked.

He sighed as she stared down at the faded writing on the envelope. 'After Dad died, we started to clear out a few of his things. Just his underwear and stuff like that. Nothing personal. But, as you would expect with Dad, it was all a bit of a muddle. In his sock drawer, there were various photos and paperwork.' His mouth tightened in a line. 'And this.'

She pulled out the handwritten letter inside and began to read.

He knew it off by heart. Knew exactly what it said and what it was. It was a love letter. From a woman called Felicity, telling Todd how much she loved him. How she would always love him. And that getting married to him had been a dream come true.

Belle looked up at Pete with wide brown eyes.

'You see?' he said. 'He was married before Mum. Maybe he still was when he and Mum were married. I don't know. But what I do know is that it proves that it was all a lie. That love is a lie. That marriage is too.'

Belle looked down at the letter again and reread it before finally folding up the paper and sliding it back into the envelope.

'I don't think that this is as bad as you think,' she said, handing it back to Pete. 'The letter isn't dated. And, to be frank, I've been stuck in the middle of a loveless marriage. Your mum and dad loved each other, deeply.' She took a deep breath. 'You need to talk to someone about this.'

He shook his head. 'I can't. It would destroy Mum.'

'What about Josh?' she asked.

He sagged in his chair. 'And destroy my brother's happy memories too? No, this one's all on me to carry by myself. I won't cause my family any more pain.'

'But you did, don't you see?' said Belle softly.

He looked at her, shocked.

'By holding yourself back,' she told him. 'By running away you did hurt them all, especially your mum. Because she didn't just lose your dad. She lost you too.'

Pete sucked in a deep breath and shook his head as he looked down at the letter he was holding. It was true. He had known it for a long time.

He wasn't sure how long he sat there until Belle leaned forward to cover his hand with hers.

'Well, whatever you decide to do, I'm here for you,' she said.

'Thanks,' he replied.

He felt an easing of the pain that he had carried with him for so long and knew that sharing the secret with Belle had been the right thing to do.

He was shocked at how bereft he felt when she suddenly withdrew her hand from his.

'Well, I think I've bored you long enough,' he said, trying to lighten the atmosphere.

She looked up and smiled at him. 'I'll send you my psychiatrist's bill in the morning,' she told him.

He was grateful for her humour. It had all got far too serious, as far as he was concerned.

But still, he suddenly found himself wanting to know more about her.

'I know you love it here but don't you find it stifling sometimes?' he blurted out.

A frown creased her forehead. 'In what way?' she asked.

'You didn't choose to come here,' he said. 'Don't you want to spread your wings?'

She was quiet for a moment before she took a deep breath. 'Actually, no. I don't. You see, you had two loving parents when you were growing up and a great big brother.'

'He was a pain and you know it,' said Pete grinning.

But Belle shook her head. 'You were, and still are, so lucky,' she told him. 'You must remember what I told you about my parents. How bad it was each and every day.'

He nodded thoughtfully. 'But your aunt and uncle...' said Pete. 'I mean, their constant arguments. Surely they're just as bad?'

'No. Because they were happy to have me here with them,' she told him. 'They couldn't have children, you see. I mean, yes, they blow hot and cold with each other, but never with me. That was the difference.'

She glanced at him and he was startled by the pain that lay deep in her brown eyes. He had a sudden urge to take her in his arms and kiss the pain away forever.

Perhaps the red wine had been stronger than he had initially realised.

It must have been, because he found himself blurting out, 'I always felt horrible about how I left things between us.' He hesitated before adding, 'After the funeral, I mean.'

It had been one kiss. One moment of tenderness from one friend to another.

And yet, some nights over the past three years, he had dreamt about that kiss. Had he imagined it? No. Had he imagined the chemistry that had sizzled between them? He didn't think so.

And sometimes, he wondered what it would be like to kiss Belle again. Properly. Not in the aftermath of an emotional day. But just because he wanted to see what it was like. And whether she felt the same way.

Belle looked at him. He thought he could see her blushing in the firelight, but it was hard to tell. Probably not when she followed up with a casual shrug of her shoulders.

'It's in the past,' she told him. 'Don't worry about it. It was an upsetting day for you and I understood and just wanted to comfort you, that's all. It really wasn't that big a deal.'

Suddenly he wanted to persuade her that it had been very much a big deal actually.

But he didn't want to confuse matters, so he too shrugged his shoulders and said, 'Okay. Well done on deflating my ego.'

She grinned. 'You're welcome,' she told him. 'Always happy to help.'

He ran a hand through his hair, feeling more confused than ever. 'I probably deserved it. Knowing me and what I'm like, I mean.'

'Yeah, you did,' she replied, still smiling.

This was crazy, he thought to himself, shifting uncomfortably in his seat. He was almost awkward around Belle and he had never felt like this before. It was as if returning to Cranbridge had thrown up a whole load of emotions into the air and he wasn't sure how they were all going to land.

He wanted his family to respect what he was doing. He wanted to prove the villagers right with his ideas. He wanted the restaurant to be a success. And, most of all, he wanted Belle to think so too. He wanted to impress her. For her to agree with everything that he had done. And for her to enjoy the change too.

'Did you ever find what you were looking for in Singapore?' she suddenly asked.

'I don't know,' he lied.

But deep down he knew that the truth was that he hadn't.

And he was beginning to think that perhaps he might find it there in Cranbridge instead. But that was impossible, wasn't it?

27

Belle glanced at the grey clouds and rain outside of the window before looking back at the sunny view through a porthole that her aunt and uncle were showing her via FaceTime.

'Lucky you,' she told them, as they turned the camera back on themselves. 'The weather's been terrible here. We lost the power last night it was so windy.'

'We've had a few choppy days out at sea,' said Uncle Mick, with a grimace. 'But it's settled down now that we're in the Caribbean.'

'Wow, sounds amazing,' said Belle.

But to her surprise, Aunty Angie was rolling her eyes. 'It's all right,' she said, in a sullen voice. 'But your uncle wanted to go on a trolley tour of one of the islands yesterday and we wasted most of the day looking at boring dockyards.'

'Oh dear,' said Belle.

'They weren't boring,' snapped Uncle Mick. 'And I said you didn't need to come.'

'So you don't want to spend any time with your own wife now you've made all these new friends onboard? Is that it?' said Aunty Angie, glaring at him. 'Right, well, it's lovely to see you, Belle, darling, but I've got Pilates at eleven so I'd better get going. Love you.'

'Love you too,' called out Belle before she heard the cabin door close.

Uncle Mick blew out a sigh. 'I dunno, love,' he said, sounding miserable. 'Maybe this was a bad idea to be stuck together day in and day out for any length of time.'

'Still, only one hundred more days to go, eh?' said Belle, with a sad smile.

Uncle Mick gave a grunt of humour in reply.

* * *

Later on that morning, Belle headed into the community hub to find out if the village had survived the bad weather. She found her friends already in there grabbing a quick coffee and a catch-up.

'There's loads of trees down,' said Molly, who, as social media manager for the local newspaper, was typing up the latest Twitter posts.

'Thankfully the power wasn't off for too long,' said Lucy, who had been making some coffee for them in the small kitchen nearby.

Belle sat on one of the sofas in the lounge area and Keith, the dog, immediately came over to lean against her and rest his head on her knee.

'So your aunt and uncle are on a luxury cruise and hating every minute of it?' asked Lucy, placing two mugs of coffee on the table between them.

'I'm not sure they're hating it,' said Belle, stroking the dog's soft furry ears. 'Just each other.'

Molly looked across at her from her nearby desk. 'Are you okay?' she asked. 'It must be really upsetting being left behind when your aunt and uncle are away for such a long time.'

Belle smiled. 'To be honest, I'm quite grateful that I'm not stuck in a cabin with those two arguing their way around the world!' she replied with a grin.

Molly shook her head. 'That's not what I meant,' she said, not returning the smile. 'It must be tough for you at the moment and, just remember, the girls and I are here for you.'

Belle smiled at her friend, grateful that they knew her so well that they expected her to be hiding her feelings as usual.

'Hey, are you still free on Monday nights?' asked Molly. 'That new Dwayne Johnson movie's out and I thought we could go and see it.'

Belle hesitated. 'I can't,' she said eventually.

'Won't Pete give you the time off?' asked Amber, with a frown. 'That's not fair. I'll get Josh to have a word with him.'

'It's not that,' said Belle quickly. 'I just can't make this Monday.'

'Why not?' asked Lucy, as all three friends turned to look at her.

'I, er...' stammered Belle. She couldn't think of a lie quick enough that wouldn't involve Grandma Tilly.

'You have a date!' said Molly, looking excited. 'Who is it?'

Belle immediately shook her head. 'Of course I don't.'

'Then what?' asked Amber.

Belle picked up her phone. 'I can't tell you,' she said.

'What do you mean?' they all chorused together. 'Of course you can tell us.'

'I just can't,' said Belle. 'That's all.'

'Well, this is all very strange,' said Lucy, looking across at Amber. 'Oh! Don't let me forget. I've got those forms for Grandma Tilly if she's in the shop today.'

'What forms?' asked Amber.

'Something to do with her pension,' said Lucy, with a shrug. 'She got muddled with the form and wanted Tom to give her a hand filling it out.'

'Okay,' said Amber. 'I'll give them to her later.'

But Belle was worried. Grandma Tilly was having trouble sewing and now filling out forms. Something was wrong and she was keeping it a secret from everyone.

She wondered once more as to whether she should talk to Pete about it. The conversation between them the previous evening about Pete's reaction to losing his father as well as finding the letter from his dad's other wife had somehow brought them closer. He had opened up to her and she was pleased that they were finally talking. Their chat in front of the fire had been nice. More than nice. It had felt right, as if they were finding their way back to each other after all the recent awkwardness.

She couldn't stop herself from smiling in memory.

She slowly became aware of the three other women staring at her in shock.

'What?' she snapped.

Amber glanced across at her friends before clearing her voice. 'It's just, I don't think I've ever seen you smile like that before,' she said eventually.

'Are you saying I'm miserable most of the time?' asked Belle.

'No, no,' said Amber, shaking her head. 'It's just that...'

'You're a fantastic friend,' said Lucy quickly. 'You're kind and generous too. And we love you, okay? But you can be a little...'

'Prickly,' said Molly, before biting her lip.

'Defensive,' volunteered Amber.

'We've just never seen you look all soft like that before,' said Lucy, with a shrug.

'I can be soft and girly,' argued Belle.

'We know,' said Amber. But her tone of voice didn't agree with her words.

'Do you want to be soft and girly?' asked Lucy, in a gentle tone. 'And if so, why all of a sudden?'

Belle hesitated long enough for the other three to break into wide smiles at her.

'Yeah, we know,' said Molly, with a giggle.

'I'm glad somebody does,' said Belle, confused. 'Would you mind telling me?'

'It's Pete,' said Amber. 'You like him.'

'In no way was the word "like" used in any context regarding Pete Kennedy,' said Belle, quickly.

'Right,' said Lucy, with a wink. 'We hear you.'

Belle suddenly found she couldn't sit still and began to pace up and down the lounge, nearly tripping over Keith, the dog, as she went.

'I mean, do I think he's a good guy? Possibly,' she said, more to herself than to her friends. 'Is he totally misguided in his attempts with this fancy restaurant? Well, obviously the man is clueless. But I think his intentions are good. I just wish he'd listen once in a while. Not that he's a bad person, of course.'

She stopped suddenly and turned to face her friends who were smiling up at her.

'But I don't like him like that, okay?' she told them in her firmest possible tone of voice.

They all nodded, still grinning.

Belle rolled her eyes at her friends.

They were all jumping to completely the wrong conclusion. Such was their desperation to match her up in a relationship.

But they were barking up the wrong tree completely with Pete, weren't they?

28

Pete was feeling optimistic for the first time in days when he rushed into the bar later that week.

'I've had a reply,' he announced to Belle. 'To the chef's position.'

'That's great,' she replied, still sounding a little hesitant about the whole thing.

'He's got a great résumé,' said Pete, anxious to reassure her. 'Says he's almost Michelin-star standard. Great reviews. It's all very promising.'

'So why hasn't he got a job already?' murmured Belle.

Pete looked at her. 'You're so cynical,' he told her, rolling his eyes. 'As it turns out, he's been working on a cruise ship and is looking to stay on dry land for a while. So the good news is that he'll be used to working in a tight galley kitchen so our little space should be a doddle for him.'

Belle narrowed her eyes but said nothing.

* * *

The following day, there was a knock on the door at exactly 11 a.m., which Pete thought was extremely promising. The man was obviously very professional.

If a little short, he realised, as he opened up the door. The man standing in front of him barely reached shoulder height. He had to be 5ft tall and not an inch more. This worried Pete who wondered whether the fancy new industrial kitchen he had ordered would be a little high for the chef.

'Hi,' said Pete, holding out his hand. 'I'm Pete Kennedy, the co-owner. You must be Andrew Deboss.'

'Actually, it's pronounced Andre du Bois,' said the man in a very plummy accent.

'Of course,' said Pete quickly. 'Do come in, er, Andre.'

The chef followed him inside and his eyes clicked open wide at the state of disarray from all the building work. The wallpaper had been stripped off and was now being plastered in readiness for a fresh coat of paint. The electrics were still being updated so there were large areas dug out in the walls hence a few dust sheets hanging haphazardly. In addition, the new spotlights hadn't arrived so there were just holes in the ceiling waiting to be filled with downlighters. And the area behind the bar was still only half painted.

'As you can see,' Pete told him. 'We're a work in progress. But this is the main lounge and over there will be the brand-new restaurant.'

'And what happens at the end of this work?' said Andre, his lips curling up in distaste.

'We will become the best gastronomic inn experience in the area,' said Pete, proudly.

Andre's eyebrows clicked up a degree. 'You will?'

'Absolutely,' said Pete, in a confident tone. 'Let me show you the plans for the restaurant area.'

He led Andre through the small opening swept aside by the plastic curtain and into the large room beyond.

Once more, the wallpaper had been stripped and the whole area needed ceiling lights, new paint and new furniture. Pete was sure that it would soon look far more modern and less like, well, a building site.

He brought out his phone to show Andre his ideas for the decoration of the restaurant and was somewhat relieved to see the chef nodding in approval.

'Very nice,' said Andre eventually. 'Now where I will create my masterpieces?'

'That too is a work in progress,' said Pete as he led the chef past the bar and towards the kitchen area. 'But it's all in hand.'

He hoped he wasn't laying it on too thick, but he felt a certain desperation at that point. Andre was the only person to have replied to the advert. The rural location had put off many potential cooks from replying. So he really did need to ensure that Andre was going to stay with them to get the place up and running.

He kept his fingers crossed as they entered the kitchen. The old units and out-of-date appliances had already been stripped away, leaving the bare bones of the room. But now that it had been plastered it began to look a little bigger, given the blank canvas that it now was.

'You have the designs for the kitchen?' asked Andre, somewhat imperiously.

Pete suppressed his snapped reply at the man's snobbish attitude. It would just take a little getting used to, that was all.

Once more, Pete showed him the plans that he had agreed with Mr Reynolds.

Andre nodded. 'It is adequate, I suppose,' he said, with a sniff.

'Of course, the menus will be entirely up to you,' said Pete, still anxious to butter the man up. 'With my approval, of course.'

'I work only by using the best ingredients,' said Andre. 'When you begin to cut corners, then the quality plummets.'

'I agree wholeheartedly,' said Pete. 'We're going to open with a gala dinner at the end of the month, inviting local dignitaries and reviewers. Give it the best possible start and press release that we can.'

'That will not be a problem when they see my food,' said Andre imperiously. 'What staff will be you providing for me?'

'Staff?' said Pete, with a small gulp. That would mean extra wages and heaven knows how the books were going to balance as it was with Andre's steep wage demands.

'I will require a commis chef at the very least to help preparations,' Andre told him. 'You cannot expect me to prepare everything, surely?'

'Not at all,' said Pete, smoothly. 'In fact, we have a local chap all ready to go. He's fully trained and keen to work.'

Whether Dodgy Del's nephew was up to the task was another worry to add to Pete's growing list.

'I'm glad to hear it,' said Andre.

'So?' asked Pete. 'What do you think? Would you like the job?'

The silence stretched out.

For one awful moment, Pete thought Andre wasn't going to accept. He was the only one that had replied to the advert. The only hope for getting the gastronomic experience he had decided on for the inn. The future of the whole inn hung in the balance at that moment.

Finally Andre nodded. 'I think we shall give it three-month trial and go from there,' he said.

'Excellent,' replied Pete, grinning with relief.

When they were back at the front door, the two men shook hands before Andre left.

Pete sagged against the door frame briefly. They had a chef! The man might be somewhat annoying in his snobbish attitude, but Pete didn't care as long as he could cook like a dream.

At last, the future looked bright. He hoped.

But still, deep down, there was the nagging thought that the restaurant would be missing something when it opened. He just didn't know what it was.

29

Belle woke up in a hot sweat. Was she ill? she wondered, as she threw off the heavy blankets that she had always slept under in the colder months.

Then she heard a small ticking noise and realised it was the radiator next to the bed. She tentatively reached a hand out and felt that it was piping hot. The heating was on. The heating was never on! It had never worked! And yet, here it was.

She lay back in bed and allowed herself a little giggle. It was ridiculous to feel luxury such as heating had made her day, but it truly had. She hadn't realised how cold she had felt for so very long. The fireplaces were all very nice, but once the fire had died out during the night, the bedroom became cold and draughty.

No wonder she felt so hot under her normal four or five blankets.

She contemplated a shower, wondering if she could face the cool water until the boiler heated up later on. Then she sat bolt upright. The boiler had been replaced. The heating was on. They now had constant hot water.

She sprang out of bed and flung open the door to rush across the corridor in her pyjamas. Then, in the sanctity of the bathroom, she realised that even the towels were now warm and toasty on the new heated towel rail. Belle laughed again and immediately stepped into the hot shower.

The water was steamy and hot and she allowed herself the longest shower that she could ever remember having. It was pure luxury.

By the time she got out, her cheeks were glowing with the steam and heat. But she found herself smiling at her reflection in the mirror. At the time, she had questioned Pete's extravagant spending, but right now she sent up a silent prayer.

In that moment, she was truly grateful for Pete taking over the inn. Maybe, just maybe, these small changes were good.

Smiling to herself, she flung open the bathroom door and came face to face with the man himself as he headed down the corridor.

'Good morning,' she said, giving him a wide smile.

'Good morning,' he said, smiling back at her. 'You're in an awfully good mood. Did you start drinking early today?'

'Ha ha,' she said, fixing the towel around her a little tighter. 'If you're speaking to Mr Reynolds today, can you tell him that the boiler is an absolute winner. That shower was incredible.'

'I'm glad you approve,' he told her. 'Personally I prefer not having frostbite on a daily basis.'

Belle nodded thoughtfully. 'I guess I just got used to the colder temperature,' she said. 'When I woke up this morning and the heating was on, I couldn't believe it. Then all that lovely hot water.' Her eyes gleam. 'Think how long a hot bubble bath I could have as well.'

Pete leaned back against the wall, his hands in his jeans pockets. 'You know, that new bathtub is big enough for two.' He broke into a grin, his eyes gleaming. 'We have to watch the pennies on the heating bills, so it's an idea.'

For some reason, Belle's cheeks suddenly felt extremely warm again. 'Well, I'd better get dressed,' she said, heading across to her bedroom.

But on the way, she tripped over one of the still loose floorboards that had yet to be fixed and fell straight against the wall.

'Ow,' she moaned, clutching her head, which was swimming a little after banging against the wall.

'Are you okay?' she heard Pete say. 'Here, come and sit down.'

She felt his hands on her bare arms as he led her into her bedroom to sit her down on the bed.

Her head was still a little fuzzy as he sat down next to her, placing his arm around her shoulders.

'Don't worry, I've got you,' he told her.

After a few moments, the swimming feeling began to pass.

'I think I'm feeling better,' she told him.

'Just keep breathing in and out,' he told her. 'I'm just going to watch your chest rise and fall to make sure.'

'Funny man,' she told him, finally standing up. 'I'm okay now.'

But his joke had raised a smile and she felt much better.

She heard Pete chuckle and turned to look at him as he stood up and headed to the door.

'What?' she asked.

'Never thought Belle Clarke would ignore a comment like that,' he said. 'Normally you would have decked me for flirting with you.'

She shrugged her bare shoulders. 'I'm in an awfully good mood this morning,' she told him, with a smile. 'So I let that one go.'

Pete nodded thoughtfully. 'Perhaps I should have installed the heating first,' he said, with an even cheekier grin.

'Perhaps you should have done,' she said, before heading over and slowly clicking the door shut.

She could hear his soft laughter as he walked away down the corridor.

The heat was still burning her cheeks and it had nothing to do with the central heating, nor the hot water. It had all to do with Pete's flirting.

In that moment, she realised that she was developing a very serious crush on Pete.

* * *

Pete was still smiling to himself as he headed down the stairs and into the inn lounge.

Funny how the small changes could have a big effect on a person, he thought. Especially Belle, of all people.

He hadn't expected to see her in just a bath towel that morning and had been a bit stunned when she had suddenly come out of the bathroom.

He stopped walking as he came into the bar. He could still smell her soft shower soap. Could still see the droplets of water on the creamy skin of her shoulders.

She had no right to look that beautiful first thing in the morning, he told himself. He was used to pretty but prickly Belle. Not the warm, giggling, semi-naked apart from a bath towel Belle.

She had never looked more desirable and he had to reach out for the counter to steady himself.

Well, this wouldn't do, he told himself. He couldn't fancy Belle. He and Josh had always referred to her as their little sister and that was how it would remain.

And yet, his quickened breath and the racing pulse told him otherwise. The vision of how good she had looked in that bath towel kept floating into his mind.

He shook his head to clear the vision, but it wouldn't go away. The trouble was, having seen her in just that towel, he wasn't sure if he would be able to think of her as just Belle ever again.

30

Later on that morning, despite the hot shower that she had enjoyed, Belle's good mood had faded somewhat.

'It may be warmer in here, but I'm so fed up of dusting each and every day,' she said, wiping the counter clean and showing Pete the results on the other side of the dishcloth. She already felt in need of another glorious power shower.

He grimaced at the dirt. 'It's the plaster,' he told her. 'The dust gets everywhere.'

'I know,' said Belle. 'I'm worried that my hair looks permanently grey,' she told him, patting her head.

'Maybe it's just turning grey from living with me,' he replied.

She smiled. 'Maybe,' she said.

He walked away and she thought how fine a pair of jeans could cling to a fine pair of legs.

She had to wake up from this dream, she told herself. Otherwise who knew where it would lead to. And she knew that the result would always be the same when it was to do with love. Pain and heartache. Neither of which she had any desire to endure.

After all, weren't her aunt and uncle a prime example of love going wrong? They were now in Florida and had rung her to chat about their trip to the Everglades.

'I got bitten to death,' Aunty Angie had said, showing her arm dotted with mosquito bites. 'And those alligators are scary.'

'That's because their mouths are almost as large as yours,' Uncle Mick had murmured.

Unfortunately, Aunty Angie had heard him and the call had finished in the midst of yet another argument.

Love was definitely something to be endured, thought Belle.

Thankfully she was spared having to think about her mixed emotions for Pete any longer as Dodgy Del turned up with his young nephew who was going to be interviewed as a commis chef.

Andre, the new chef, wouldn't be returning until a fortnight's time. Belle was secretly quite pleased. Her first impression when they had met briefly had been of a pretentious snob and she wasn't sure that her opinion was going to change at all.

But Pete had tried to reassure her that Andre's credentials were excellent, so perhaps his food would put pay to her concerns about his personality.

Dodgy Del's nephew, however, was almost non-talkative as he stood there, arms crossed in front of his chest. He glanced up every once in a while, his eyes screwed up as if trying to suss out whether or not he could escape.

Belle recognised the look as one she had worn when she had first arrived in Cranbridge all those years ago. It was a look of total mistrust from the twenty-one-year-old Brad. Life had dealt him a hard hand and he didn't trust anyone.

'So, Brad, you want to be our commis chef?' said Pete, in an amiable tone of voice.

Silence followed, so Del gave the lad a nudge in the ribs.

'Ooof,' said the young man, rubbing his torso. 'Not so hard.'

'Well, speak up,' said Del, rolling his eyes at Pete and Belle. 'They ain't psychic, you know.'

'Suppose I do,' said Brad eventually.

He had dark hair which was almost hidden under his beanie hat and a beard which was concealed under the collar of his battered Puffa jacket. But Belle thought that it was a good-looking face which was still scowling back at them.

'Excellent,' said Pete, his tone faltering somewhat. 'And where have you worked before?'

Brad gave a shrug. 'Here and there,' he mumbled.

Del sighed heavily. 'Sorry about this,' he told them, looking embarrassed. 'The truth is that he's struggled to get a job since he left college.'

'And what course did you do?' asked Pete.

Finally Brad came to life. 'Commis Chef standard apprentice- ship after Level Two Food and Beverage diploma,' he replied. 'Passed them both too.'

Belle could hear the pride in his voice and her heart nearly burst at the young man who was so desperate to be given a hand up in life.

'Well, that's great,' she found herself saying, looking to Pete. 'Isn't it?'

'Er, yes,' he replied. 'So if we give you the job, you'll be working for a world-renowned chef. We're planning big things for the restaurant here so you'll need to work hard. The hours won't be that sociable as it'll be in the evenings.'

'He doesn't mind,' said Del, quickly. 'That'll keep him out of mischief at night anyway.'

'I don't make mischief,' said Brad. 'It was all a mistaken identity thing, weren't it?'

'Yeah,' said Del. 'And the moon comes out during the day and the sun at night. Anyway, they don't need to hear about all that. You keep your nose clean here otherwise you'll hear about it from me.'

Brad shrugged his shoulders again. 'Don't care,' he muttered.

Belle knew he was lying and looked at Pete with desperately pleading eyes. 'Well, I think we should at least give him a trial run,' she said. 'Same time as Andre seems fair.'

Pete's eyes widened, but he seemed to give in to some kind of internal struggle as he turned to Brad and said, 'Well, the job's yours if you want it.'

Brad looked up at them, shocked, with piercing blue eyes. 'For real?' he asked.

'Absolutely,' said Pete. 'I'll be in touch with a date and I'm sure Andre will want to meet you before the big opening, but yeah, welcome to The Black Swan.'

He held out his hand for it to be shaken, but Del stepped forward and shook it instead.

'You won't regret it, mate,' said Del, shaking Pete's hand so violently that Belle thought it may dislocate his shoulder.

'Let's have a drink to celebrate, shall we?' asked Belle.

'We'll just give his mum a call and then you're on,' said Del, tugging Brad over to a far corner as he brought out his phone. 'She's going to be made up that you've got a job at last. Especially one working for Todd Kennedy's son.'

'Who?' asked Brad.

Del rolled his eyes. 'Youth of today,' he muttered before turning back to his nephew. 'He was a famous guitarist, lad.'

Brad shrugged his shoulders. 'I only listen to rap.'

'Of course you do,' said Del, blowing out a long sigh.

Pete and Belle walked back to the bar in silence before he turned to look at her with raised eyebrows.

'What have I done?' he asked.

'You've given someone a helping hand,' she told him. 'I don't think you'll regret it.'

She hoped he didn't hear the hesitation in her voice.

'Hmmm,' said Pete. 'Well, I guess time will tell.'

'Just give him a chance,' she urged him. 'He looks like he needs it. And we all need a chance now and then.'

She glanced over to where Brad was muttering down the phone presumably to his mother.

As she looked back, she found Pete studying her with his green eyes.

'What?' she asked.

'You're a good person,' he said softly, reaching out to brush a stray lock of hair out of her eyes.

She caught her breath as his fingers briefly touched her face. Her skin felt as if it were on fire.

Then he abruptly let go as Del and Brad headed over to the bar for their celebratory drinks.

And Belle was left even more bewildered than ever before by Pete.

31

There remained one last test for Brad, the new commis chef, to overcome. Unfortunately it was quite a big one, thought Belle as she introduced the young man to Andre.

Andre gave Brad a narrow-eyed stare as he looked him up and down, although it was mainly up as he was so short and Brad was quite tall.

'Hands,' he snapped.

Brad looked bewildered and glanced at Belle for help with wide eyes.

'Show me your hands,' said Andre, rolling his eyes. 'I need to check them for cleanliness. I won't have bad hygiene in my kitchen.'

Brad clenched his hands briefly by his side as if he was going to throw a punch at Andre. And who could blame him, thought Belle. Having only met him twice, the new chef had brought on her own daydreams of accidentally dropping a large saucepan over his head. She was hopeful that his credentials were true and that he really was a talented chef. But his people skills left an awful lot to be desired.

Finally Brad held out his hands for inspection. Andre leaned forward to study them closely before straightening up with a nod of approval.

'Well, that at least is acceptable,' he replied. 'But your clothing is not.'

Brad was wearing jeans and a green sweatshirt. 'I don't wear this when I'm cooking,' he said, his tone sullen. 'I have my own chef's jacket and trousers, of course.'

Andre's eyebrows rose slightly, as if almost impressed. 'I'm glad to hear it,' he replied. 'Now, let's see if you are worthy of the title of being my commis chef.'

Belle felt her nostrils flare in irritation. 'We have already employed Brad and he will be here for a three-month trial, just like you,' she snapped.

Andre turned to look at her. 'But this is my kitchen. My empire,' he said smoothly at her.

'It's okay,' said Brad quietly. 'I'm good enough.'

Belle glanced over at the young man, who was suddenly looking very determined.

'Well then, let's see,' said Andre, walking towards the long kitchen counter. 'I need these vegetables finely chopped.'

Brad grabbed the small rucksack he had brought with him and produced a couple of expensive-looking knives.

'Good brand,' said Andre with a nod of what appeared to be approval.

'Saved up for them 'specially,' said Brad, looking proud of himself.

Brad almost strutted over to the counter, thought Belle. He was confident of his abilities, she realised, with hope filling her heart. He just needed to be given a chance.

But even she was amazed when his knife flew over the vegetables in a matter of seconds. It was as if a film had been sped up, such was the speed at which he prepared the vegetables.

Having completed his instruction, Brad stepped back, a smug look on his face.

Andre leaned down to study the chopped vegetables in silence before straightening up once more. 'Not bad,' he said eventually.

Brad appeared to grow taller in that moment at the unexpected praise. Belle thought that Brad hadn't had much encouragement in his life so far. He looked proud of himself, as well he should.

'Of course, there are better techniques out there,' carried on Andre. 'I myself was trained at the Iles de Paris by none other than Pierre Madiot. One of the finest chefs in the world. So, in his eyes, you would be doing it completely wrong.'

At once, Brad deflated back down in front of Belle's eyes. She groaned inwardly. Andre was awful. The man didn't have any idea how to motivate or give people confidence. He would be a completely useless mentor to Brad.

She spun on her heel and marched out of the kitchen, leaving Andre still regaling stories of his glamorous days in a Parisian kitchen. She wondered why he hadn't stayed there. Surely The Black Swan was a major comedown for someone whose ego could hardly fit through the door?

She found Pete in the new restaurant where the new spotlights were being placed either side of the oak beams overhead.

'I need to talk to you,' she hissed.

He looked surprised at her angry tone. 'What's up?' he asked, letting her take his arm and drag him over to a quiet corner.

'It's about Andre,' said Belle, through gritted teeth.

Pete leaned against wall and crossed his arms. 'What now?' he asked, with a heavy sigh.

'I don't like him,' said Belle.

'Why am I not surprised?' murmured Pete. 'Is it because he's male?'

She glared at him. 'No! I have some very nice male friends actually,' she told him.

His eyebrows shot up. 'You do? Who?' he asked.

Belle was perplexed by his surprised reaction. 'Well, your brother for a start. Look, can we get back to talking about Andre?'

'If we must,' said Pete, who was also frowning now.

'I just feel like he's looking down his nose at us the whole time,' said Belle.

Pete shook his head. 'No,' he told her. 'I think that's just his whole chef demeanour.'

'Yeah, right,' she drawled. 'Listen, he was pretty awful to Brad when I was in the kitchen with them. Shouldn't he be mentoring him? Encouraging him? Rather than putting him down.'

'Haven't you seen those Gordon Ramsay shows?' said Pete. 'He's not exactly all warm and fuzzy, is he?'

'No, I suppose not,' said Belle, biting her lip as she considered whether Pete was right.

'Just give Andre a chance,' urged Pete.

'I will if he gives the rest of us the same courtesy,' said Belle before sighing heavily. She looked around the space which was still a work in progress. 'Do you really think we're going to be ready for the first of November?'

It looked a mess and she wasn't sure how on earth it was going to turn into the dust-free, gorgeous restaurant that Pete had promised her.

'Mr Reynold's team seem to have it all in hand,' said Pete. 'Look, let me deal with Andre. He might be a diva, but if his food is as good as I'm hoping it will be, he can be as awful as he likes in the kitchen. Just as long as it translates into reservations and lots of bookings.'

'Is that all that matters to you?' she asked.

He looked down at her with his eyes suddenly serious. 'It's business,' he told her. 'If you want encouragement and a spirit of togetherness then the community hub is right over the other side of the river.'

'Why can't we have both?'

'Because that won't balance the books and then The Black Swan will close forever,' he told her in a solemn tone. 'So just trust me, okay? A quarter of all inns have shut down since the year 2000. I don't want The Black Swan to join that number.'

'Me neither,' said Belle.

'Good,' said Pete with a nod. 'Then for once we're in agreement.'

As he walked away to discuss something with the electrician, Belle sighed again. She was seriously worried.

What if the inn was successful but lost everything that she had always held dear about it? What about the community and village as a whole? What if the inn no longer felt like home at all?

She knew that she had to trust Pete and hope it was all okay. Otherwise last orders would be called on her time at The Black Swan forever.

32

Pete's initial rush of confidence about the way the renovations for the inn had been going had begun to fade somewhat. Standing outside the inn and looking down at Mr Reynold's estimate for the huge costs so far, that hope kept disappearing.

The initial budget had gone way over the projected sum as further problems continued to be discovered. This time it was the water pipes that had corroded and needed replacing.

Perhaps Mick and Angie had the right idea to sell up before they were declared bankrupt, but it was too late now. Pete had sunk every penny into The Black Swan and he had no choice but to keep going forward towards the grand opening of the restaurant.

He had surprised himself by being so worried about it. Not that he let on to anyone about his concerns. Especially Belle. She was already concerned enough without him adding to her unease.

That was it. Perhaps it was just unease. After all, this was an entirely new business venture for him. But it felt more than that. It felt like make or break, as if there was far more riding on the success of the renovation than just a run-down inn in a village that he had used to call home.

But he had never failed at anything before. And he wouldn't fail this time either, he decided.

But when he looked down at his iPad again, rereading the email that Andre had just sent him, there it was again. That tiny pinprick of unease.

He hitched his mobile under his chin, still looking at the iPad with a gnawing sense of worry in his stomach. Perhaps it was just the thought of all the food and he'd only just had lunch.

'Hi, Andre,' he said, when the call was answered. 'It's Pete. Thanks for the sample menus. They're, er, certainly interesting.'

'They're very of the moment,' said Andre, almost purring down the line in his smooth way.

'Are you sure? They seem pretty fancy,' said Pete.

The expensive ingredients whirled in front of his face. Foie gras. Lobster. Wild boar. Scallops.

'Could we not use a few items that don't cost as much?' asked Pete, scrolling past the sample menus that Andre had provided and on to the costing for the actual food. It was an eye-watering amount, far more than he had anticipated having to spend.

'I'm afraid, in culinary terms, you get what you pay for,' said Andre.

'I see.' Except, despite his words, Pete was having trouble under-standing.

'You did want a gastronomic experience?' prompted Andre down the line. 'The best gastro restaurant in the area?'

Pete nodded. 'Yes,' he said. 'I believe I did say that.'

'Then these are the menus that will gain you the best possible outcome,' said Andre. There was a short silence before he added, 'And the best reviews from popular food critics as well, of course.'

That ended Pete's hesitation almost immediately. Reviews were vital in getting a new restaurant up and running. The classier the establishment, the better in his opinion.

'Of course,' carried on Andre. 'If you wish to go back to the kind of food that they had there before...'

His voice drifted off, leaving Pete with the memory of the horrible food that Angie had used to cook. If indeed cook was the right description for the inedible mess that he had found on his dinner plate the one time that he had dared to eat there.

'Yes, you're quite right,' said Pete quickly. 'Okay, well, if you think that this will all taste as good as it sounds than let's go with this new menu. We can always tweak it as time passes, depending on how well it goes down.'

'Absolutely,' said Andre, sounding smug. 'I thought you'd agree that going upper class is really the way forward. All this back-to-earth, good grub just fills me with absolute horror. I shall get going on ordering the food and send you the invoices, okay? Toodles.'

The line went dead and Pete sagged back against his chair.

Upper class? In Cranbridge? For a second, his unfailing confidence wavered. Had he pitched it right? Would it be okay?

Of course it would, he reminded himself. Just because The Black Swan had started off run-down and rustic, it didn't mean that was how it was destined to continue. After all, wasn't that the reason the place had been nicknamed The Mucky Duck?

Not that it had a name at all, at the moment. Behind the shroud of the scaffolding, the old letters spelling out half of the name of The Black Swan had finally been removed in preparation for the outside of the building being painted the following week.

'Hey,' said Josh, heading across the small pedestrian bridge. 'How's it going?'

'Okay, thanks,' Pete said, his breath visible in the cold morning air. It was mid-October already and the autumn colours were vivid all around them, as well as being reflected in the river. 'I was just checking out the menus for the restaurant,' he added. 'Do you want to see them?'

Josh shook his head. 'Let it be a surprise when me and the family come for the big opening night,' he said. 'Not long to go now.'

Pete nodded. 'I know. Hey, thanks for the tip-off about the local brewers. I've got some great local wines and gin on order. The beer's already been delivered.'

It was the one change that Pete was most confident about. The locally brewed drinks were of excellent quality and he had been very impressed when he had tasted them all.

'Great,' said Josh, looking pleased. 'That will help local business.'

'As will a good restaurant,' added Pete.

Josh cleared his throat. 'Look, I know you've had this great idea and I agree that it should be good for the community...'

'We've been through this before,' said Pete. 'I do have experience in running a place like this.'

'Only in Singapore,' replied Josh. 'And Cranbridge is no sophisticated city.'

'I know. That's why I've sourced all local drinks.'

'Okay,' said Josh with a shrug. 'I'm sure you know what you're doing.'

At that moment, Pete wasn't sure that he did.

They both looked up at the scaffolding once more.

'It's going to look so much better than before,' said Pete.

'Couldn't have looked much worse,' said Josh, with a grin. 'If I forget to tell you next week, I'm proud of what you've achieved.'

'Thanks,' said Pete, pleased to have his brother's support.

'That's quite enough of the touchy-feely stuff for now,' muttered Josh. 'I'm off to the cash and carry.'

'See you later,' called out Pete as his brother headed off.

Josh had agreed to help out behind the bar to allow Belle her night off.

Pete was beginning to enjoy seeing his brother on a daily basis. His mum and Grandma Tilly too. In addition, he was beginning to enjoy standing behind the bar each evening and talking to people. He realised that he had actually been quite isolated and lonely in Singapore.

The only slight fly in the ointment was that people often talked about his dad. It had hurt so much initially, but perhaps the pain was easing a little with each passing mention.

He wondered what his dad would make of him buying The Black Swan. Would he have approved? Pete hoped so.

He knew that Belle had tried to persuade him to talk to Josh about the letter that he had found, but there had never been an opportune time. And besides, he was still apprehensive about upsetting his brother.

He looked up at the façade of the inn once more. It was time to tear out the old memories and feel of the place and bring in the new. He liked to think that he was breathing new life into this old place.

At that moment, he saw Belle through the windows cleaning the tables for opening time. She was still unsure about the restaurant, but he was hoping that its success would help her see differently.

Of course the restaurant wouldn't fail. Failure, as NASA said, wasn't an option.

Not when there was so much else on the line as well as the inn, he thought, flicking another glance towards Belle.

33

Belle was deep in thought as she left the inn that evening to head to Grandma Tilly's bungalow.

The Black Swan sign coming down had affected her more than she cared to admit. It wasn't even The B ck Sw n any more. The inn had been stripped of its identity and she felt as if hers had gone with it.

She snuggled her face further down into her scarf against the cold wind. The rustling of dried leaves crunched under her boots as she walked along the riverside.

At least her ideas for doing up the lounge seemed to have gained Pete's approval. The old lampshades with the fringes had been thrown out, along with the faded wallpaper, the threadbare rugs and the stained velvet that had covered the bar stools. It was now a blank canvas and the years of old stale cigarette smoke had finally cleared.

Despite all her tension, she was looking forward to spending the evening using her sewing machine and chatting to Grandma Tilly.

However, she had barely sat down with her mug of tea when the doorbell went.

Belle and Grandma Tilly looked at each other in surprise.

'Who on earth can that be?' asked Grandma Tilly, getting up from her armchair.

To Belle's surprise, there sounded like quite a few voices at the front door, most of which she recognised. But she was still amazed when Grandma Tilly came back into the living room, closely followed by Amber, Lucy and Molly.

'What are you all doing here?' asked Belle.

'We could ask you the same thing,' said Lucy, sitting down next to her.

'How did you know I was here,' said Belle.

'We followed you,' said Molly, looking sheepish.

'Only because we were worried about you,' added Amber, quickly.

Belle sighed and looked at Grandma Tilly. 'It looks as if the cat is out of the bag,' she said.

Grandma Tilly nodded. 'I'd better get some more biscuits,' she said.

A little later, everyone was settled in the small living room and still waiting for answers from Belle and Grandma Tilly.

'So what's going on?' asked Amber, looking at the sewing machine.

'That's mine,' said Belle. 'I was just helping out with the quilts, that's all.'

'I didn't even know you could sew,' said Molly, frowning.

Belle shrugged her shoulders. 'I never told you, so why would you?'

'I thought you went to bingo on a Monday night,' said Amber, looking at Grandma Tilly.

'I lied,' said the pensioner, looking uncomfortable. 'Belle wanted it to be a secret.'

Belle shook her head and smiled. 'I did not,' she said. 'This is all on you.'

'Humph,' said Grandma Tilly, frowning.

Belle sighed and leaned forward to take her hand. 'Look, I think it's a good thing that the girls came over tonight. It's time to be honest, don't you think?'

Grandma Tilly shuffled in her seat. 'I don't know what you're talking about.'

Belle squeezed her hand. 'There's something wrong with your eyes, isn't there? That's why you can't thread the needle any more.'

Amber gasped. 'And you were peering closely at a price label in the shop the other day and still said the writing wasn't clear enough.'

'That was just poor penmanship,' replied Grandma Tilly, still frowning.

'I think you should go to the optician,' said Belle. 'It's probably nothing.'

'I don't want to,' said Grandma Tilly, positively sulking by this point.

'I'll go with you,' offered Amber, softly. 'We're going to be family, aren't we?'

Grandma Tilly's bottom lip began to wobble. 'We already are, my dear,' she said in a tremulous voice.

'Well then, that's settled,' said Lucy, with a nod. 'No more secrets.'

'Not even of the heart?' asked Grandma Tilly, giving Belle a wink.

Belle blushed and busied herself cutting up some more squares of material that had already been laid out.

'So who wants to learn about quilting?' asked Grandma Tilly. 'We need to get at least half a dozen more done in the next month.'

The girls watched Belle demonstrate how to join the pieces of material together and then eagerly began to sew, in various levels of competence. In the end, Lucy was given the job of cutting up the material as her stitching was so appalling.

'These colours are so lovely,' said Amber, looking at the material that she had in front of her. 'Where did you get all this material?'

'Some were old blankets and whatnots,' said Grandma Tilly. 'Some of it came from Belle's grandmother.'

'She liked to sew?' asked Molly.

'She was a wonderful seamstress,' said Grandma Tilly. 'And you should see the clothes she made. The cut was marvellous. You'd think that they were vintage designer or something.'

'You've still got the clothes that she made?' asked Lucy, with wide eyes. She had a particular love of fashion.

Belle nodded. 'Of course,' she said.

The girls then demanded that Belle show them, so she had no choice once they had left Grandma Tilly's bungalow but to head back to the inn.

They waved at all their partners and friends in the bar but carried on upstairs, where Belle led them to her bedroom.

'These are beautiful,' said Molly, holding up a pretty flowered skirt.

'Look at that material,' gushed Lucy, touching a silk top. 'It's real quality.'

'Why did you never tell us?' asked Amber.

Belle blushed and shook her head. 'I never thought about it,' she said.

Lucy held up a pretty summer dress. 'You could totally wear this,' she said.

But Belle shook her head. 'You know me,' she told them. 'I'm happiest in my dark colours.'

Her friends looked at her but didn't press the matter further.

Later on, when Belle went to bed, the clothes were still piled up where the girls had lovingly looked through them all. The colours were so beautiful, she thought, heading across to draw the curtains.

She glanced outside briefly at the trees in the street lights. As the world changed to rich oranges, fiery reds and earthy browns, maybe it was time for her to have a touch of colour as well.

But could she transform herself?

Belle reached out to stroke the brightly coloured silk, trying to imagine herself standing out in the colour. Then she snatched her hand away and began to place the clothes back in their protective bags.

34

'So here's the menus that I'm going to get printed up,' said Pete. 'They look good, don't you think?'

Belle looked down at the printout that he had just handed her and stared at the words in disbelief. Those that she understood, that was.

'Jus of what?' she read out loud, peering at the piece of paper. 'And what on earth is a daikon?'

'It's a radish,' said Pete smoothly.

She looked up at him. 'I'll give you £5 if you didn't have to google what that was when you first read this,' she said.

He swiftly broke the eye contact. 'It's good to learn new stuff,' he replied with a shrug. 'Anyway, what do you think?'

Belle glanced once more at the menu. 'Wild boar, langoustine,' she read aloud. 'Don't you think that it's a bit over the top for our little village?'

'I thought we were trying to bring The Black Swan into the new century,' he told her.

'Yes, but it's still in Cranbridge,' she told him. 'The inn hasn't moved to Kensington in the last few hours, has it?'

'There are some wealthy folk around here that would love to have some fine dining in the area,' he said.

Belle looked at him. 'And you really think they're going to want to come here for it and not head into London for the weekend instead?'

'Why not do both?' he said with a smile. 'We may even get some out-of-towners coming here to specifically sample our cuisine.'

Belle sighed. 'It's an inn,' she said, trying to keep her voice level. 'It doesn't have fancy cuisine, it has atmosphere and roast dinners and a comfortable, warm vibe about the place.'

'Actually we're not planning on having any roast dinners on the menu,' he told her.

Belle was shocked. 'We're not? I thought you were a business-man! How can we be an inn if we don't serve Sunday roasts?' she asked him.

Pete looked away again. 'Andre says that he can't cook them,' he muttered.

'*Won't* cook them more like,' said Belle. 'He's too busy stoking his own ego with his,' she glanced at the menu, 'lobster with jus grass, rather than a good old roast beef with Yorkshire puddings which would fill the place up as well as people's stomachs.'

'If we need to, we can always expand the menus,' said Pete. 'But for now I'm trusting Andre's instinct. We have to try it out, don't you agree?'

The trouble was, Belle didn't agree. It was all so out of place and out of sync with the inn.

But some changes she had got used to and was almost enjoying. The bar and lounge were finally completed and looking so much better. The wall lamps had been upgraded to more modern fittings but still gave off a warm light. In addition, she had wrapped fairy lights around the oak beams to create a pretty effect, especially in the darker nights. The peeling wallpaper had been replaced by some soft green paint and the walls looked far crisper but still in keeping with the centuries old inn.

Finally, Pete had insisted that the bar stools and comfy chairs be reupholstered and Belle had chosen a dark brown leather which would be both practical and comfortable.

The new lighting behind the bar worked far better and the whole place looked fresher but still with a comfortable atmosphere.

She had swapped photos with her aunt and uncle after they had sailed through the Panama Canal. They had both been impressed by the new fittings and their reaction confirmed what she had felt. She had thought that she would hate the different feel of the place, but actually she always found herself smiling when she entered the bar area as she was so pleased with the result.

Belle had begun to think that a few changes weren't a bad thing, after all.

Although she was still worried about Pete's plans for the restaurant, she had decided to place her trust in him.

He had looked quite shocked when she had told him so.

'Really?' he said. 'No more arguments?'

She shook her head. 'No, I'm all argued out.'

He looked at her for a long time before finally speaking, 'Well, then, maybe we can start being friends again.'

She nodded. 'That would be nice,' she had replied.

But not nearly enough, she realised.

The only thing she could think of was when he had caught her in just a towel outside the bathroom a week or so ago. Then he had looked at her in such a way that breathing had become almost impossible.

But it was crazy. It was just a crush. After all, there was no way that Pete was ever going to think of her like that.

35

Four days before the official opening of the inn's new restaurant, Belle was busy sorting out the tableware.

There was so much still to organise, but Pete was adamant that they opened that Saturday night. The much-hyped restaurant reviewer had been booked, as had a couple of the other tables. Friends and villagers were going to make up the numbers so that the restaurant would be full.

Belle looked around the restaurant area. It looked so different now to the abandoned, dusty room it had been only a short time ago. With the raised ceiling revealing the oak beams that rose to an apex into the roof, it should have felt much more light and airy, but the new furniture did much to offset that airiness. Pete had chosen dark brown tables and chairs, which were quite stark to look at. In addition, he hadn't used either her suggestion of a candle on each table, nor coloured napkins. Everything was either dark brown or grey. But maybe that was the fashion, thought Belle. After all, she had never eaten at a fancy restaurant.

Neither had their new restaurant staff, she suspected. But at least they now had a waiter and waitress to help serve the customers. They were Brad's friends, a blonde girl, Cassie, and a guy with ginger dreadlocks called Aaron.

A tap on one of the front windows made her look up. Amber waved at her through the glass whilst Josh appeared to be carrying a rather large box.

Belle headed to the other end of the restaurant where the new patio doors had been installed to let them in. She was looking forward to the summer when the doors could be flung open and more tables could be arranged on the patio space outside. Admittedly, it still needed fixing as the patio was so wonky that customers were likely to trip over the uneven paving slabs. If the inn was still in business by then, she reminded herself. As well as whether she would even be living there.

There were so many uncertainties that all Belle felt she could do was to concentrate on each day, otherwise her anxiety would be sky-high.

She unlocked the door and let Josh and Amber inside.

'It's pouring out there,' said Amber, shaking her long blonde hair out from under the hood of her anorak.

'Right, where shall I put this?' asked Josh, still carrying the huge box.

'Down here is fine,' said Belle, pointing to the floor. 'Was today Grandma Tilly's appointment at the opticians?'

'Tomorrow,' said Amber.

'Can't believe she didn't tell any of us how much she was struggling,' said Josh, rolling his eyes.

'Hopefully it'll be something easy to sort,' said Belle, repeating the same words she had told Pete. 'So, is that box what I think it is?'

Amber smiled and nodded. 'It is.'

Belle clapped her hands together. 'How exciting.' She went

forward and pulled open the box that Josh had placed onto the oak floorboards. Inside were lots of handmade napkin rings in various intricate designs of silver.

'I didn't know which ones you wanted so I just went for it,' said Amber.

'She's been working hard every evening on them,' said Josh. 'And ignoring me at the same time.'

Amber gave him a nudge and shushed him. 'Belle appreciates the work and, besides, you were watching the football.'

'I am so grateful,' said Belle. 'I'm sure we can pay you something for them.'

But Amber shook her head. 'No need,' she said. 'If you can use them, then that's great. If not, we might sell them in the shop!'

Belle laughed. 'Not a chance. They'll work perfectly.'

Josh looked around the place. 'It's okay, if a little stark for my tastes. I didn't think my little brother could pull this together, but he might just have.'

'With a bit of help from Belle,' added Amber in a pointed tone.

Josh grinned. 'A lot more help than just a bit, I would say. Here's hoping it all goes well at the weekend.' He suddenly frowned. 'You might have to change the music though.'

Belle had hardly been taking any notice of the radio that she had on in the corner until that point. Then she realised that some irritating pop song was currently playing.

'I'll switch it off,' she said, heading over.

But just as she reached the radio, the song changed and on came Beyoncé's 'Crazy In Love'.

'Oooh!' said Amber from behind her. 'Did you see that girl from *EastEnders* on *Strictly Come Dancing* this weekend? She did a salsa to this.'

'I think you'll find it was the samba,' said Josh.

To which Amber and Belle both turned around laughing.

'I didn't know you were studying it that carefully,' said Amber, giggling.

Josh shrugged his shoulders. 'With all those female dancers in their little dresses?' he said, with a grin.

'Oh really?' said Amber, putting her hands on her hips.

'I only have eyes for you,' said Josh, taking Amber into his arms and beginning to sway. 'I think we could show them a few moves.'

Belle found herself smiling as the couple swayed back and forth, attempting a few steps. They were so in love and it was wonderful to see, she thought.

'Maybe we can do this for our first dance at the wedding,' said Josh, before he tripped over his own feet and nearly catapulted them into a nearby table.

'I'm not sure about that,' said Amber, who was still laughing as Josh took her back into his arms to attempt another move.

'What is this?' asked Andre, suddenly appearing next to Belle in the doorway.

'It's called dancing,' drawled Belle. 'You should try it some time. You know, you might even break into a smile.'

'That is not dancing,' said Andre, with a sneer. 'That is not how you samba.'

'Oh, really?' laughed Belle. 'And how would you know?'

'Because my mother made me take lessons when I was growing up,' he told her, reaching out to take Belle's hand. 'I will show you.'

To Belle's surprise, she suddenly found herself in Andre's arms as he swayed his hips alarmingly in a provocative fashion. She couldn't stop herself from bursting out in laughter at the shock.

'You need to move your hips like this,' said Andre, reaching out to hold her and moving her torso back and forth.

It took a couple of minutes, but eventually Belle found that she could make out a few steps and with a few sways here and there, she began to get the knack of the samba.

She was so busy concentrating, however, that she didn't see Pete staring at them in shock from the doorway.

36

Pete felt as if his feet had been nailed to the floor. The shock continued to run through him as he watched Andre, of all people, do some kind of sexy Latin dance with Belle in the restaurant.

It had been a busy morning and he had felt relieved to get back to what he had thought would be the peace and quiet of the inn. He was finding being around Belle more and more calming.

Except for right at that moment. Right now he could quite easily punch his hand through the brick fireplace, such was the unexpected anger surging through him.

'Hey,' said Josh, crashing to a breathless halt in front of him, holding a giggling Amber in his arms.

'Is this some kind of village initiation?' drawled Pete to his brother. But his eyes never left Belle as he spoke. 'I didn't know you had it in you.'

'It's just a bit of fun,' he heard Josh say. 'You do remember how to have fun, don't you, bro?'

'Of course,' snapped Pete. But he had lost all sense of humour and his world had decreased to where he could only see Belle still being spun around in Andre's arms.

Her long dark hair whipped around her face as if in some kind of tornado. Her eyes were lit up as she laughed.

She looked both gorgeous and sexy. And she was dancing with another man.

'Are you okay?' asked Amber, staring up at him.

Pete finally blinked back to life and turned to look at her. 'I'm fine,' he replied.

Next to Amber, Josh was frowning at him. 'You're grinding your teeth,' he said.

'I missed my last dentist appointment,' replied Pete automatically.

'Uh-huh,' he heard Josh say.

But Pete's eyes had been drawn back to Belle again. He was completely mesmerised. Her cheeks were flushed. Her eyes were flashing. She was laughing. She was magnificent.

He slowly became aware that he was gnashing his teeth together. He had known that Andre had some kind of Mediterranean blood coursing through his veins, but this was really going too far. He ought to be professional and not be dancing with Belle.

But Pete was feeling distinctly unprofessional himself and was currently running through various daydreams, all of which resulted in Andre lying on the floor and Pete dragging Belle away like some kind of caveman.

None of these were thoughts or feelings that Pete had ever encountered before now. It was pure rage, pure jealousy.

He was jealous? Of Andre?

Pete couldn't believe it. It was obviously just some kind of reaction to Andre flirting outrageously with his friend. He and Josh had always been very protective of Belle over the years. That was it. He grasped onto the thought like a man drowning hangs on to a lifebuoy. He just needed to protect her, that was all.

But when Andre suddenly pulled Belle into him and they were

joined groin to groin, Pete had reached the limit as to what he could endure. He strode over to where the radio was and switched it off, fighting against the urge to fling the damn thing into the fireplace.

The dancing abruptly stopped as Belle turned around in surprise at the sudden silence.

'What's going on?' she asked, still breathless and laughing.

Pete stared down at her. Her face was lit up, glowing almost and Pete had a horrified thought. What if she had fallen in love with Andre? What if he were her dream man?

The pain that suddenly struck him was so awful that he could barely breathe.

He just about managed to gather himself together long enough to say, 'Shouldn't we all be getting back to work? I was under the impression we had an inn to open in a few days' time.'

Belle stopped laughing and stared up at him with wide eyes. 'What on earth's the matter with you today?' she asked.

He honestly had no idea at that moment, so found himself pretty much speechless.

'I will get back to the kitchen,' said Andre, walking away.

Finally Pete found his voice again. 'It just wasn't very professional of him, that's all,' he said, his voice coming out as some kind of croak.

'Oh he didn't mean anything by it,' said Belle, smiling as if it were no big deal. 'Right, I'll go dig out those napkins we had delivered. Amber's made us some beautiful napkin rings.'

She wandered away out of sight, leaving Pete standing by the fireplace still trying to gather himself together.

Nearby, Josh and Amber exchanged a look.

'Well, I suppose we'd better get back to the shop now that Pete's broken up the party,' said Josh. 'Never known you to be a party pooper before, bro.'

'There's just a lot to do before we launch, that's all,' snapped Pete.

'I'm sure that's all your overreaction was about just then,' drawled Josh.

Pete barely heard his brother's response so merely nodded and walked away with the intention of making sure that Andre had actually returned to the kitchen and wasn't initiating yet another move on Belle.

He was already in the lounge and out of earshot when Amber turned to Josh and asked, 'Do you really think Pete's overreaction was just the stress about the grand opening?'

To which Josh smiled at his fiancée as he shook his head. 'I don't think that's what that was about at all.'

37

'So how's it going?' asked Lucy as the four friends gathered around a table next to the fireplace in the inn on Friday evening. 'Are you all set for the big opening?'

'I guess so,' said Belle. 'But I've only got time for a quick drink as there's still so much to do.'

The inn was even quieter than usual as everyone was booked in for a meal the following evening. Even so, there were still napkins to fold, cutlery to polish and tables to finish setting.

'Is everything okay?' asked Amber.

'It's fine,' said Belle, quickly.

But it wasn't quite true. She couldn't relax and be herself whilst Pete was behind the bar. Even now she could feel him glancing over at the table once in a while. He had been like this for the past few days and she had no idea why.

'Swap with me, will you?' she said to Molly. 'I'm getting too hot here by the fire.'

'Okay,' said Molly, amenable as always.

'Are you sure it's the heat from the flames?' said Lucy, with a wink as Belle sat down next to her. 'Not from your hot man behind the bar?'

'He's not my hot man,' said Belle, grateful that she was now sitting with her back to Pete and that he couldn't see the blush she could feel on her cheeks.

'You're blushing,' said Lucy.

'I was too warm next to the fire,' said Belle.

'Did you notice she didn't dispute the hot man comment?' said Lucy, turning to look at Amber.

Amber nodded and smiled softly to herself as she sipped her drink.

'I never said...' But Belle just let her voice drift off in the end. It was too exhausting to keep fighting her friends' wave of opinions all the time.

Instead she gave a start as she felt a furry body bump against her knees. She peered under the table and found Keith had settled down by their feet.

Feeling Belle's gaze, he lifted his grey shaggy head to stare up at her adoringly. But that was most likely because she had a bag of crisps in hand, she realised. So she fed him a couple under the table, which caused his tail to thump and thus give the game away.

'I hope you're not begging,' said Lucy, giving Keith's head a stroke. 'He'll have to go on a diet if he carries on this way.'

'Nonsense,' said Amber, smiling sweetly at the dog. 'He's perfect just the way he is.'

Belle had a sudden thought. 'We'd better make sure that we have some dog-friendly tables in the new restaurant, don't you think?'

Her friends nodded their approval.

'That's a great idea,' said Amber encouragingly.

Belle made a mental note to mention it to Pete. She slowly became aware of Molly looking at her. 'What?' she asked.

'You said "we",' said Molly, with a soft smile. 'I presume you meant you and Pete?'

Belle shrugged her shoulders. 'Nobody else I'm stuck with in this place is there?'

She realised all three of her friends were now grinning at her and sharing knowing looks.

'Yes, we're a "we" where the inn is concerned,' she snapped. 'So you'd better get used to it.'

'Well, that's a step in the right direction at least,' said Lucy, nodding her head in approval. 'So does this mean that you two are getting on better these days?' Lucy looked up at the bar before looking back at Belle. 'Or should we still be removing all sharp objects in the vicinity whenever we mention his name?'

'You'd be amazed what damage can be done with just a teaspoon,' said Belle with a smile. She hesitated before adding, 'But yeah, I suppose I'm getting used to him.'

The others exchanged knowing looks once more.

'That doesn't mean that I now believe in love or any of that soppy stuff,' she added, bringing out her mobile. 'I mean, look at this text from Aunty Angie. Does this look like love conquers all?'

'We're in San Francisco,' read Molly out loud. 'I should have left your uncle in the cells on Alcatraz.'

'Sheesh,' said Lucy, with a grimace.

'Exactly,' said Belle, before looking at Amber. 'Now, tell us about Grandma Tilly's optician's appointment.'

'It's cataracts,' said Amber, with a huge sigh of relief. 'They're quite bad but entirely fixable, thank goodness.'

'That's such good news,' said Molly, smiling.

'I shall have a word with her tomorrow night about giving us all a fright,' said Belle.

'And you're all set to go?' asked Amber.

Belle nodded. 'More or less.'

'And what are you wearing?' asked Lucy.

Belle glanced down at her dark top and jeans. 'My usual stuff,' she replied.

The girls sighed and looked at each other, shaking their heads.

'Why don't you wear one of your grandmother's pretty tops?' said Molly.

Amber nodded in agreement. 'That's a great idea,' she said.

But Belle was frantically shaking her head. 'There's too much to worry about tomorrow already.'

Secretly, she longed to have the courage to wear one of the beautiful tops, but the fear of rejection was still strong, a hangover from her wretched childhood.

'Stop nagging,' said Lucy, with a sigh. 'She'll do it in her own time.'

'I'm sure Pete would appreciate seeing you in something different,' murmured Amber.

Belle frowned at her. 'Just because we're getting along that doesn't mean I have to transform into one of the usual glamour girls that he goes for.'

'But you are getting along better,' said Molly, with a beaming smile.

'Yes, but he hasn't had a personality transplant, has he?' She picked up her drink but before taking a sip, added, 'I mean, Pete Kennedy is just as arrogant as he has always been. He doesn't listen to anyone else's opinion. He's cocky, did I mention arrogant...?'

Hoping for at least some kind of agreement from her friends, she suddenly realised that everyone was looking over her shoulder.

Belle sighed. 'How long has he been standing behind me?' she asked.

'Long enough,' she heard Pete say.

Everyone else around the table tried not to smile as Belle

squirmed on her chair in embarrassment. In the end, not knowing what else to say, she turned around to where Pete was standing and said, 'Excellent timing. We want to order another round of drinks.'

She managed to look him in the face but didn't quite meet his eyes.

'Of course,' he said smoothly. 'I'm sure you can help me carry them back to the table.'

She sighed as he walked away. 'I'm so going to pay for this, aren't I?'

Her friends nodded.

'Possibly,' murmured Molly. 'But what a way to go.'

Belle got up and marched over to the bar but stayed determinedly on the customer side. If anything, the barrier helped her feel safer.

'I was saying to Lucy that we need to factor in some dog-friendly tables in the restaurant,' she said, as he poured out their drinks. Her nervousness made her prattle on further to counter the awkward atmosphere. 'I mean, think about it. That could attract quite a few people walking their dogs who decide to pop in on the off chance for a drink and see the new restaurant. It's really coming along, isn't it? The girls were just saying so.'

All four drinks were placed on the bar in front of her and Belle finally managed to lift her head to where Pete was looking at her, bemused.

'I think it's a good idea about the dog-friendly tables,' he told her before leaning across the bar further to add, 'Never let it be said that I don't listen to anyone else's opinion.'

'Good. Great,' she muttered, picking up the glasses from the counter. 'Glad to hear it.'

She rolled her eyes to herself as she headed back across the bar. But as she placed the drinks onto the table she realised that she had said the word 'we' again when referring to the work on the inn. Maybe the girls were right. Maybe she was getting used to being a team with Pete.

To her surprise, she found the idea wasn't so bad after all.

They were all still grinning inanely at her as she sat back down.

'What?' she said, rolling her eyes at the soppy grins on their faces. 'We're just friends, that's all.'

'I've seen the way he looks at you and it's not as a friend,' said Amber softly.

'Rubbish,' said Belle before swiftly changing the subject.

But as they talked about the latest village gossip, she wondered whether Amber was right.

She was just about to smile to herself but caught it just in time before her friends noticed and jumped to any more conclusions.

* * *

Later that evening, Belle locked the front door at 11 p.m.

'That was even quieter than normal,' said Pete, who was kneeling down in front of the fireplace, ensuring that the flames were dying down.

'Everyone's coming to the restaurant tomorrow night,' Belle told him. 'So I guess they're all enjoying a night at home tonight.'

'Doesn't do much for the profit margins though,' he said, straightening up.

Belle rolled her eyes. 'You and your profit margins,' she murmured, switching off the main lights.

Only the lights in the hallway remained as they made their way across the floor and away from the bar.

'Are you nervous about tomorrow night?' she asked, as they headed upstairs to the apartment.

'Not especially,' he told her.

'Glad someone's not,' she said, turning to look at him as she reached the top floor.

'There's no need to be nervous,' he told her with a smile. 'We've got a top-class chef, the staff are trained and we have an exceptional menu.'

She was still worried about the pressure on Brad's friends who had been employed as waiting staff. Neither Cassie nor Aaron had experience in serving customers, let alone with Andre's fancy meals.

'At least the building work is finally finished,' she said, more to reassure herself than Pete.

The scaffolding had finally come down and what a transformation! Belle hadn't quite been able to believe her eyes as she had stared at the building that afternoon. The fresh coat of paint had made the outside gleam again. The white walls showed off the shiny black window frames and flower boxes. No more peeling paint or wonky roof tiles.

She had sent a photo to her aunt and uncle who were now heading across the Pacific Ocean. They had sent back their own shocked reaction to the difference to the place they had called home for so long.

Belle yawned. 'I need to get an early night. I think tomorrow's going to be a busy one.'

They reached the doorway to his bedroom first, the master bedroom. She glanced in it, half expecting to see Aunty Angie's brightly coloured clothes strewn across the bed. But it was pretty empty apart from the guitar case in the corner.

Belle gave a start. 'I never noticed that before,' she said, looking across the room to where the guitar case was propped up against the far corner. 'Do you still play?'

'No.'

In his voice, there was real pain and she spun around to look up at him. There was pain now in his eyes as well and she wished she could take it away from him.

'I can remember you playing with your dad on the veranda of the shop,' she said softly.

But her words only seemed to make him more upset and he shook his head. 'That's a long time ago now,' he said, his tone almost harsh.

'Surely it would be a good thing to replicate those happy memories,' she told him, reaching out to squeeze his hand.

But Pete merely shook his head in reply.

'Did you ever talk to anyone about that letter you found?' she asked.

'I wouldn't even know how to start a conversation like that,' he said, looking back at her.

'Then perhaps it might help to have a friend with you,' she told him, with a soft smile.

She went to let go of his hand, but suddenly he was holding hers with his instead.

'Is that all we are?' he asked. 'Just friends?'

She had been planning to say goodnight and walk away, but suddenly her feet wouldn't move. Pete was watching her, his eyes dark in the unlit room.

The air suddenly shifted. It was heavy and she found herself catching her breath.

She opened her mouth to say something, but she couldn't find the words.

Pete's gaze lowered to her lips and when he raised his eyes back up, they were filled with desire.

They came together instantly in an embrace, stepping forward to wrap themselves around each other.

His lips came crashing down onto hers and for a moment, there was nothing but Pete and his kiss.

She moaned against his mouth at the feel of his lips on hers. She had dreamed about this ever since that day three years ago. Had wanted this for so long, maybe even longer than that.

She knew he felt it too. She knew from the way his lips assaulted hers, the way his breath had become ragged and the way he was crushing her to him.

Finally they broke apart, both breathless and wide-eyed as they stared at each other.

She knew that he had felt the connection between them as well. She'd never been kissed like that before. She wasn't sure she ever would again.

Gradually coming out of her daze, she realised that they had both let go of each other.

'I don't want to hurt you,' he finally said.

Her lips were still bruised from their passionate kisses. And yet, she felt that he was holding back again.

'It doesn't matter,' she told him, feeling déjà vu all over again as history repeated itself from the day of the funeral three years ago.

'It does,' he said, going to reach out to take her hand in his.

But Belle's self-defence mechanism had already kicked in. She shook her head and said, 'Get some sleep. We've got a big day tomorrow.'

It took every piece of strength that she could find to walk away from him and out of the bedroom, knowing that sleep was unlikely to come that night.

Nothing had changed in the three years. Her feelings for Pete and the way she had reacted to kissing him had been exactly the same.

And yet, everything had changed. Her aunt and uncle were

halfway across the world. The inn had been sold. Even her home had been transformed and given a different look.

As she sank down onto her bed, she looked across at the pile of her grandmother's clothes and wondered whether she too should be brave enough to give herself a new look as well.

And whether that would change anything at all.

38

Pete stood outside looking at the inn early in the afternoon on Saturday. Just in time for the grand opening of the restaurant that evening, the scaffolding had finally come down from around the building and the place had been transformed.

'Thanks,' he said to Mr Reynolds, reaching out to shake his hand. 'It looks really great.'

'My pleasure,' said Mr Reynolds. 'It's always so satisfying taking a run-down place such as The Black Swan and making it look like new again.'

After they had said goodbye, Pete continued to stand outside staring up at the new sign.

The Black Swan Inn was now officially his. The paperwork for the sale had been signed off the previous day. The inn licence had been granted in his name too. There was no going back now.

The new commercial kitchen had been finished just in time and had been signed off an hour earlier by the health and safety officer. Having the approval on the day the restaurant opened was sailing pretty close to the wind, but he hoped it would all be worth it.

Everything was ready and yet he wasn't excited. He was almost a little nervous, something he had never felt before. Or at least, since he had been a child.

It was a strange feeling. He had always been so confident, so sure of everything, including himself and his choices.

But somehow suddenly he wasn't sure about anything.

He was afraid that his choice of going down the gastronomic route for the restaurant was wrong. He was worried about the chef. He was concerned that he had been overambitious by inviting the restaurant critic to the opening. He was nervous about the young staff he had hired and their lack of waiting abilities and experience.

But more than anything, he wasn't sure about his feelings for Belle.

Somehow, the previous evening he had kissed her. He hadn't been able to stop himself. She had glowed in the soft light of the bedroom and her soft perfume, the lustrous dark hair, her kind heart, all of it had robbed him of his sense of rationale and reason.

He should have been ashamed about his lack of control, but he had since realised that she had responded to his kisses with some of her own. As if she too desired him as much as he desired her.

Strangely, it hadn't made things awkward between them that day. They had said good morning and then the preparations for the restaurant had overshadowed everything else.

He would try to speak to her later to apologise. To tell her that it wouldn't happen again. And yet, some part of him was adamant that it should happen again and soon. That her kisses weren't to be forgotten, as precious as they were.

And how much he wanted to feel her lips on his again, over and over.

Pete shook his head, as if trying to deny himself the sweet thoughts of having Belle in his arms.

Thankfully he was momentarily distracted by the arrival of Cassie and Aaron, the young waiter and waitress.

'Hi,' he said, his heart plummeting at the sight of them.

Cassie gave him a shy smile.

How would she even begin to interact with the customers? At least most of them were local and would be kind, but she looked as nervous as her heavily bitten fingernails.

But Aaron gave him more worry.

'I see you've dyed your hair for the occasion,' said Pete, trying and failing to smile.

Aaron nodded. 'Needed to try out green,' he replied, solemnly. 'The ginger just wasn't working for me.'

'I see,' said Pete. 'Well, at least it won't clash with the black uniforms.'

'Are you sure we can't just dress as we are?' asked Aaron, glancing down at his jeans.

Pete shook his head. 'Shall we just try out the uniforms for tonight and see how we get on?' he said. 'I mean, I don't want you to get that T-shirt ruined.'

They all looked down at his T-shirt which appeared to be mainly swear words.

'Good point,' said Aaron. 'It's one of my favourites.'

'I can see why,' said Pete, turning away to open up the door for them both.

His heart was already sinking.

Belle was giving the place one last wipe down and check. She looked up and said hi as the youngsters came in.

Pete wandered over to her as they disappeared towards the kitchen.

'Did you see his hair?' asked Pete.

Belle laughed. 'I like it,' she said. 'It's a bit of colour around here. Those black uniforms you've chosen for them are pretty bland.'

'Bland is good,' said Pete, still frowning.

Belle's eyebrows shot up. 'Are you really the same Pete Kennedy who once wore cut-off jeans with a lime green T-shirt?' she asked, smiling sweetly at him.

Pete couldn't help but smile at the memory. 'I did love that T-shirt,' he said, almost to himself.

'Well then,' she told him. 'You weren't much younger than those two.'

He blew out a sigh. 'It's going to be okay, isn't it?'

Belle gave a start. 'You mean tonight? Of course it is.' She looked at him concerned. 'Why? Where's this sudden dip in confidence come from?'

Pete shook his head. 'I don't know,' he told her. 'Just a feeling.'

'And there was me believing that invincible act that you've had up until now,' she said.

He fixed her with a look. 'At some point we need to talk about last night,' he said softly.

She looked away, her creamy cheeks filling with blush. 'I suppose,' she said, a little hesitantly.

He reached out to hold her chin gently to bring her gaze up to his.

There it was again. The zinging chemistry that surged whenever his eyes met hers. He caught his breath and saw that she had too.

It was no use. She was like some kind of drug to him. He went to step forward to kiss her again, but at the sound of a sudden footstep behind him, he took a step backwards instead.

Belle smiled and chatted to Cassie as she came around the corner, fussing over the dark uniform and telling the girl how great she looked.

Leaving Pete as confused and mixed up as he had ever been.

He had to get his act together, he told himself. Self-doubt wouldn't help anyone.

Tonight would be a roaring success and then he and Belle would decide where their futures lay. And he found himself hoping that it was together.

39

Belle put on the new waitressing outfit so that she matched the others and checked herself in the mirror. It was pretty sombre, but perhaps it did look more professional than she usually did in her jeans and top.

She glanced over at her brighter clothes and figured that they would have to wait a while longer yet. Anyway, wasn't black her signature colour?

She had been worried about the restaurant opening, but it hadn't really hit home until that evening. She was nervous, but it was mixed with excitement as well.

Perhaps change really was good. Perhaps it would all be all right. And perhaps this could be a new beginning, not only for The Black Swan but for her and Pete as well.

The kiss had stayed with her. Although upset that Pete had once more pushed her away, she had hugged those memories close to her all night and had woken up smiling. She didn't think it was an act this time. Nobody could pretend whilst kissing her with such passion. His feelings for her were real. She just wasn't quite sure what they were. After all, he had kissed many women before her.

But there was no time to worry about that now, she told herself, as she slicked on some lipstick. She checked that her hair was back in its ponytail with no stray locks. She looked okay. Better than okay, she told herself. She looked, dare she say it, pretty?

She nodded at her reflection and then rolled her eyes at herself. What on earth was she turning into?

But she was still smiling as she headed down the stairs.

She found Lucy and Tom standing behind the bar, where Pete was showing them the ropes. They were going to be running the bar whilst Belle and Pete were hands on inside the restaurant that evening.

'All set?' she asked.

Lucy nodded. 'No worries,' she said. 'We'll have it all under control.'

Tom gave her his usual wide smile. 'Trust us,' he told her, with a wink. 'I've spent many nights in this bar. I think we can handle it.'

'And we're only in the restaurant if there's a problem,' said Pete.

'Exactly,' said Tom, laughing. 'So you two go and do your stuff. Me and my beautiful girl will hold the fort here.'

Belle smiled at Lucy's blushes. They really were the sweetest couple, she thought. And wistfully found herself wishing that someone talked about her in the same way at some point in her life.

As Pete told them how the till and credit card machine worked, Belle wandered into the kitchen to check on how the preparations for the evening meals were going.

Unfortunately she found the atmosphere somewhat stressful.

'I said julienne!' shouted Andre. 'Not sliced!'

'This is better for the recipe!' Brad shouted back, holding his ground.

'That's enough,' she snapped, coming to stand between them. 'You're not helping anyone by ranting at each other.'

'My kitchen, my rules,' said Andre.

Belle took a deep breath. *Let's just get through tonight,* she thought. *Then I'll get Pete to have a word with him.* Andre's attitude was truly awful.

'Right,' began Belle in a calm voice. 'The customers are going to be arriving any moment and I'd rather they enjoyed the new décor rather than hear you two going at it hammer and tongs!'

Andre and Brad both took a deep breath at the same time but continued to glare at each other.

'It's important that you're a team tonight,' she said, looking directly at Andre. She knew that he was the problem. He had no man-management skills and he was borderline rude and bullying towards Brad most of the time. 'Everything is riding on this being a successful opening,' she said. 'So let's keep the hysterics to a low-level simmer until later, okay?'

Both men gave a grunt in reply and Belle shook her head.

'Look, nothing's going to go wrong tonight,' she carried on. 'Everything will run smoothly.'

At which point, the lights flickered on and off.

Thankfully they came back on after only a few seconds, but the brief power outage had caused Andre to go from smooth operator to complete slightly hysterical diva, shouting at both Belle and Brad.

He was almost incoherent by the time Pete joined them in the kitchen.

'What the hell is this?' Pete shouted.

Belle turned to him. 'Andre is having a meltdown,' she told him, rolling her eyes.

'So I heard,' he said. 'Along with everyone else.' He turned to look at his chef. 'Look, the electricity is always a problem around here. Get everything prepped and ready. Just concentrate on the cooking and leave the hysterics for later, okay?'

Andre gave a hissy humph under his breath and turned his back on them to continue to prep the meat.

Brad was looking as if he were about to bolt, so Belle nodded reassuringly at him. 'You okay?' she mouthed.

He shrugged his shoulders and returned to chopping up the vegetables.

Belle and Pete walked back out into the narrow hallway.

'What do you think?' whispered Pete. 'Are we going to be all right?'

'I honestly have no idea,' said Belle, smiling at his lack of assurance for once. 'But it's too late now as the first customer has just arrived.'

'Well then,' said Pete, with a grimace. 'Bring it on.'

But he didn't move, instead looking down at her, before leaning in to kiss her gently on the lips. 'For luck,' he said before walking away.

Belle touched her lips as she stood alone in the hallway, figuring they might just need all the luck they could get.

40

Despite his rare nerves, Pete was feeling proud as he showed his family to their table in the restaurant. It really did look great, he thought. The new lighting was bright and cheerful. The dark tables and chairs looked stylish and offset the beams tremendously well.

'Oh, this is nice,' said his mum, in an overly forced cheerful tone of voice. 'Don't you think so, Tilly?'

Grandma Tilly was looking all around her in amazement. 'It's very pleasant,' she said, waving across the room to where Frank and Stanley were sitting. 'If a little stark in here.'

Pete gave a start at his grandmother's criticism. 'Stark's a bit harsh, isn't it?' he said, laughing. 'It's called modern, Grandma.'

'Just saying,' said Grandma Tilly. 'Place could do with warming up a bit. That's all. Both in temperature and those bright bulbs.'

They all glanced up at the bright white LED lights that Pete had wanted so much.

'It's not the most flattering of lighting for one of advanced years,' said Grandma Tilly, as she sat down. 'It certainly won't do my dating prospects any good.'

'At least the fire's nice,' said his mum, with a nod of approval.

Pete spun around and saw that Belle had indeed just lit the fire.

'I thought we were going to leave it tonight,' he whispered to her.

Belle gave him a shrug of her shoulders. 'People were complaining of feeling cold,' she replied before walking away.

'It looks great,' said Amber, ever the peacemaker and smiling up at Pete from the table. 'You've worked so hard.'

'He didn't do anything,' said Josh, pulling a chair out of the table for his mother to sit on. 'It was the builders and Belle that did all the hard work.'

Pete looked at his brother and raised his eyebrows.

Josh gave him a wide grin. 'Just kidding, bro. You've done brilliantly to get it ready in time.'

Pete grinned back. 'Thanks.'

He hadn't wanted his brother's approval, or any of his family's, to start with. But now he realised that he did want them to approve of the changes to the restaurant. This was to be their local restaurant in the local inn. He wanted it to be good. Better than good, in fact.

He glanced around the room, but there was no sign of the restaurant critic yet. Just what appeared to be local families and couples who had all been invited for the launch. The place was filling up and the chatter of conversation began to fill the air.

Once his family sat down, Pete handed them all the brand-new menu.

'Shall I get you all a drink?' he asked, as they all looked down at the menu.

'How about some wine?' said Amber, beaming around the table before looking back at her fiancé who was sitting next to her.

But Josh was frowning down at the menu. 'What's this?' he said, looking up at his brother with incredulous eyes. 'Wild boar? Langoustines?'

'What's a langoustine?' asked Grandma Tilly, making a face. 'Is that, whatsername, vegan?'

Amber gave Josh a nudge with her elbow, but Josh ignored her. 'Where's the local food?' he asked.

'Every ingredient has been sourced from top suppliers,' Pete told him in a lofty tone of voice.

'Yeah, about 300 miles away from the looks of it,' said Josh.

'I'm sure it'll all taste lovely,' said his mum, glancing between both her sons. 'Now, shall we go for white or red wine?'

Josh crossed his arms in front of him and scowled whilst his mum and Amber decided on a bottle of wine.

Pete decided that once they had chosen their wine he would be quite grateful to leave the somewhat awkward atmosphere at his family's table. His big brother had always been environmentally conscious and had carried on that ethos in the shop, always trying to source as many items as locally as he could. Pete wondered if perhaps he should have gone down the same route with the food, but it was too late to change everything now. He was sure it would be all right.

Just then his nerves ratcheted up a notch as he spotted a single man, smartly dressed, who had just headed in the door and walked directly to the restaurant area.

'Well, I'd better check on the front of house,' said Pete. 'I'll leave you in Cassie's capable hands.'

'Good luck,' whispered Amber before he left.

'Thanks,' he said, before fixing a smile at the gentleman who was waiting, a little impatiently, at the entrance. 'Good evening. Can I help you?'

'Yes, I have a reservation in the name of Mr T Faulks,' said the man.

'I thought so,' said Pete, holding out his hand. 'Welcome to The

Black Swan. I'm the proprietor, Pete Kennedy. We spoke on the phone.'

'Ah yes.' The critic looked down at Pete's hand which was still held out as if to be shook but instead placed his coat into it instead.

'Let me show you to your seat and then I'll hang up your coat,' said Pete. Everyone else had hung their coats on the back of the chairs, which wasn't really giving the desired effect, he realised. He seemed to recall Belle mentioning something when they had got rid of the old coat stand in the inn lounge, but it had then completely slipped his mind. So he hung the coat next to the entrance to the restaurant by the cutlery and then headed straight back with the menu.

The critic had naturally been given the best seat in the house, which was by the window, overlooking the river. Which, Pete now realised, was a huge mistake because it was dark outside and perhaps he should have placed him nearer the fireplace as it was such a wild night out.

The lights flickered once more and Pete prayed that they would stay on. Maybe Belle's other idea about some tea lights on the table would have helped calm his nerves as well, if the lights went out.

He mentally crossed his fingers before handing the menu to the restaurant critic.

Oh well, he thought. It was too late now.

The restaurant was officially opened.

41

Belle looked around the restaurant and thought that it was going to be okay. Everyone had their drinks and were smiling and chatting away.

Although she had to admit that quite a few people appeared to be shuffling on their bottoms, quietly complaining about the hard seats.

The dark wooden chairs were not a huge hit, she had to admit. And with the darkness outside, along with the dark tables and chairs, the whole place felt even more stark than before.

The restaurant desperately needed colour, but everything Pete had chosen was dark wood and grey. But at least the fireplace was giving some cheer with its pretty flames. And some much-needed warmth as well, as the starkness made everything feel colder, especially with the rain hammering against the windows.

She was pleased to see Cassie and Aaron were doing really well waiting on everyone and nobody appeared to be without drinks or a bread basket to keep them going until the food arrived.

Pete sidled up to her. 'That's the restaurant critic from *The Times*,' he said out of the corner of his mouth.

Belle glanced over to where a solitary man was sitting and studying the cleanliness of the wine glass that he was holding up to the light.

She grimaced. 'Okay,' she whispered back. 'So are you going to be the one to serve him?'

He nodded. 'God, yes. I don't want Aaron to start chatting about compost heaps or whatever.'

'He means well,' she said.

Pete rolled his eyes. 'Just not tonight,' he said, looking stressed. 'Tonight we've got to get the best start ever to get ahead profit-wise.'

Belle sighed. 'Can't we just enjoy the fact that we're actually open for business and not worry about profits for just one evening?' she said.

She walked away to head over to the table where Stanley and Frank were sitting with another man.

'Good evening, all,' she said. 'So what do you think of our new restaurant?'

'It's marvellous,' said Stanley, as affable as always. 'You remember my grandson, Logan?'

Belle smiled down at the man sitting opposite. 'Hi, yes of course I do,' she said. 'It's been a while since you've been in Cranbridge, hasn't it?'

Logan nodded. 'It certainly has, but you've clearly been working hard in the meantime,' he said, looking around the room. 'This all looks great.'

'Thanks,' said Belle. 'Are you staying in the village for the weekend?'

'Actually there might be exciting news in that regard,' said Stanley, looking pleased. 'Logan may be joining our happy community on a permanent basis.'

'How wonderful,' said Belle.

Newcomers were always welcome to the village, especially ones in their early thirties like Logan. They brought life and hopefully business back to Cranbridge.

'Are you all right for drinks?' she asked. 'And I see you've got the bread basket as well.'

The three men nodded.

'Good thing too,' said Frank. 'I don't normally eat this late, but as it's a special occasion.'

'I'll get the kitchen to hurry up your order,' said Belle, giving his shoulder a squeeze.

Frank waved away her concerns with his hand. 'It's fine,' he said. 'No fuss required.'

'I'll be right back,' she said, giving him a wink.

She headed into the inn lounge, checking that Lucy and Tom were okay behind the bar, before going on to the kitchen.

The atmosphere in the kitchen was frantic, borderline hysterical. Brad was rushing around, trying to ensure everything was prepared, but Andre was fussing over every plate to ensure that it looked like an artistic masterpiece.

'It doesn't matter what it looks like,' she said, as he wiped off a swirl of some kind of sauce and replaced it with yet another swirl which looked almost identical. 'The customers are getting restless out there.'

'Have you got the order for table five?' asked Cassie, as she joined them. 'They say that they've got to get back to the babysitter at 9 p.m.'

Andre gave a huff of irritation. 'They'll have to wait,' he snapped.

Cassie raised her eyebrows at Belle but didn't reply.

Belle also noticed that with Andre fussing over the presentation of the plates Brad had been left to juggle various pans and was actually doing the majority of the cooking.

'I need you to check this wild boar,' said Brad, looking down at the pan. 'I don't know how it should be done.'

'Oh, leave it to me,' said Andre, abandoning the plate he was working on and going over to the smoking hob. 'You've charred the edges, you stupid boy.'

'I don't know how to cook it,' said Brad, walking over to the plates. 'They're good to go,' he told Belle. 'That's table five.'

'I need to check the look of everything before it goes out!' said Andre, rushing back over and abandoning the wild boar once more.

'Too late,' said Belle, picking up the plates and handing them over to Cassie. 'Go,' she said softly. Then she turned back to Andre. 'Please hurry up,' she urged him before leaving.

But as the evening wore on, Andre appeared to have totally ignored her instructions and more and more customers were looking at their watches before asking when their food was likely to be appearing.

Belle fixed a smile on her face as Pete headed towards the kitchen to see what was going on.

At least some of the food had been served, she thought, walking over to where Stanley, Frank and Logan were sitting and eating their fancy food.

'How is everything?' she asked, smiling down at them all.

'Very, er, interesting,' said Frank, after swallowing hard. 'I've never tried wild boar before.'

He didn't sound as if he would be wanting it ever again.

But at least he was eating what had been served, as opposed to Logan who still had an almost full plate.

'Is everything okay?' she asked him.

Logan looked up at her with a grimace. 'It's a bit rare for me,' he said.

'Oh dear,' she said quickly. 'But perhaps that's how it's supposed to be served. It's gastronomic cuisine, I've been told.'

'It's not rare when pork is not cooked properly,' he said, showing her the raw meat inside his steak. 'It's officially classed as food poisoning.'

Belle was aghast. 'I'm so sorry,' she told him, picking up the plate and praying that nobody else had eaten the undercooked pork.

But as she carried the plate towards the kitchen, she was stopped by another customer on the next table.

'Have you any water?' asked the man. 'My wife's just swallowed what tastes like half a pound of salt. There's something wrong with that sauce.'

'Of course,' said Belle, looking over to where the woman was sitting, holding her throat and with watering eyes. 'I'll get you a glass.'

She asked Aaron to fetch the glass of water for the lady and was about to head back to the kitchen again when the critic called her over. Feeling she had no choice, she went up to him.

'How can I help?' she asked, fixing a smile on her face.

'You can help by taking this monstrosity away,' said the critic, pushing his half-eaten plate away from him. 'The boar was almost inedible in its toughness, the potatoes were burnt, the jus was inexplicable and I'm not sure what on earth that brown mush is supposed to be in the corner.'

'I'm so sorry,' said Belle, just as Pete came up to join them.

'Is everything all right?' he asked, smiling down at the man.

But his smile quickly faded.

'No, it most certainly is not,' replied the critic, pushing his chair back and standing up. 'The food is a disgrace. This is not a gastronomic experience. This is a disaster. The food is inedible and quite revolting. I cannot believe you have wasted my time like this.'

Belle was horrified to hear a smattering of applause agreeing with the critic's words.

'I'm sorry to hear that,' said Pete, looking stunned.

'Not as sorry as I was to have agreed to come here in the first place,' said the man, glaring at him. 'Now where is my coat?'

To add insult to injury, the man's coat which had been hung up next to the cutlery and condiments appeared to have some kind of mustard spilled up the sleeve.

As he marched out, a few more people also got up and left without paying their bills. Belle really didn't blame them. Why should they pay for disgusting food which was inedible?

There was no doubt. The restaurant was a qualified disaster. And the inn looked more likely to close down than ever before.

42

After the last of the customers had left and the inn was officially closed, Belle sat down in the cosy lounge next to the fireplace with her friends. She felt utterly exhausted by the whole, disastrous evening.

'Well,' said Lucy, sitting down at the next table with Tom. 'Erm...'

But even she seemed lost for words and looked to Tom to say something positive.

He gave Belle a smile that she noticed didn't quite meet his eyes. 'It could be worse,' he said.

'I don't see how,' said Belle with a sigh. 'The restaurant critic walked out, we may have given half the village food poisoning from uncooked food and those that aren't ill walked out because they never even received their food which, apparently, was disgusting and they wouldn't have enjoyed their meal anyway.'

'See? Doesn't that mean that less people will be ill if they walked out?' said Tom with a gentle smile. 'Every cloud and all that.'

'And we don't feel ill,' said Amber, who was sitting next to Belle. She reached out and squeezed Belle's hand.

'That's because you didn't have the pork,' said Belle. But she was grateful for their support.

'I'm not sure what I had,' said Josh, frowning. 'It was supposed to be wild boar or something, but it was just chewy. Really really chewy.'

'I wouldn't even give that food to Keith,' said Grandma Tilly, sneaking a crisp under the table to where the dog was sitting. He took the crisp gently and seemed to enjoy it more than anyone else had enjoyed their food that evening.

The food had looked very pretty on the plate, thought Belle, but, according to nearly everyone, it had been almost inedible.

She couldn't believe that all the effort and hard work had been for nothing.

'The waiter and waitress did well to handle it all,' said Cathy, obviously trying to find something positive about the whole disaster.

'They really did despite everything,' said Belle.

Cassie and Aaron had left only a short time ago after being told not to bother tidying up. She would do the washing-up and clearing away tomorrow. It wasn't as if the restaurant would be in use after that evening. It would never be used again, she suspected. Nobody would want to eat there now.

Poor Brad, she thought. He would be out of work again and heaven knows what that would do to his fragile confidence and trust in people.

'Well, we really enjoyed pulling a pint behind the bar,' said Lucy. 'So if you ever need a break for an evening, then we're happy to step in.'

'Thanks, but I don't suppose I'll be around much longer anyway,' Belle told her in a dull tone.

'What do you mean?' asked Cathy looking startled.

Belle rolled her eyes. 'The restaurant is a disaster. It's not going to make any money, so Pete will have to sell the place and then it'll go to a new owner. Or be pulled down to make some flats or something, I suppose.'

'Pulled down?' Grandma Tilly looked shocked. 'Of course not. It's the only thing in the village that's been here as long as I have.'

'Apart from the church,' drawled Josh before looking back at Belle. 'But I agree with my grandmother. It's not the end of the world.'

'Thanks everyone,' said Belle, standing up. 'It's been really kind of you to stay behind and try to cheer us up, but I think we'll call it a night. It's been pretty exhausting, to be honest.'

She looked around as her friends stood up, but it was just them in the bar.

'I saw him head out into the garden,' said Josh quietly. 'If I know my brother, and I'm afraid to say that I do, he'll be sulking in a corner somewhere. Although this time I feel he may deserve some of the blame.'

Belle nodded. 'Me too, to be honest.'

Josh gave her a quick hug. 'Tomorrow will seem better, I'm sure,' he said.

'Thanks,' said Belle, with a grateful smile. 'Goodnight.'

She unlocked the door to let them all head out and received hugs and goodnights from her friends before they left.

Finally it was just Belle standing alone in the lounge. She could hear Andre still clattering around in the kitchen. She had no idea what he could still be doing as the customers and staff had all left, but she didn't want to see him now.

She needed to see Pete. Although she had no idea what she was going to say to him. But she guessed that he would be the only one who was feeling as bad as she was at that moment.

* * *

Pete sat in the dark garden, not even feeling the cold night-time temperature which had dipped to almost freezing.

He knew that he should be in the inn with Belle, trying to talk to his family and friends. But he had nothing to say. He was out of words and out of excuses.

All he knew was that it was all his fault. The evening had been a disaster, but surely he should have seen it coming? It was his responsibility. He had hired Andre. He had insisted on the fancy menu and booked the restaurant critic. And now the review would be fatal for the inn.

'Hi.'

On hearing her voice, he turned his head to find Belle standing nearby, her arms clutched around her as she shivered in the cold night air.

'Hi,' he replied, quickly looking away.

'I just wanted to check where you were,' she said.

He gave a grunt of humour as he stared down at the ground. 'Why, are you thinking of pushing me in the river?' he asked.

'It's not the worst idea you've ever had.'

His whole body sagged under the weight of responsibility. 'I know,' he replied. 'And I've had some pretty awful ones recently.'

'Yes. You have.'

He finally willed himself to look up into her dark eyes. 'I'm so sorry,' he said.

She nodded her acceptance but remained quiet, her arms still wrapped around her as she stood in front of him.

'So what happens now?' he asked.

She shrugged her shoulders. 'We open up the bar again tomorrow and then it's the village bonfire night celebrations. There are always a few more customers on that night so that will help takings.'

'And then?' He couldn't stop himself from asking. From needing to hear it from her.

'And then I don't know,' she said simply. 'I guess we'll take it one day at a time. That's what I normally do after a failure.'

He'd never failed at anything before. Except, he suddenly realised, that he had. He'd failed at being supportive to his family. He'd failed in staying true to the family name. He'd failed at ensuring that The Black Swan would succeed.

Most of all, he'd failed to help Belle keep her home.

'I was wrong,' he told her.

'About what?' she asked.

'About all of it.'

She nodded. 'Yes. You were. But at least you tried. Don't stay out here too long. It's freezing.'

She hesitated before turning to walk away. He knew what the unspoken words meant. It meant that she would never forgive him.

But what she would never realise was that he would never forgive himself either for causing her so much pain and letting her down.

43

Belle had walked away from Pete. He seemed happy to be drowning his own sorrows in the garden and she needed to secure the inn and close up.

In truth, she also didn't want to talk to him at that moment. She was filled with disappointment about how his insistence on the gastronomic experience that he had wanted for the restaurant had always been destined for disaster. It didn't fit with Cranbridge and it certainly didn't fit with The Black Swan. Or her.

That was her deepest worry of all. That he was looking for something glamorous. Something far more stylish than she could ever hope to be.

And she felt worse than ever. Because it was also just possible that Pete had put the death knell on The Black Swan for good. Without a restaurant, they couldn't make the money they needed to survive in business. Which meant that she was about to lose her home.

She pushed open the back door to the inn, still deep in thought. So she was startled to hear a noise coming from the kitchen.

She wondered if perhaps they had mice, but when she went

into the kitchen, she realised it was just a big rat in the form of Andre.

'What are you doing?' she asked, as he was poring over some written notes in a book.

'I'm planning the menu for tomorrow,' he told her in a sarcastic tone.

'What are you talking about?' she asked.

'Yes, what *are* you talking about?' asked Pete coming to stand next to her. He had obviously followed Belle inside.

Andre looked at them both with raised eyebrows. 'I am the head chef, am I not? Then I must plan the meals for tomorrow's dining experience.'

Pete blew out a sigh of disgust. 'Tomorrow?' he said. 'There is no tomorrow. The restaurant is closed for good. Your awful food saw to that. Among other things, I admit.'

'My awful food?' Andre's voice had risen several octaves. 'I don't agree.'

'The pork wasn't cooked properly,' said Belle, her own anger flaring up. 'You may very well have given quite a few of our customers food poisoning.'

'Nonsense,' said Andre. 'My food is always cooked and delicious.'

'Dear God, you are delusional!' said Pete, running a hand through his hair. He looked at Andre in disbelief. 'Did you not check the food before it left the kitchen?'

Andre lifted his chin in an apparent smug gesture. 'Of course I didn't,' he said, almost preening. 'My work is excellent.'

'It was awful,' said Pete. 'I cannot believe a man with such glowing references could cook so poorly.'

Andre gulped in the silence that followed, at which point Belle's mouth fell open in shock.

'You faked your CV,' she said.

'I did not!' said Andre, shaking his head at her.

'Crikey, you did!' said Pete, now agog as he stared at his chef. 'It makes sense now. Your attitude stinks, your cooking is awful. Of course you made up the references!'

'Only because the cruise line wouldn't give me a reference!' shouted Andre.

A short silence rang out before Belle heard Pete take what appeared to be a calming breath.

'Leave,' he said, quietly but firmly. 'Leave our inn now and never come back.'

'You cannot do this!' blustered Andre.

Pete said nothing but took a step forward instead.

Andre appeared to panic at this point and grabbed his coat, wallet and phone which were nearby. 'I am too good for this crummy little inn!' he announced, with a sneer.

Pete grabbed him by the collar and frogmarched Andre out of the kitchen.

Belle followed to watch Andre unceremoniously thrown out of the front door before Pete locked it and leaned against it.

Belle watched as his body appeared to sag.

'I can't believe it,' said Pete, almost to himself. 'I'm such an idiot. How naive am I? He had me totally fooled and I had no idea.'

He looked up at Belle with haunted eyes and her heart plummeted for him. Yes, he had mucked up on an enormous scale. But he hadn't meant to. None of his mistakes had been deliberate.

She found her feet moved automatically until she was standing in front of him.

His head had dropped in despair. So she reached out to touch his cheek and bring his face up to hers.

'I've made everything ten times worse,' he said, his voice hoarse with despair.

'Yes, you have,' she told him.

His eyes widened in alarm so she reached out to touch his other cheek and held his face in her hands.

'But it was all done with good intentions,' she said. 'You're an idiot, Pete Kennedy, but you haven't got a bad bone in your body.'

'I've let you down,' he said.

But she shushed him by lifting her face until their lips were almost touching. 'You tried,' she told him. 'That was enough.'

Then she closed the final small gap and kissed him. It was a soft kiss to begin with to ease his pain. As it grew deeper, she felt his arms close around her to hold her close.

But something held her back from letting herself go completely. The fact remained that the inn was still in peril and the hurt was too deep for her to think about anything else that evening.

So she took a small step back to smile softly at him.

'Maybe it'll all seem better in the morning,' she said.

He nodded, still looking somewhat dazed after her kiss.

So she said goodnight and then walked away whilst she still had the power to do so.

Because all she really wanted to do at that moment was rush back into his arms and stay there, preferably forever.

44

Pete woke up late the following morning after tossing and turning for most of the night. The guilt of the failure of the restaurant lay heavy on him.

He could hear movement downstairs and figured it was Belle tidying up the mess of the night before.

He sighed heavily as he lay in bed, willing himself to get up and help her. He thought back to when she had kissed him the previous evening. It had seemed like a kiss between friends, but the reaction from his hammering heart on having her lips touch his had been anything but friendly. He had wanted more. He had wanted to never let go of her.

And yet she had walked away. If the restaurant had been a success, perhaps she might not have, he mused. But it had and so she had walked.

He finally got up and dressed, not having the stomach for breakfast, so he headed downstairs and found Belle clearing away the tablecloths in the restaurant.

'Morning,' he said, hovering by the doorway.

She spun around and raised an eyebrow at him. 'I think it still is, just.'

'Sorry,' he said, dragging a hand through his hair. 'I should have got up earlier to help.'

She shrugged her shoulders. 'It's okay. I can handle it.'

'I didn't sleep very well, so I think I'll go grab a coffee from the shop,' he said. 'Do you want one?'

She nodded. 'Sounds good.'

Outside, he found the air had cooled significantly overnight and there were signs that there had been a frost. It was barely above freezing and he could see his breath in the air as he walked across the narrow pedestrian bridge towards the shop.

The river had slowed down and was reflecting the blue sky overhead. It had remained clear, but the sun was now low, still hidden behind the trees in the distance. A few people were out walking, but thankfully not anyone he recognised as friends or family.

He hesitated before heading inside, not wanting to face his brother or Amber quite yet. But the thought of a decent coffee finally made up the decision for him, so he went up the steps and pushed the door open.

Grandma Tilly was standing by the till alongside Amber. 'Well, look who decided to finally get up,' she said.

'How did you know?' asked Pete, nonplussed.

'Josh tried to call you earlier,' said Grandma Tilly. 'When there was no reply, he checked in with Belle to make sure that you were okay.'

They were always looking out for him, he thought, his family. That would never stop, Pete realised. And he didn't want it to. It gave him a warm feeling inside that somebody cared for him. But he had let them down.

'I had a bad night's sleep,' he told his grandmother.

'I'm not surprised,' she replied, picking up her knitting. 'Was it the pork?'

'You weren't ill, were you?' asked Amber, looking concerned.

Pete shook his head. 'No. Has anyone reported being ill?'

Both Amber and Grandma Tilly shook their heads, which caused Pete to let out a sigh of relief. 'Thank goodness for that.'

'They were all probably just hungry,' said Grandma Tilly. 'I think most folks went without dinner altogether.'

'Well, they don't need to worry about eating in The Black Swan ever again,' Pete told them both, attempting a smile. 'I gave Andre the sack, so that's the end of that.'

'There are other chefs, you know,' said Amber softly.

But Pete shook his head. 'Not around here. Anyway, that doesn't matter. What matters right now is that I badly need caffeine. Can I help myself to a coffee? And one for Belle too?'

'I'll make them for you,' said Amber. 'The machine can be a little temperamental at times.'

'Much like my brother,' said Josh, coming out from the back room. 'Add another one to that order, would you please? We'll take them outside.'

The brothers headed outside to the veranda.

Pete sat on the bench and enjoyed the view. Watching the river slowly make its way downstream and listening to the nearby bird-song was giving him a sense of peace he hadn't felt for a long time.

Josh sat down next to him. 'How are you doing today?' he asked.

Pete realised that there was no malice in his brother. He was just looking out for him as he had always done. 'Bit weary but okay,' said Pete. He paused before saying, 'I've got a lot of bridges to build.'

Josh nodded. 'Maybe, but the foundations are already there.'

Pete blew out a long sigh. 'I'm sure it'll be just fine,' he said. 'If I ignore the overriding sense of shame and regret, plus the frustration about a total lack of plan going forward.'

'So it's a mess,' said Josh, nodding. 'Well, it was about time you joined me and Dad, to be honest.'

Pete turned to look at his brother. 'What are you talking about?' he asked. 'Look at what you've achieved here. Look at what Dad achieved throughout his life.'

'Yeah!' laughed Josh. 'Just look! You think all this,' he gestured at the shop behind them, 'was easy? You think we didn't make mistakes along the way? I nearly lost the shop and Amber before we finally got straight.'

Pete watched as Josh's face became more serious.

'And it was Dad that left both the shop and the family finances in near ruin,' said Josh. 'I mean, I loved him. We all did. But he sure as hell wasn't perfect. Come on, I mean, the unexpected trips out that ended who knows where. Don't you remember how stressed it would make Mum worrying where we would all sleep if we went too far? Let alone all the crazy stuff that he bought for the shop when we first moved in before getting bored with it and playing the guitar on the veranda instead.'

There was a long silence whilst they both went back in time. Pete then wondered whether he should tell Josh about the letter but in the end decided against it. Everything was already hard that day and he couldn't face any more heartbreak, let alone upsetting his brother.

'He's a tough act to follow though,' Pete eventually said.

Josh nodded. 'Yeah. He is,' he said, in a softer tone. He turned to look at his younger brother. 'Have you played the guitar recently?'

Pete shook his head. 'Not sure I ever will without him,' he confessed.

'Well, you'll get no pressure from me if you can't face it,' said

Josh. 'But I think it would be a sad thing not to hear you play again. You were pretty good.'

'Is that a compliment?' asked Pete.

'Only one you're going to get from me today,' said Josh, smiling. 'But I do have a question for you, now I come to think about it.'

Pete looked at him, his eyebrows raised in query.

'Will you be my best man?' asked Josh.

Pete was touched but troubled by the question. 'I'm not sure I'm a best anything at the moment,' said Pete. 'I don't want to mess up again.'

'You won't,' said Josh. 'But you're my brother and I want you up there with me when I get married.'

Pete nodded. 'Then, of course I'll be your best man,' he said, his voice thick with emotion.

Josh gave him a brief hug before slapping him on the back.

They both leaned back in the seat and concentrated on the lane and river once more.

Pete's eyes strayed towards the inn.

'It'll be all right,' said Josh, who had turned to look at him. 'The inn, I mean.'

'How?' asked Pete.

Josh gave a shrug of his shoulders. 'I have no idea, bro,' he replied. 'But you've got Belle and she's pretty special. You'll both think of something, I'm sure. Have you got any kind of plan going forward?'

Pete shook his head. 'Not yet.'

'You'll think of something,' said Josh before laughing as he stood up. 'You always do.'

'Maybe this time I'm out of my depth,' Pete told him.

Josh shook his head. 'Then take some time to work it out,' he said. 'We didn't fix the shop overnight. And we didn't get the right mix of stuff at the beginning. It takes time. So spend the winter here and enjoy it.' He hesitated before adding, 'I'd enjoy having you around too, to be honest.'

Pete looked at his big brother who was shuffling from foot to foot in embarrassment.

'But if you make me say it again, I'll push you in the river,' said Josh.

Now it was Pete's turn to laugh. 'Dream on, bro. You know you'll never be as strong as me.'

'You want to find out?' asked Josh.

Pete knew he was only joking. 'Would love to prove you wrong as always, but I need to go and give Belle her coffee. She's been stuck tidying up all morning whilst I've been wallowing in my own misery.'

'Maybe she'll be the one to push you in the river instead,' said Josh hopefully before giving his brother a wink and walking off.

But for all their banter, Pete felt a little lighter in spirits suddenly. He felt closer to his brother than he had done for weeks, maybe even years. Slowly they were starting to become friends again. And perhaps all the pain would be worth it if they did.

Perhaps it was time to make amends with Belle and ask for her help. He just hoped she wanted to listen to him after everything that had happened.

45

Belle had waited until after lunchtime to call her aunt and uncle with the bad news.

'The restaurant was a disaster,' she told them, as she sat on her bed. 'A total and utter failure.'

'Oh, love,' said Aunty Angie. 'I'm so sorry. But it'll work out fine, you'll see.'

'How?' asked Belle.

'Because it always does, doesn't it?' said Angie, looking at her husband. 'And we should know.'

'That's right,' said Uncle Mick, laughing. 'We've had so many failures over the years. The beer that flooded the cellar due to that dodgy pipe.'

'The rats in the early days,' said Aunty Angie with a shudder.

'The electricity shorting out and causing the whole village to go dark,' added Uncle Mick.

'I'd forgotten about that one,' said Aunty Angie.

'What we're trying to tell you is that there's always a second chance,' said Uncle Mick. 'I mean, look at where we are.'

The phone screen spun round to briefly show an endless ocean and blue sky before swinging back to show her aunt and uncle's faces once more.

'We've just crossed the international dateline,' said Aunty Angie. 'Do you know what that means?'

Belle shook her head.

'It means that today's date is the same as yesterday,' Uncle Mick told her. 'Tomorrow doesn't arrive for another twenty-four hours.'

'It means we've got a chance to rewind the last day and do it over,' said Aunty Angie. 'Do it even better.'

'A restart,' said Uncle Mick.

Belle watched as her aunt and uncle suddenly turned to look at each other.

'Never thought we'd get another chance,' said Uncle Mick.

'Never thought we'd ever have a chance to do anything like this,' said Aunty Angie.

'Maybe a restart is what we all need,' murmured Uncle Mick.

Belle watched them as something passed between the couple. Tenderness. Perhaps even love.

'So what will you do with your groundhog day?' she asked.

'We'll do it better,' said Aunty Angie. 'And do it right, for once.'

Uncle Mick nodded in agreement. 'And you can do the same, love,' he told Belle.

Belle was still mulling over her uncle's words when there was a tap on the door.

Molly's friendly face peered around the corner, closely followed by Amber and Lucy.

'Pete said you were up here,' said Molly.

'We just wanted to make sure that you were okay,' said Amber, as they all sat on the bed with her.

Belle gave a shrug of her shoulders. 'I don't know how I feel really,' she said. 'So I'll just keep going until I do.'

'Is this all going spare?' asked Amber, looking at the rolls of cloth in the corner.

Belle shook her head. 'All reserved for Grandma Tilly's quilts,' she said. 'Although I don't think she's got enough for the Christmas fete yet.'

'We can help,' said Lucy.

So they spent an hour cutting up the spare cloth into squares until Belle declared that she really had to get back to work.

'I still can't believe you didn't tell us that you were this good at sewing,' said Molly, looking at one of the unfinished quilts.

'And that you were meeting Grandma Tilly in secret,' added Amber in a pointed tone.

'A girl's got to have some secrets,' said Lucy with a smile.

'It's just that I always thought we were honest with each other,' went on Amber.

Belle shrugged her shoulders but stayed silent.

'It is good to talk about yourself sometimes,' added Molly in a soft tone.

Belle went to shrug her shoulders again and managed to stop herself. Perhaps she was a bit like Pete in that regard. And maybe she needed to open up too.

'It's only sewing,' she finally said. 'I didn't think it was that important.'

'But it's important to you and that's what matters,' said Lucy.

'And it's not just sewing,' said Amber, taking the quilt from Molly. 'I mean, look at your stitches. They're so tiny and perfect.'

Belle looked away, feeling her cheeks blush. She wasn't used to compliments.

'You do know how amazing you are, don't you?' said Lucy.

But Belle found she was shaking her head. 'Look, I'll be blunt,' she began.

'How will we tell the difference?' murmured Lucy.

'Shut up,' said Amber. 'Go on, Belle.'

'I know you all think I'm super strong, but it's all a lie. I'm afraid of everything. Because without Cranbridge I don't think I'd have anything, or anyone, in my life. I don't even want to bring any attention to myself when it's just us. I've always preferred the attention on everyone else but me.'

'Of course you have,' said Amber. 'You were a target for your parents when you were growing up and that must have been terrible.'

'But that was twenty years ago,' said Belle, hanging her head.

'Oh, Belle,' said Molly, giving her a teary smile. 'Pain doesn't disappear that easily, trust me.'

'But perhaps it's time to trust us and be brave,' said Lucy. 'Because you're just as beautiful on the inside as you are on the outside.'

'I don't know about that,' said Belle quickly.

'You could start with a few brighter colours,' said Amber.

'I thought you liked the pastels,' said Belle, frowning at the cut-up pieces of material.

'I meant for you,' said Amber softly.

Belle took a deep intake of breath and automatically glanced down at her dark clothes.

'It would be nice to see you in something brighter, for a change,' said Molly.

Belle hesitated, unable to find any words. She had hidden away for so long that she wasn't sure how.

'Why don't you start off with just one piece,' said Lucy, nodding her head in encouragement. 'Like a pretty top.'

'Or even a brightly coloured scarf whilst the weather's so cold outside,' added Amber.

As her friends all nodded in agreement, Belle found she was hoping that their encouragement would rub off on her.

'Maybe even Pete will notice,' muttered Lucy.

Belle blushed and pretended not to have heard. She might only just be brave enough to wear a slightly brighter top. She certainly wasn't brave enough to confess how she really felt about Pete yet to her friends.

Because, despite everything that had happened, Belle knew that if Pete left, she would be completely heartbroken.

46

Pete was emptying out the bins later that afternoon before realising how much darker it was becoming now that the clocks had gone back an hour.

He had felt a little better after the conversation with his brother, and although he felt as if he didn't deserve his support, Pete was truly grateful that he had it in any case.

But how to move forward now with the inn? Sooner or later, he was going to have to face everyone outside of his family. What would he say to their many questions? He had no idea.

He was so deep in thought as he went to head back inside that he didn't notice Ned sitting on the bench nearby until he hollered at him.

'Oy! Cloth ears!'

Pete looked around startled and then smiled at the old man, turning in his tracks to walk over to him.

'Never seen a chap look as if he had the weight of the world on his shoulders before,' said Ned.

'Mind if I join you?' asked Pete.

'Be my guest,' said Ned, gesturing at the bench. 'I should think you need to sit down with all those thoughts going on inside your head. Take the weight off, son.'

Pete sat down and relished the silence as they looked out across the river. It was a truly beautiful afternoon in Cranbridge, but it gave him no solace whatsoever.

'Have you ever failed at anything, Ned?' he found himself asking.

The old man sitting on the bench beside him laughed. 'Of course I have! Life is all about failure, don't you know that?'

Pete was shocked. 'What do you mean?' he said, nonplussed.

'I mean,' began Ned. 'That there's a fortunate few, normally those who have been blessed with infinite wealth, to whom life is easy. And then there's the rest of us. We can only learn from our failures, lad. Not our successes. But that's the key. You've got to earn your success.'

Pete thought about his job in Singapore. Yes, he'd worked hard but mostly he had been in the right place at the right time. Had he learnt anything? Only that money hadn't made him particularly happy.

He felt Ned watching him as they sat on the bench. 'What about you?' he asked the pensioner. 'What failures have you learnt from?'

Ned laughed again. 'How much time have you got?' His smile faded a little though as he carried on. 'Two marriages, neither of which were particularly happy experiences. That was my fault. They were good women and didn't deserve a scoundrel like me. A son whom I never see. Doesn't want to see me and why should he? I was a terrible father, never had time for him. And in my career too, I failed many times over, mostly due to my own arrogance. To be honest, that's how I met your dad.'

Pete looked at him in question.

'I was just through with my second divorce and partying too heavily when I met Todd at a gig,' Ned explained. 'He saw a fellow musician with huge problems in his personal life and we became kindred spirits, in a way. He helped me get clean and we went from strength to strength.'

'I didn't know that,' said Pete.

'Oh yes,' said Ned. 'Todd mentored quite a few musicians who were battling various addictions. He'd partied too hard and knew how it could affect both your personal life as well as your playing abilities.'

Pete nodded to himself. There had never been any chance of bragging with his father. His talent came naturally to him and it was just there. The fact that he had been a famous musician had never impacted their childhood either. Todd had been a normal dad to Josh and himself. He realised in that moment how special his dad had truly been.

He wondered what Todd would make of his younger son's decisions in life. Would he have been as accepting of failure as Ned said he would have? Pete didn't know. All he knew was that somehow he had to start afresh.

'So what do I do now?' asked Pete, to himself more than to the elderly pensioner sitting next to him.

'You pick yourself up and start over,' said Ned, slowly standing up. 'Are you going to let one failure dictate the rest of your life? Are you going to let one mistake stop you from being happy forever? Then buck up, lad. Stand up and get going. Life passes by in the blink of an eye and you're only young once.'

Pete stood up. 'Thanks, Ned,' he said softly.

Ned smiled at him. 'I see it as repaying a favour to your dad for debts a long time ago,' he said. 'And if it gets through to you that you're capable of so much more, then even better.'

'I'll do my best,' Pete said.

Ned nodded. 'That's all anyone can ever do, son. See you around.'

Pete watched him as he walked off, his heart aching in that moment for his father. He would have given every penny in the world to see him once more.

But all he could do was cherish the family that remained and take his dad's friend's advice.

* * *

Belle was behind the bar when he arrived back at the inn, so Pete found his feet automatically moving upstairs.

There, in his bedroom, he went and stood next to the guitar case. He stared at it for a long time before finally reaching out and clicking open the locks.

As he crouched down in front of it, the sweet smell of mahogany hit him. It was a beautiful guitar of polished dark wood.

He reached out to feel along the smooth wooden body all the way up to neck and fingerboard.

Finally, his fingers hovered over the strings until he plucked just one. The tone rang out, deep and warm, and he felt it filling his heart as well as his ears.

Perhaps there would be a time in the future when he would play again, he thought. Perhaps he could face it after all. Just not quite yet.

He felt his heart lift a little as he headed back downstairs.

'You look cheerful,' said Belle, sounding surprised, when they met at the bar.

'I feel more cheerful,' said Pete, going to stand in front of her. 'I've decided we're going to save the inn.'

Belle blinked a couple of times as she looked up at him. 'We are?' she asked. 'How do you propose to do that?'

'I have no idea,' said Pete, dragging a hand through his hair. 'But I'll think of something.'

She smiled at him, as if trying to believe that it were true. But as she walked away, Pete's smile faded. He just hoped he would have enough time to think up a way of saving the inn. For everyone's sake.

Because now that his dad was gone he had to step up, just like Josh had done. He might be three years too late, of course. And he had missed his chance to help his brother out in the shop. But maybe, just maybe, he could somehow keep the inn open for the village instead.

And for Belle too.

47

Bonfire night arrived along with a northerly wind which made everyone rush into the inn to warm up beside the fireplaces once the festivities were over.

Belle noticed that as everyone came in, wrapped up in woolly hats, scarves and thick coats to offset the cold air, nobody was mentioning the fiasco of the restaurant opening night. She was just grateful that they were still coming into the inn at all.

It was even busier than the previous year, Belle thought, later that evening. Perhaps the clear, dry night had helped, especially as snow was forecast for the coming week.

All Belle knew was that her feet were beginning to ache by the middle of the evening and they still had a couple of hours to get through.

Lucy had managed to push her way to the front of the bar with Tom. 'Hi,' she said, smiling at her friend. 'How's it been tonight?'

Belle looked at her friend and smiled wearily. 'Incredible. You?'

Lucy nodded. 'Oh yes,' she said, grinning. 'The community hub has been mobbed with people wanting to know about the craft classes and what we do. There's been a huge uptake. We've only just shut the doors now.'

'Lucky you,' said Belle, looking across the still busy lounge. 'I reckon it's going to be like this until we close tonight.'

'Have you had a break yet?' asked Tom, looking concerned.

Belle shook her head. 'You're joking,' she said, with a laugh. 'I haven't even eaten anything since lunchtime.'

'That's terrible,' said Lucy. 'Do you want me to grab you some food?'

But to Belle's surprise, Tom shook his head. 'Tell you what, why don't you let me and Lucy hold the fort. Go get a break. And take Pete with you. I don't suppose he's had a break either.'

On hearing his name, Pete wandered over to join them. 'What's going on?' he asked.

'You're having an overdue dinner break,' said Tom in firm tone of voice. 'There's a stall out there selling the most amazing burgers. Go out and grab one whilst he's still there. Then you'll be all set for the rest of the evening.'

Pete hesitated. 'Are you sure?'

'Go!' urged Lucy.

Belle looked at Pete, who nodded at her. 'I could do with some fresh air, to be honest,' he said.

'And my stomach's rumbling,' she replied.

So they both grabbed their coats and headed outside.

The rush of cold winter air hit Belle's lungs as soon as they stepped out next to the river. It was dark now, but the lane was lit up with fairy lights and lanterns, giving everything a special glow.

Josh, Dodgy Del and a few other villagers had built the tall bonfire only that morning out of old pallets and discarded shrubbery cuttings. It was a fairly good size for such a small village and everyone had turned out to join in the festivities.

All the children were wearing Day-Glo bracelets that Dodgy Del had procured from somewhere – not that anyone was asking their origins. Everyone appeared to have sparklers and hot drinks, as well as various decorated cupcakes which Molly had made.

She and Pete headed straight to Molly's cake stall first but were disappointed to find her packing away the tablecloth.

'Have I missed it?' Belle asked. 'I was hoping for one of your cupcakes,' she said, licking her lips.

'Oh no!' Molly looked upset. 'I should have kept one back for you. I've sold every last cupcake and the big cakes as well. It's been unbelievable.'

'That's because your cakes are amazing,' Belle told her.

No matter how many times they assured their friend that she was an incredible baker, Molly never seemed to quite believe them.

'Pity though,' said Pete, who was standing next to her. 'I'm starving.'

'Tom said something about a burger stall?' said Belle, looking around.

'He's at the other end of the lane,' said Molly, pointing in the right direction. 'Everyone says they're really yummy.'

'Then lead the way,' said Pete to Belle. 'Or else I'm going to faint from hunger.'

'Do you want to come?' asked Belle, looking at Molly.

Suddenly she didn't want to be alone with Pete. It was all too romantic. The crackle of the fire. The pretty fairy lights causing a romantic glow everywhere.

'I've got to clear away, but I'll see you in the inn later,' said Molly, smiling.

'Okay, we'll see you back there,' said Belle, putting her hands in her coat pockets. 'It's freezing tonight.'

'They were saying on the radio today that it might be a white Christmas,' said Molly. 'How lovely would that be?'

Belle had a fleeting memory of making snow angels with her aunt and uncle and missed them terribly in that moment.

However, crossing the international dateline and forcing them to relive the same day twice appeared to have had some effect. She had text them to make sure that they hadn't pushed each other overboard, but to her surprise the photos she received in return from one of the tropical islands in the Pacific Ocean were full of a smiling couple in front of a waterfall.

Perhaps the cocktails were extra strong that day, she thought.

They said goodbye to Molly and began to weave their way through the bonfire which was still aflame.

Belle had always enjoyed bonfire night. It had been the very first event that the village had celebrated when she had arrived all those years ago. Bruised and battered emotionally from her traumatic childhood, she had found the convivial atmosphere of the Bonfire Night celebrations almost surreal. At first, she hadn't been eager to talk to anyone, such was the level of distrust that she had felt. Surely they were all being so nice towards her for a reason, she had thought. Having been used as a weapon between her parents for so long, it was hard for Belle to understand that people were just being friendly and wanted to welcome her, with no hidden agenda.

Since that first time, the smoke and crackle of a bonfire always gave her a glow inside as well as out. But it had still taken until Christmastime that year for her to open up to anyone, especially the Kennedy brothers.

They had cajoled her into helping them decorate the lane with strings of fairy lights, as well as decorating the tree that their dad had set up outside the shop. In typical Todd fashion, it was almost too wide and far too close to the entrance, so for the whole month of December, everyone had had to sidle into the shop sidewards.

Not that anyone ever complained, of course. Todd did everything with such ease and charm that nobody ever wanted to put down his grand plans.

Pete had been like that at one time, thought Belle. She could still remember him persuading Josh to hold a plastic duck race down the river for charity years ago. It had gone slightly awry when the ducks had moved a lot quicker than expected, causing a rescue plan to spring into life further down the river. But everyone had just laughed and said that Pete was a chip off the old block.

But since the failure of the restaurant a few days ago, he had been quiet. Too quiet for a Kennedy, she thought.

Winter always made her feel somewhat wistful, she found. Yes, she had her family. She had her friends as well. And yet, there had always been something missing.

And as she walked along with Pete, she knew that she had been missing Pete all these years. That it had always been Pete.

And he didn't think of her that way at all, she thought, sadly.

But perhaps it was for the best. They were friends again and maybe that would just have to be enough for her. After all, to be friends with Pete was better than not having him in her life again.

48

Pete couldn't believe the success of the bonfire night, nor how busy it was.

Thinking about it, the inn had been packed, but he had figured that everyone had just naturally migrated towards where the alcohol was. But they were still surrounded by couples and families out on the lane and it was a happy atmosphere.

He glanced at Belle as they walked along and was pleased to see that she was also smiling and enjoying their walk.

The smell of a barbeque began to fill his senses and his stomach groaned in anticipation. Having skipped lunch, he was hungry and just hoped that the food was as good as Molly had told them it was.

When they finally arrived at the barbeque stall, Pete was shocked to find Brad standing behind the barbeque.

'Hi,' said Belle, also sounding surprised. 'How are you?'

'Not bad,' muttered Brad, not quite meeting their eyes.

Who could blame him? thought Pete. With the restaurant failing, Brad was also out of work.

'Has it been busy?' she carried on, trying to lure the young man into conversation.

'Yeah.'

'So how about two burgers?' Belle looked at Pete in question, who nodded his reply.

'You'll find none better,' said Dodgy Del, appearing in front of them. 'Surprised to see you two over here. The inn looked packed.'

'We needed some food,' said Pete.

'Well, you'll get none better than our Brad's burgers,' said Del, throwing his nephew a smile.

But Brad was too busy to spot his uncle's proud look as he was loading up two burgers with sliced onions, lettuce, tomatoes and cheese. Finally, he handed them over to Belle whilst Pete gave him the money.

Belle gave Pete his burger before taking a bite out of hers.

'Oh my God,' she mumbled, her mouth full. 'This tastes amazing.'

'It's good, ain't it?' said Del, grinning at her. 'Told you so.'

They all looked at Pete, who had been deciding how to best fake how much he was going to enjoy the burger. Brad had already lost his job, thanks to Andre. Pete didn't want to dent his tender confidence any more.

But it turned out that he didn't have to lie or act at all. With the first bite, the flavours exploded in his mouth. The burger was well cooked but tender, almost crumbling in his mouth. There was a kind of seasoning which he didn't recognise but it brought the burger up to a whole new level.

'What's the bun?' asked Belle, before taking another bite.

'Brioche,' Brad told her.

'And what have you done to the onions?' she asked.

'Just caramelised them.'

Pete took another bite out of his burger just to make sure that he hadn't been hallucinating.

He wasn't. The burger was incredible.

'Where did you get the burgers?' he said, when he was finally able to speak.

Brad looked at him with a scowl. 'Sam's farm,' he said shortly.

'Sam makes burgers now?' asked Pete, surprised. The local farmer's meat products were of superb quality, but he didn't know that they produced anything other than steaks and other raw items.

Brad looked at Pete as if he were mad before shaking his head. 'Sam gave me the mince,' he said. 'I make the burgers myself.'

'And the seasoning?' asked Pete.

'My own recipe,' said Brad, sounding the tiniest proud. 'And the burger sauce too.'

Pete looked at him aghast. 'Why didn't you tell us you could cook like this?' he said, still shocked.

'You never asked,' came the sullen reply.

Pete felt instantly guilty for underestimating him.

'You're absolutely right. Well, I'm asking now,' said Pete, leaning forward. 'What else can you cook?'

Brad shrugged his shoulders. 'Shepherd's pie. My risotto is pretty good. I do a mean chicken pie. Make my own puff pastry too.'

'And he makes the best roast I've ever had,' said Del.

'Not fancy enough for your place though,' muttered Brad.

'Well, let's just say that I was the one that was totally wrong,' Pete found himself saying. 'I want to offer you your job back.'

Brad crossed his arms and shook his head. 'I'm not working for that idiot again,' he said, making a face.

'You won't need to,' said Pete. 'I gave Andre the sack. I want you to be head chef at the inn.'

Belle looked across at Pete with wide eyes. Pete nodded at her and her face lit up.

They both looked back at Brad.

'So what do you say?' Pete asked him.

There was a long silence when Pete wondered whether he had managed to lose the single best chef in the area.

Finally, Brad spoke. 'I want to cook decent proper food,' he said. 'None of that fancy stuff.'

'I agree,' Pete told him.

'I'll need to hire a commis chef and I have first choice,' said Brad. 'Aaron is good enough.'

'Agreed.'

'I get to decide on the menus,' said Brad, who appeared to be growing in confidence by the minute.

'With my agreement,' added Pete.

There was another long pause before Brad finally said, 'I won't let you down.'

'Of course you won't,' Pete told him. 'I trust you.'

Brad appeared to grow a foot in height at this before nodding.

'This is great news!' said Del, beaming from ear to ear as he clamped an arm around Brad's shoulders. 'We must ring your mum.'

'I'll see you in the morning,' said Pete. 'We've got lots to do.'

Brad nodded. 'I'll be there,' he replied.

Pete led Belle away towards a nearby bench which had just become empty and sat down to finish their burgers.

'Are you sure?' she asked.

He nodded. 'I am,' he said. 'What about you?'

Suddenly he was concerned that his own ego had taken over once more.

To his relief, she smiled. 'I think it's a brilliant idea. Proper inn grub.'

'I should have listened to you in the first place,' he told her.

'Well, that's all in the past,' she said. 'And if there's any way you can save the inn, please please please do it. For the village.'

Pete shook his head as he looked at her. 'If I do it for anyone, I'll do it for you,' he murmured.

Her eyes filled with tears as she looked up at him in wonder.

'Don't cry,' he told her. 'I get it now. This is your home. And mine too. We won't let it go without a fight.'

She gave him a teary smile and nodded her head.

Pete smiled back at her, suddenly unable to tear his eyes away from hers.

He had known her for so long, but had he ever really looked at her before? Up so close, where he could see the length of her dark eyelashes and the fleck of gold amongst the brown of her eyes.

She took his breath away.

He'd held her at arm's length for so many years, but now she was everywhere in his life and he was having to hold himself back for her sake, not his. Because all he wanted to really do was kiss her. And keep kissing her.

In that moment, he knew that she was so much more than a friend.

But he had just begun to lean forward to kiss her when they were suddenly interrupted by Del appearing beside the bench.

'My sister's beside herself with excitement,' he said, giving Pete a nudge with his elbow. 'Budge up, will ya?'

So Pete shuffled along whilst Del chatted away about his family and Brad. But all Pete could think about was the fact that his leg was now pressed up hard against Belle's.

And how he wished that they were alone right now, as the snow began to fall.

49

The snow flurries over the week had become heavier and heavier as the days had passed until the village was in danger of becoming cut off due to impassable roads.

'We haven't had snow like this for years,' said Belle, looking out of the front window of the inn.

Outside, only the river and clear sky remained a different colour from white. The paths and roads, trees and riverbanks were all laden with snow and along by the riverside various snowmen had been built.

The temperatures had remained below zero and the forecasters were predicting that there wouldn't be a thawing for at least a week.

'Something about the jet stream,' said Pete, coming to stand next to her. 'It means that the cold air from the Arctic is sweeping over the whole country, along with a whole heap of snow.'

The snow had quietened down the village as people had mainly stayed indoors out of the bitingly cold wind. Cars were barely visible under a foot of snow. Only a few hardy souls were wrapped up and walking alongside the river towards the shop.

Belle turned back to look at the lounge. At least the fires were all lit and, along with the excellent new boiler and windows, the heat from the radiators was staying inside and it felt cosy and draught-free.

But that still left the problem of the restaurant décor.

Belle stood at the entrance to the restaurant with Pete.

'So we need to change this,' she said.

Pete turned to face her. 'What's wrong with it?' he asked.

'It's bleak,' she told him, simply. 'It might look cool and trendy under the glare of hot sun outside, but this is the English country-side on a dark and cloudy day. It just looks wrong.'

He sighed. 'Any ideas on how we can fix it as cheaply as possi-ble?' he asked.

'Let's start at the top,' she began, looking up at the ceiling. 'The lighting is way too harsh. It's bright and unflattering. It makes it seem colder in here. We need warmth and softness. So see if you can change the downlighters to a warm white instead of bright and glaring. And maybe a dimmer switch so we can adjust it accordingly.'

He nodded. 'Okay. That doesn't sound too dramatic. Or expensive.'

'And on the tables we should have some tea lights,' she carried on. 'Candlelight is soft and romantic. It'll help with the atmosphere.'

'If you insist,' said Pete.

'And a few fairy lights wouldn't go amiss.' She took a deep breath. 'And now for the tables and chairs,' she began.

As expected, Pete spun around to look at her once more, shaking his head ferociously. 'We cannot change them,' he told her. 'They cost me a small fortune.'

'And are terribly uncomfortable,' she replied. 'Have you even tried sitting on one for the duration of a meal. They're rock hard.'

He faltered in his protestations. 'Belle,' he told her. 'We can't return them. They've been used. And, for what it's worth, my savings are seriously depleted.'

'We don't have to return them,' she said. 'I can make some seat cushions to soften them up. They can still look stylish without being hideously painful to sit on.'

'Okay,' he said, still sounding unsure. 'Just don't put a whole load of pink bows everywhere, that's all I'm asking.'

Belle rolled her eyes. 'Yes, because I'm known for my love of bows and pastel colours, aren't I?'

Pete chuckled. 'Okay. Fair enough.'

She looked around the room once more. It could work, she thought. With just a few more homely touches, perhaps it would work out all right.

She turned to find Pete staring down at her.

'I should have listened to you from the beginning,' he said softly.

'Yes, you should have,' she told him. 'But if we start to make a few changes now then maybe something good can come from this.'

Change was certainly on the way with regard to the menu too.

Belle sat down with Pete and Brad that afternoon to discuss the choice of food. She took heart from the fact that Pete was including her in the meeting. That finally he trusted her opinion regarding what the inn needed.

They both looked down at the menu that Brad had made on his phone. It wasn't ambitious nor particularly long, but it covered all the basic inn food requirements, such as a burger, steak, vegetarian pie, pasta, pizza and, on Sundays, a choice of roasts.

'This looks great,' she said, smiling at Brad. 'Really great.'

He gave a shrug of his shoulders. 'It's just stuff that I'd wanna eat, you know? If I came to the inn.'

Belle looked across at Pete.

'This is really good,' said Pete, to Brad's obvious relief. 'Let's keep the menu short to start off with until we find our feet. I'm aiming to start this weekend.'

'Okay, boss,' said Brad.

'I want to source all the produce for the menu locally,' carried on Pete, who gave Belle a knowing look. 'That should please my brother.'

'And the local farms too,' replied Belle.

'I'll need to get back in touch with Cassie and see if she has a friend to help staff the restaurant again if Aaron is to be your commis chef,' said Pete. 'But there's just one problem with this menu,' said Pete. 'Where's the desserts?'

Brad broke into a wide grin. 'Apple pie, mince pies and you haven't lived until you've tasted my death by chocolate,' he said.

As it happened, he was right because he spent the rest of the day preparing and serving them testers of all the various recipes in the kitchen. Each one was delicious.

'Have you tasted Brad's pizza yet?' asked Pete.

Belle clutched her full stomach. 'I have and if I keep eating everything, I'm not going to be able to fit through the door soon,' she replied.

Pete's eyes softened as he looked at her. 'Let me keep an eye on your figure, okay? And you're looking mighty fine today.'

She couldn't help but smile back at him. 'You're so corny,' she told him. 'How on earth did you manage to date so many women?'

'I have a cheeky grin,' he told her, breaking into a wide smile before walking away.

After he had left, she walked slowly to the window. Outside, she could see that the snow was falling quite heavily now. Everything was being wiped clean by the snow.

Maybe they could do the same with the restaurant, she hoped.

Rather strangely, there appeared to be a new start happening on the other side of the world. She had just received a video of her aunt and uncle out on one of the speed boats which had them both roaring with laughter. Then there were the accompanying photos with their arms around each other and even one of them kissing. They both looked happy. Really happy.

And Belle thought that perhaps love could find a way for most people after all. Maybe even for her too.

50

Pete had braved the freezing-cold air to grab a few supplies from the corner shop and had bumped into Tom inside.

'How's business in the hub?' he asked.

'We've ventured onto Zoom, which is always an interesting experience, especially with some of our older residents,' he said, with a grin. 'Although your grandmother is remarkably quick on the uptake for her age. Please don't tell her that I said that. It'll be more than my life is worth!'

'Yeah, I think she still only agrees to people talking about her age if they say that she's fifty-five,' Pete told him with a grin.

'The good thing is that people are beginning to rally around the older residents these days,' said Tom. 'Some of these cottages are lovely and old but particularly draughty.'

Pete thought back to how cold he had been living in the apartment before he had organised for new central heating to be installed.

'I've been trying to advise a few folks about how to keep warm,' carried on Tom. 'Especially at the moment. Thankfully, most of them have families looking out for them.'

Pete nodded, but as he headed outside into the freezing temperature, he thought about Ned. From what he had told Pete, he didn't have any family. Nor did he like joining in at the community hub. Ned wasn't like his own grandmother who had the whole family to keep an eye on her and make sure that she was warm and dry. Ned was a loner and that made him more vulnerable.

Also, Pete realised that Ned hadn't made it into the inn the previous night for his weekly pint. He hadn't thought about it at the time, but he wasn't sure anything would cause Ned to miss his pint.

So he found that his feet were automatically heading towards Cherry Tree Lane where Ned lived.

Pete stood on Ned's front doorstep and waited for an answer to his loud knock on the door. Even at almost lunchtime, he could see his breath in the freezing cold air. The path had been icy to walk along and he had slipped a couple of times, even in his big boots.

Slowly the door opened.

Ned looked surprised to find Pete standing there.

'Morning,' said Pete, with a nod. 'Just wanted to check and see if you needed anything.'

'What would I need?' asked Ned, frowning. He gave a little puffed-out sigh and said, 'Well, at least come in so we can shut the front door and keep what little warmth there is in the house.'

After Ned had moved away from the door, Pete stepped over the threshold and quickly closed the door behind him. It was a tiny cottage, two up and two down, with barely any room in the hallway, which was presumably why Ned moved into the front room to allow Pete a bit of space.

'It's pretty nippy out there,' said Pete, thinking that it wasn't that much warmer inside the cottage.

Over Ned's shoulder, he could see the fireplace wasn't lit.

'Well, that's winter for you,' said Ned. 'So what can I do for you, lad?'

'Here,' said Pete, finding that he was holding out the bag that he had just filled at the corner shop.

Ned took it from him with a look of surprise before staring down at the contents. 'What's all this for?'

'I figured you might not have made it to the shop in the last few days,' said Pete.

Adding silently to himself that Ned wasn't the type to order his groceries online either. In fact, Pete couldn't even spot a mobile phone, let alone a computer or iPad.

There was a silence whilst Ned continued to stare down at the bag before finally bringing his head up to look at Pete. 'Well, that's kind of you,' he said. His voice was its normal gruff tone, but there was a wobble in the words which made Pete realise how emotional his gift had been for Ned.

'We'd best get that milk in the fridge,' said Pete, suddenly deciding that he needed to ensure that Ned had enough food in the house.

The back room, which comprised a tiny dining room table and kitchen, wasn't much more promising. It was tidy but pretty bare.

Pete followed Ned into the kitchen and tried not to stare as the pensioner opened up his fridge. To his dismay, the fridge was as empty as the fireplace in the front room. The elderly man was obviously struggling but had his pride and wasn't going to ask for help.

Ned closed the fridge door once he'd put the milk away and turned around to find Pete studying him.

'It's only me,' said Ned. 'I don't need much.'

'But you do eat and drink something, I hope,' Pete told him.

'Can't make it to the inn at the moment so it's not as if I'm using much energy up, listening to the radio,' said Ned.

Ned needed help. But he was proud and would probably refuse it if offered. So Pete decided that there didn't need to be a question, just a statement in his next move.

'Right,' he said, with a firm nod. 'Well, I'll be back in a while.'

'Whatever for?' asked Ned.

'Because otherwise I would miss your cheery smile,' said Pete.

Which at least made Ned give him a small grunt of humour.

Pete headed out the front door with determination in his step. His first stop was back at the shop.

'Are you getting forgetful in your old age?' asked Josh, laughing as he stood by the till counter with Tom. 'You bought these same things only an hour ago.'

But Pete wasn't in the mood for banter.

'I've just popped in to check on Ned,' he told them. 'There's no fire in the hearth and no food in his fridge.'

Josh's laughter came to an abrupt halt. 'That's not good,' he said, frowning.

'He's not the only one from what we've heard at the hub,' said Tom, with a sad shake of his head.

'So I gave him our milk and bread,' said Pete. 'Next I'm going to grab some logs from the inn.'

'Good idea,' said Josh. He looked at Tom. 'You're good at this kind of stuff. Any more ideas?'

'We started a list on the website for people who need help,' said Tom. 'A lot of the people struggling can't afford high heating bills. So if they've got a safe chimney to use, then logs will definitely help. Sand or salt for the pathways too, so that they can get out if they want. Extra blankets and a decent meal would help as well.'

Pete looked at Tom for a moment. 'A decent meal,' he said. 'I wonder...'

'What?' asked Josh.

'Brad is trying out all these new recipes at the moment,' said Pete. 'I wonder if he could whip up a few more so we can hand them out.'

'That's a great idea,' said Tom, beaming. 'Hold on whilst I go and grab the numbers that we need.'

As Tom dashed out of the shop, Pete found Josh looking at him.

'What?' he asked.

'I'm impressed,' said Josh. 'It's a great idea.'

'Well, I was probably overdue for one,' said Pete, rolling his eyes.

'Only by a decade or two,' said his big brother, his smile softening his joke.

Tom came back into the shop with his notebook.

'Okay,' he said, staring down at his written notes. 'We've worked out that we have just under a dozen vulnerable people or families living in the village. Around two-thirds are pensioners. The rest have young families. Unfortunately, there's quite a few folks around here that have got hardly two pence to rub together.'

'Right,' said Pete, quickly collecting his goods off the counter. 'I'll get Brad started on some meals. Pizzas and lasagne for the families. Maybe some kind of pie for the elderly.'

'I'll organise a team to deliver them,' said Tom.

'We'll add milk and bread to each order,' said Josh.

'Excellent,' said Pete. 'I'll check back with you in a couple of hours when we're good to go.'

As he left the shop and began to walk over the narrow bridge to the inn, despite the circumstances, Pete felt lighter in spirit than he had done for days.

He realised that it was because he could actually help someone out who was worse off than himself, for once. And he realised how selfish he had been over the last few years. And how determined he was that things definitely had to change.

51

Belle was just finishing restocking the bar when Pete strode in, carrying a shopping bag.

'Hey,' she said. 'That took a while.'

He had left almost an hour previously.

'I stopped in to check on Ned,' he told her as he crossed the floor towards her.

'How is he?' she asked.

'Not good,' said Pete, shaking his head. 'Have you got a minute?'

She followed him towards the kitchen, where Brad was still conjuring up his taster menu, full of delicious flavours.

'Right,' said Pete, when they were all standing inside the kitchen. 'I've had an idea and I need both of you to give me a hand.'

Brad, who had been chopping up some vegetables, finished his work and then looked at Pete in surprise.

'So,' began Pete. 'I need some individual meals to hand out to some villagers who are struggling.'

Belle looked at Pete. 'Who?' she asked.

'Ned, for a start,' he told her, his mouth set in a grim line. 'But it turns out that he's not alone. Apparently there are about a dozen pensioners and families who are struggling to feed themselves this winter.'

'That's terrible,' said Belle, shocked.

'The weather's awful, so a lot of them haven't been able to venture too far,' said Pete. 'I'm going to grab some of our logs and get them delivered, but they're going to need hot, nourishing meals that they can heat up easily without it costing too much.'

Belle and Pete both turned to look at Brad.

'What kind of thing did you have in mind?' asked Brad.

'For the elderly, I don't know,' said Pete, with a shrug. 'Something plain, I guess.'

Brad frowned. 'I don't do plain food,' he said.

'Okay,' said Pete. 'But what do you cook for your grandparents? That's the kind of thing I'm talking about. Oh and if you've got anything going spare, you know, like the trial meals you've been cooking, that would be great. We need to get some hot meals in some empty stomachs today, if at all possible.'

Brad tapped the worktop, deep in thought. 'Right,' he said finally. 'We'd better get to work.'

Whilst Pete headed outside to load up some logs into a wheelbarrow, Belle stayed in the kitchen to help Brad.

As her cooking skills weren't up to scratch, she was happy just to dash about and grab whatever ingredients he needed and do the washing-up as required.

It was quite incredible to watch him whizz up so many meals so quickly. They still had some empty microwave dishes that Aunty Angie had used, although not quite so skilfully and certainly not as deliciously. But at least that meant that individual portions could be easily divided up.

After what felt like no time at all, there were already a handful of shepherd's pies, chicken pies and lasagnes all cooking in the oven. Meanwhile, Brad was making his pizza dough for the families to enjoy.

Soon, there were a number of meals of substantial portion sizes to be distributed around the village. Word had obviously got out as a few villagers arrived at the inn as willing volunteers.

Working out each individual family requirements, they distributed the meals inside various insulated bags and headed into the snowy village to deliver them.

Pete followed them with a wheelbarrow full of logs which could be handed out where necessary.

Belle had agreed to meet Pete over at Ned's cottage. And she had added one more thing to her load – the first quilt that she had made. One evening with scraps of material left over, she had begun to piece together the different patterned cloth until she had a pretty quilt of blues and purples. She thought that perhaps Ned would approve and hopefully use it.

She arrived at Ned's front path at the same time as Pete. He looked tired from wheeling the laden barrow all around the village but also pleased, his cheeks rosy in the freezing-cold air.

'I told you I'd come back,' he said to Ned as soon as the front door was opened.

'I wasn't expecting company,' said Ned, peering around Pete to look at Belle.

'Well, we'll forgive you that you're not in your Sunday best,' Pete told him, picking up a large armful of logs from the wheelbarrow. 'Anyway, let's get these indoors.'

Belle followed him inside and closed the door.

'I've got some meals for you,' she told Ned.

Ned looked slightly alarmed. 'Your Aunt Angie didn't make this food, did she?' he asked.

Pete shook his head. 'Don't worry,' he said with a smile. 'We wouldn't do that to you.'

Ned was still frowning. 'Don't need no charity,' he said gruffly.

'It's not charity, it's a gift,' Belle told him. 'Big difference. Our new chef is trying out some recipes and Pete and I can't eat it all.'

'Humph,' he said, before sniffing the contents of the bag that she had given him. 'Smells good, I'll grant you.'

'There's both a chicken and a shepherd's pie in there,' she told him.

'A real chicken pie? With pastry?' he asked, with eyes wide.

'And home-made gravy,' she replied.

At which point, she was pleased to see Ned's eyes gleam. 'Not had proper pastry for a long time,' he said.

'There's a note with each meal telling you how long to warm them up, but it shouldn't take long,' she said.

He nodded. 'Well, I'm grateful,' he said in a gruff tone.

'Good,' she told him. 'And there's something else. I made it, so if you don't want it then I won't be offended. I just thought it would give a bit of cheer.'

He drew out the quilt, staring at it. 'Well, isn't that something,' he said. 'I haven't seen one like this for many years.'

'But if you don't want it...' began Belle.

'Why wouldn't I want it?' snapped Ned, clutching the quilt to his chest. 'Never said that, did I?'

Belle was still smiling to herself as Pete came into the kitchen.

'Got a nice fire going,' he said, leading them into the front room.

Instantly, Belle could see that the fire gave out both warmth and some cheer into the small room.

Ned settled himself down into his armchair, just staring at the flames. He was still clutching his quilt in his hands, but then he carefully unfolded it and lay it over his legs. He gave a small sigh of satisfaction, obviously grateful to be warm and comfortable at last.

Belle and Pete exchanged a smile to themselves.

'Well, it looks like you're settled for today,' said Pete. 'I'll start to clear your path in the morning and get some salt down.'

Ned looked up at him. 'Maybe you're more like your dad than I gave you credit for,' he said, with a nod of thanks to them both.

'If that's a compliment, then I'll take it,' said Pete, with a smile. 'Do you need anything else?'

'The only thing I'm missing is my pint of beer,' said Ned.

'Done,' said Pete. 'I'll bring it over later. Don't suppose we'll be too busy in the inn tonight.'

'Bring one for yourself, if you've time,' said Ned, turning back to look at the fire.

'I'll make time,' Pete told him before they left.

On the way back to the inn, Belle looked across at Pete who was deep in thought.

'That was a good thing you did today,' she told him.

He gave a shrug of his shoulders in response, almost embarrassed, she felt, by the praise.

'Maybe you're not the bad guy you think you are,' she said, reaching out to give his hand a squeeze with hers.

'Maybe not,' he murmured.

With neither of them reluctant to let go, they stayed holding hands all the way back to the inn.

52

Pete parked his car next to the inn and clambered out of the driving seat. He then stood back to look at the second-hand Range Rover he had just bought. It had cost him almost the last of his savings but not having any kind of transport was getting problematic.

Life was so much busier than he could ever remember it being before. As well as preparing the restaurant for the reopening, Brad was still making additional meals and Pete was delivering them around the village. He had even enjoyed his pint with Ned in his cottage.

The snow was still deep on the ground, but there was a thaw on the way, thank goodness. The recent snow had reminded him that whatever vehicle he bought, it needed to be used in all weathers and conditions so a Range Rover had seemed the best option.

He allowed himself a wry smile. He was wearing wellington boots and he drove a Range Rover. He was certainly living in the country now.

But as he waited for the ping of disappointment or even disproval from his inner critic, it didn't come. All he felt was a kind of peace that had been missing for a long time.

'Nice wheels,' said a voice from the other side of the river.

Pete looked up to find Josh at the end of the bridge so he walked over to join him.

'How's things?' asked Pete.

'Busy but all good,' said Josh. 'I know it's been a pain for most people, but I do love the snow. Do you remember that winter when Dad tried to convert his old motorbike into a snowmobile?'

Pete smiled in memory. 'He nearly ended up in the river on his test run,' he said.

Josh laughed. 'Yeah. He was pretty hopeless but always optimistic, you know?'

Pete's smile faded as the secret that had weighed him down for so long remained deep inside.

'What is it?' asked Josh, gently. 'I know you're keeping something from me. Talk to me. You can trust me.'

Pete hesitated, not wanting to hurt his brother nor the memories of their dad.

'Let's go and sit down,' said Josh, heading up the steps of the shop.

Pete followed him and sat down on the bench next to his brother. He was quiet for a moment before finally speaking.

'I don't want to upset you,' said Pete. 'But I found out something about Dad.'

'What is it?' asked Josh.

With a heavy sigh, Pete brought out the letter that he had carried in his wallet for so many years.

'I found this amongst Dad's things after we lost him,' said Pete.

Josh looked at him quizzically before staring down at the envelope, frowning at the unfamiliar writing. He then drew out the letter and began to read.

All the while, Pete watched and waited and worried, holding his breath.

'I don't understand,' said Josh, finally looking up. 'Who is this Felicity?'

'That's a name I haven't heard for a very long time,' said a soft voice next to them.

They both jumped and found their mum standing next to the veranda, looking at them.

'Mum!' said Pete, leaping up from the bench. 'I didn't know...' His voice trailed off.

This was awful. The last thing he had wanted was for his mum to find out. Now he was going to break her heart all over again.

'Sit down,' she said, coming around to walk up the steps to where her sons were. She appeared very calm. 'May I see what you're reading?'

Josh looked at Pete before finally handing it over to their mum.

She looked down at the envelope first. 'Gosh,' she said quietly. 'I haven't seen this address written down for a very long time.'

Then she read the letter.

Pete watched, more concerned about his mum's reaction than his own feelings. What would his mum think when she realised that her husband had been unfaithful?

But her reaction when she finally looked up at them wasn't hysterical or even angry. She just looked sad.

'Poor Felicity,' she said, shaking her head. 'She was such a sweet, beautiful girl. Almost unworldly, you know? Ethereal, that's what I meant.'

'You knew her?' asked Pete, amazed. 'I mean, you knew about her?'

Their mum nodded. 'Your dad was still married when we met. I know you've heard the story about how he came to stay in the hotel where I was working when he was on tour. But what I never told you boys was that he was married at the time.' She sighed. 'It wasn't a good time for your dad. The tour was endless and Felicity was very unwell by that point. Addiction is a terrible thing. She was so sweet but just not strong enough to fight the whole drugs culture. Why do you think your dad only ever drank and never touched any drugs? He'd seen the damage first-hand as to what drugs could do.'

Pete suddenly recalled a serious talk that his dad had given him before he had gone to university, warning him against the evils of getting involved with drugs.

'Your dad tried over and over to help her, but by that stage it was just too much for Felicity,' his mum carried on. 'They'd married on a whim, but it didn't mean that he didn't care for her any less. Sadly, her poor heart gave out a few months later. He mourned her, of course. And, in time, we turned from friends into something more.' She smiled to herself. 'It's hard to describe, really, the connection between us. It felt like a once-in-a-lifetime thing when I met your dad. I know it's hard to understand if you've never felt that.'

Pete was as still as a statue. He was pretty certain he had, he thought, glancing over to the inn.

'Anyway, the loss helped focus your dad on helping other people with similar struggles,' his mum said. 'He liked to give everyone a hand where he could.'

Pete thought of Ned and how grateful he had been for the friendship with Todd.

'Your dad was a good man,' she added, holding out the letter for Pete to take.

But he shook his head. It wasn't his to hold on to any more.

'I didn't know,' he told her. 'I thought, well, I thought the worst. The worst of him, I guess. And I've been so wrong.'

'You should have asked me,' his mum said.

Pete nodded. She was right, of course. Instead he had run and made things worse.

'Your dad would be so proud of what you've achieved since you've come back,' she added. 'The both of you, I mean.'

Pete laughed. 'What? Making a mess of the restaurant, you mean?' he said.

But she didn't laugh and reached out to take his hand. 'I mean, the good things that you've done for people around here,' she told him. 'I've heard what you did for Ned and the others. How the inn has been providing meals to the families in the village that needed them. Maybe you're more like your dad than you give yourself credit for.'

Was it true? Pete liked to think so. Or at least, hoped so.

'She's right,' said Josh, standing up next to them.

'Well, I must check on your grandmother,' said their mum. 'She's been going on about how they used to skate on the frozen river and I need to nip that idea in the bud before she breaks both her hips.'

'I'll come with you,' said Pete, holding out his arm for his mum to take. 'I've got time for a quick coffee with you both before getting back to the inn.'

She looked pleased. 'Well, that would be lovely,' she said, putting her hand through the crook in his elbow.

He looked over to find his brother smiling at them and nodding his approval before heading back into the shop.

'That's new, isn't it?' she said, nodding at the Range Rover as they gingerly made their way across the slippery stone bridge to the other side.

'Be careful,' he said.

'Thank you, son,' she said, stepping off the bridge. 'But I've been crossing this river for nearly all of my life, I'll have you know.'

'So, what do you think?' he asked as they walked towards his new car.

His mum looked at him. 'I like the colour,' she said. 'Green is, after all, very suited to the country.'

He laughed. 'Yeah, I like to camouflage myself as much as I can these days,' he told her.

She smiled. 'So,' she began, clearing her throat. 'Buying a car.' She hesitated before adding, 'Does this mean...' Her voice ran off before she could finish her sentence.

Pete knew what she was going to ask him. She wanted to know if this meant that he was staying.

'Come on,' he said, beginning to walk in the other direction towards Grandma Tilly's bungalow. 'It's a beautiful day.'

The grey, snow-filled clouds had finally cleared and been replaced by deep blue endless skies. And Pete felt as if his own personal storm cloud had begun to disappear as well. He had got things so wrong these past few years and suffered because of it. He felt sad that he had ever doubted his father and that he had run away instead of talking to his mum. But after their chat, he felt lighter, as if a weight had been lifted from his heart.

'By the way, Mum,' he said, as they walked alongside the river. 'Yes.'

She looked up at him confused. 'Sorry, love, what do you mean?' she asked.

'I mean, yes,' he told her. 'I'm staying in Cranbridge. Indefinitely.'

She broke into a wide smile, the tears pricking her eyes. 'Well,' she said in a shaky voice. 'That's wonderful. It truly is.' She paused before asking, 'Does this mean you're finally happy?'

He glanced back at the inn behind them before looking at his mum. 'I think it does,' he told her, squeezing her hand before they carried on walking alongside the river.

53

Belle was quite nervous before the reopening of the restaurant that evening.

But she wasn't worried about the food. That was proving to have exceptional feedback from all the grateful residents to whom various meals had been donated over the past week.

She wasn't even worried about the new décor, she thought, looking around the restaurant with a sense of achievement.

True to his word, Pete had left her in charge of making the changes to the original stark colour scheme. So she had had the spotlights changed from a bright white to a far softer and more flattering light which could also be dimmed to help with the atmosphere.

The soft lighting continued with the fire, which was now permanently lit, as well as tea lights in jam jars on every table. In addition, wrapped around the oak beams overhead, she had placed some pine branches and holly, along with many strings of fairy lights. The whole ceiling seemed to now give off a magic glow and softened up the place.

Also softer were the new seat pads she had made, which helped make the chairs far more comfortable. In their pastel shades with matching napkins on the tables, it looked modern but welcoming. Soft, cosy, warm and inviting. And, hopefully, it made the place look just a little bit special. Or at least, Belle thought it did.

She even had confidence about the return of Aaron and Cassie. Aaron was doing a great job as the new commis chef and Cassie's friend, Rachel, would be a great addition as waiting staff. They were far more excited and enthusiastic about Brad's cooking than they ever had been about the dreaded Andre's haute cuisine.

So, all in all, she was hopeful that the trial run that evening with Pete's family and friends would be a success.

So why was she nervous? She glanced down at her blue wrap-around top. It wasn't even dark navy. It was a beautiful turquoise which she had admired for ages in her pile of handmade clothing but had never had the courage to wear. But with the girls' encour-agement, and with everything else that had happened in the past few months, she had decided that enough was enough.

After all, maybe it was finally time to embrace change for herself. She had told Pete he needed to change, so wasn't it right that she follow her own advice?

But that didn't stop her nerves rattling as she waited for Pete's reaction since he hadn't seen her before she had changed for the evening.

So she held her breath as he came to stand next to her, looking at the restaurant.

'Well,' he said. 'I have to admit defeat. You've got this exactly right.'

'Thank you,' she said.

He glanced down at her. 'So are we all set?' he asked.

'I think so,' she told him. 'Everyone should be arriving in about ten minutes' time.'

He nodded. 'Excellent. I'll go check on Brad.'

But just as he turned to head towards the kitchen, he stopped and looked back at her.

Belle took in a sharp intake of breath as he stared at her for a moment.

'Have you done something different with your hair?' he finally asked.

She touched her head where her long hair was tied back in a messy bun. 'I don't think so,' she replied, still keeping her smile fixed on her face.

'Well, something's different,' he said, before shrugging his shoulders and wandering away.

Belle let out her held breath with a long sigh. He hadn't even noticed that she was in a new colour, she realised. All he knew was that she was looking different. Which left her wondering whether that was a good or bad thing.

The one thing she didn't need to wonder about was the success of the restaurant. The small group of family and friends had nothing but praise about the new décor and the new menu.

'This pie is tremendous,' said Cathy, finishing off the gravy by pouring it over her mash.

'You should try the steak,' replied Josh. 'It's so tender. I've never had steak that good.'

'And it's all local too,' said Pete, who had been hovering nervously nearby.

'Excellent,' said Josh, before giving his fiancée a tender slap with his fingers as she reached over to try one of his home-made chips. 'Oi! Get your own.'

All in all, the future was looking up, thought Belle as she headed over to the bar to pick up some more drinks for the tables.

The inn had a few more customers as well, she realised. Now that the snow had thawed outside, people were anxious to get out and about once more.

'We've had quite a few enquiries about booking a table for the restaurant,' said Lucy, as Belle came to order the drinks that they needed.

Lucy and Tom were manning the bar for that evening, just in case there had been a problem. But it was almost as if Belle had nothing to do as Cassie and Rachel had everything under control.

'That's great,' Belle told her.

Lucy looked at her. 'What's the matter?' she asked softly. 'Is everything going okay?'

'It's fine,' said Belle, with a sunny smile. Too sunny, in fact.

Lucy immediately frowned. 'Stop faking it,' she said. 'It's me. What's going on?'

Belle sagged briefly. 'I'm wearing my top like I promised,' she said in a dull tone.

'Yeah, I told you it looked great, didn't I?' said Lucy, before comprehension appeared to dawn. 'Ah. I get it. He didn't like it, did he?'

Belle shrugged her shoulders. 'How would I know? I don't think he's even noticed.'

Lucy rolled her eyes. 'Men,' she muttered. 'They're hopeless. Look, you're going to have to be a little more obvious. Flirt with him a little.'

'Flirt?' whispered Belle, horrified. 'I'm not sure I can.'

'Just try,' said Lucy. 'What harm could it do?'

Belle thought that it could do a great deal of harm actually. Especially if he laughed at her, or worse, rejected her.

But still, something had to give. Neither of them had mentioned the kisses that they had both seemed to enjoy only a few weeks ago. Surely Pete hadn't forgotten about them already?

It was driving her crazy, the not knowing. So when their family and friends had left for the evening and they were alone, Belle knew that now was her chance.

'That went great,' said Pete, with a wide smile as he locked the front door. 'I think the restaurant might just make it after all.'

'Well, the bookings are coming in thick and fast,' she said, watching as he went over to the restaurant.

Her feet automatically followed him and she came to stand next to him just as he switched off the main lights.

'Is everything okay?' he asked, frowning. 'Did I forget to do something?'

He looked over the restaurant, which was now only lit by the hundreds of fairy lights in the oak beams above.

'No,' she told him, before clearing her throat and trying a more husky tone of voice. 'Everything's wonderful,' she added.

He looked at her. 'Are you getting a cold?' he asked.

'No,' she said, frantically shaking her head. She rolled her eyes to herself as he headed over to the other side of the room to turn off the fairy lights by the switch on the wall.

She could hear Lucy egging her on in her mind but didn't have a clue what to do next. In the end, she leaned up against the doorway in what she hoped was a seductive, sexy look. She even threw her hand above her head, to show off how good her figure looked in the top.

At least it slowed Pete's walking down as he neared her.

'Are you sure you're okay?' he asked. 'You're, erm, being a little odd.'

'Only a little?' she drawled before she could stop herself.

Pete broke into a smile. 'That's better,' he told her. 'I was worried that you'd gone soft on me.'

But as he began to walk away, she blurted out, 'I can be soft when I want to!'

He turned to raise an eyebrow at her.

'Okay,' she said, with a sigh. 'I really can't.'

He shook his head as if she had made some sort of funny joke and then went to walk away once more before stopping to look back at her.

'Nice top, by the way,' he said, with a wink before walking off.

She smiled to herself. He'd noticed after all!

But still, they were just joking as friends, as they'd always done. Maybe she was too late. Maybe they'd missed their moment. Maybe their stolen kisses had been just that. A fleeting moment in time when they'd both needed each other and now the time had passed. He obviously wasn't interested in her that way. She was just a friend to him.

Perhaps he would even revert back to type now that he seemed like the old Pete. Perhaps she would have to witness another long line of girlfriends arriving before being dismissed after a short time.

But she really wasn't sure her heart could cope. Because now she finally knew how she felt about him. It was love, pure and simple. And it made her just as miserable as she had expected it to.

54

'That's such a lovely top,' said Molly, looking at Belle's green long-sleeved top appreciatively.

'Yeah, you look great,' said Lucy.

A week after the reopening and with the restaurant up and running and almost full every night, Belle was finally able to meet the girls for a catch-up.

Once more they were upstairs in Amber's apartment where they could relax and chat in peace.

'Thanks,' said Belle, feeling pleased at the compliments.

It had become a habit to wear a different, brighter top or even one of the skirts each day. Customers in the inn had commented on it, even asking where she had bought them from. She was pleased that her grandmother's clothes were finally getting the recognition they deserved.

And, unexpectedly, the compliments made her feel better about herself as well.

'Where are your aunt and uncle?' asked Amber.

'In the Far East,' Belle told her. 'They loved the Great Barrier Reef.'

She showed them the photos that they'd sent, pleased that they were still looking so happy and in love.

'They look ten years younger,' said Lucy.

'Did you tell them about the restaurant?' asked Molly. 'You're the talk of the village and the newspaper too. Everyone is raving about the food.'

'You're going to be so busy at the Christmas fete this weekend,' said Amber. 'Us too.'

'It's going to be freezing if this weather doesn't warm up,' said Lucy.

'But so pretty,' said Molly, with a smile. 'Christmas and snow go together like, I don't know, something!'

'Mistletoe and wine?' said Amber.

'Christmas trees and fairy lights?' said Molly.

'Belle and Pete?' said Lucy, with a grin.

Belle could feel her three friends smiling as they watched her, but the only emotion she could muster was heartbreak.

'It's no use,' she told them, with a soft sigh. 'It's not going to happen.'

'Why not?' asked Amber.

'Because we had our chance three years ago,' she said, finally opening up the last of her secrets.

Her friends were stunned for a brief second before exploding with questions for her.

'When?' asked Amber.

'How?' asked Lucy.

'What happened?' asked Molly.

'I kissed him,' Belle told them. 'After his dad's funeral. I don't know why.'

'Yes, you do,' murmured Lucy.

'Okay, maybe I do,' said Belle, dragging a hand through her hair. 'It was Pete. It's always been Pete, I think. But I blew it by kissing him and he walked away. He doesn't think of me that way.'

'And so he's never kissed you again?' asked Amber.

Belle blushed.

'So maybe he does feel that way about you,' said Lucy.

Belle shook her head. 'He's backed off again. And this time I think it's for good.'

Molly reached out to squeeze her hand and Belle was grateful for the warmth of her touch.

'You're always telling me that there's plenty more fish in the sea,' she said gently.

At which point Belle burst into tears. 'But there's not,' she wailed. 'Not for me anyway.'

Her friends all leapt forward with hugs and arms around her as if a group hug could heal her heart from breaking. And, in a small way, it helped.

'So he's the one,' said Amber, nodding. 'You love him.'

'Yes, I love him!' said Belle in between sobs. 'And it's completely ridiculous! Can't you slap me out of it or something?'

'I'd love to, but I don't think that will help,' said Lucy, with a soft smile.

'And what's wrong with you falling in love with him anyway?' asked Molly.

'Because he's not planning on staying here,' said Belle. 'And he won't even look at me. Not like that, anyway. I'm just a barmaid to him.' She looked up at them and wiped away the tears from her cheeks. 'I'm sorry. This is supposed to be a happy party, not a pity party. Quick, somebody help me pull a cracker or something.'

The girls were kind enough that they changed the subject and they did at least manage a few laughs as the evening wore on. And Belle was grateful for their hugs as they all said their goodbyes.

Once back out in the cold night air, she could feel how much she had had to drink, but still, it had been nice to open up to her friends finally.

Were they right about her and Pete? Was there hope?

She looked up into the clear night sky and found the North Star to wish upon. She knew it was a fantasy that could never come true, but even someone as cynical as Belle was allowed a Christmas wish, she hoped.

55

Pete stood behind the bar, pulling a pint of beer feeling every inch the inn landlord.

Surprisingly, he found that it was a nice feeling.

The inn was busy that evening with customers, full of laughter and festive cheer. Everyone seemed to appreciate the new armchairs but that it still felt cosy and warm with the fireplaces all lit.

In addition, the restaurant was almost full once more. Cassie and Rachel were doing a great job handling all the customers by themselves so that Pete could remain behind the bar. In the kitchen, Brad and Aaron were doing an amazing job and it was wonderful to watch Brad grow in confidence with each passing day.

Pete was proud of what they had accomplished in the face of disaster. Bookings were full for every night until Christmas and even between then and new year as well. He was determined to give the staff Christmas day off though to spend time with their families. However, he and Belle would open the inn in the evening in case anyone in the village needed some company.

He had popped back to check on Ned each day until the snow

had begun to melt and had enjoyed their chats. Ned had returned for his weekly pint on a Monday night looking a lot more cheerful than Pete could remember.

'Evening all,' said Dodgy Del, coming to stand in front of the bar.

Tom and Josh both greeted him as he slid onto a bar stool next to them. They had been there all evening whilst the girls had got together.

'About the Christmas tree you sold us,' began Pete.

'No refunds or returns, I'm afraid,' said Dodgy Del quickly.

'What's wrong with it?' asked Josh.

'One soft nudge with your little finger and every last pine needle is going to drop to the floor,' said Pete, nodding at the nearby offending tree.

They all turned to look at the decorated tree, which was almost bare as it had lost so many pine needles over the past week.

'It'll be lucky to make it to Christmas without ending up on the compost heap,' said Pete.

'Just unlucky I reckon,' said Del. 'I've had no other complaints from anyone else.'

'That's because you never answer your phone,' said Tom.

'This is a very unfestive conversation,' said Del. 'And I'd like to move it along to far more Christmassy matters. Such as donkeys and how you can help out with them.'

They all stared at him before Tom finally spoke up.

'Donkeys?' he asked, somewhat incredulously.

Del nodded. 'The vicar wanted one for the nativity service on Sunday. I think she meant a toy one but, of course, I've managed to find her a real one. Or rather two for the price of one because donkeys get lonely and Ethel wouldn't be separated from Fred.'

'How am I going to be able to help out with your donkeys?' asked Pete. 'We're an inn, not a zoo.'

'Depends on the clientele some nights,' murmured Tom.

'Well,' said Del. 'The trouble is that Ethel and Fred just need a bit of shelter for the Christmas fete and before we stroll to the church on Sunday afternoon. So I was wondering if they could maybe camp out in your backyard. As it's not in use due to being winter, that is.'

Pete stared at him. 'You want to put a couple of donkeys in our garden?' he said in disbelief.

'That's about the sum of it, I reckon,' said Del with a nod.

Pete looked at Josh, who was grinning at him.

'Never a dull moment around here,' said his big brother.

'But it's freezing cold at night,' said Tom, frowning. 'Shouldn't they be in a barn or something?'

'Well, Angie's got that old summer house around the back,' said Del. 'I reckoned that would do the job for a couple of nights.'

Pete dragged a hand through his hair, for once quite at a loss as to what to say.

'Excellent,' said Del, taking his silence as confirmation of the deal. 'I'll ring the vicar. She'll be dead chuffed that you're helping out.'

Before Pete could protest, Del had disappeared off his stool and out of the inn.

Pete looked at Josh and Tom. 'Did I just imagine that conversation?' he said, still somewhat flabbergasted.

'I'm afraid not,' said Tom.

'Nice to know that we're not the only ones to suffer at the hands of one of Del's schemes,' said Josh. 'Maybe you could make a bit of extra money by charging some families to come and pet the donkeys.'

Pete blew out a sigh. 'If they don't eat everything in sight first.' He had another thought. 'Angie's prize garden pots,' he said, looking in them in horror. 'You know what she's like about her gardening.'

Josh nodded. 'She's always been a keen gardener.'

'And I must say that her hanging baskets always look pretty good,' added Tom.

'Not sure how good they're going to look once Ethel and Fred have finished with them,' said Josh, raising an eyebrow at his brother.

Pete shrugged his shoulders. 'Oh well,' he said, with a grin. 'Luckily she's the other side of the world at the moment.'

They all smiled before going on to chat about football.

Pete was finding himself enjoying the company of his brother and friends more and more. Even Del, despite his obvious short-comings. They were good people, he found. Where he'd been concentrating on earning money, there were people like Tom and Josh too who were out there giving everything to their neighbour-hood. By providing some extra meals and logs, Pete felt that, at last, he too had stepped up and was helping as well. It was a nice feeling, he found.

In fact, he was enjoying his time at The Black Swan so much that he and Belle had decided to throw a New Year's Eve party for the village. Nothing fancy, just canapés and drinks, but everyone had agreed to come.

The subject of conversation at the bar had moved on from foot-ball to Del's disastrous love life.

'If I bring my next date in here for a meal, you're gonna need to put up some mistletoe,' said Del. 'At least that might give me half a chance.'

'Unless Belle gets the wrong idea,' said Tom, laughing.

Pete frowned and Josh immediately picked up on his brother's reaction.

'Don't worry,' said Josh. 'I don't think you need to worry about Del as competition for Belle's affections.'

Pete rolled his eyes. 'You're all mad. We just drive each other crazy, you know that.'

'Why?' said Josh, laughing. 'Because she doesn't agree with you and hang on your every word like all your other girlfriends.'

'She's not my girlfriend,' Pete told him.

He quickly turned away with the excuse of grabbing another box of crisps, hoping his brother didn't see what felt surprisingly like blushes.

But Josh's words played on his mind for the rest of the evening and he found himself wondering what it would be like to have Belle as his partner. She was feisty and beautiful. Life certainly wouldn't be dull.

Especially when she came home a bit tipsy as she did that evening when he had closed up the inn.

'Did you have a good evening with the girls?' he asked.

She gave him a slightly lopsided smile and giggle. 'Too good,' she told him, placing a hand on his chest to steady herself.

Her hand seared warmth against his skin and he was suddenly overcome with the urge to kiss her.

'I'd better go upstairs whilst I can still walk,' she told him with a soft smile.

After she had gone, Pete shook his head, at himself mainly. He had backed off ever since the disaster of the restaurant. Emotions had got heated and he had become unsure of everything.

But as time had gone on, and the restaurant had turned into a success, he found himself still holding back to protect Belle. She didn't need an ex-playboy ruining her reputation and he sure as hell didn't want to hurt her in any way. He cared about her too much. More than he had ever cared for anyone, he realised.

56

Belle woke up early on the Saturday before Christmas and flung open the curtains with bated breath. Thankfully the day had dawned chilly but bright, the sky a brilliant blue with no clouds.

It was the perfect day for the Christmas fete, she thought. And thank goodness because the success of the fete meant that the inn would be busy and they needed all the help they could get.

She looked across to where the empty trestle tables were all lined up along Riverside Lane. Normally so quiet first thing, there were already people about beginning to set up their stalls.

Last year, the first year the fete had been held, had been a roaring success and looked as if this year would be as well.

Amber was outside on the veranda of the shop, placing some poinsettias up either side of the steps. There were already a couple of miniature Christmas trees on either side of the front door.

The shop would be serving hot chocolate, tea and coffee, but Belle needed to get going on the mulled wine. A chilly day meant that people would need warming up.

She also needed to make sure that the fires stayed lit so that the

inn was a warm welcome for visitors. She turned away from the
windows to get dressed. It was going to be a busy day.

She found Pete already downstairs, sorting out the till.

'I'm going to get going on the mulled wine,' she told him. 'And
then get all the extra glasses lined up. If it's anything like last year,
it's going to be a bumper day.'

'Hee-haw,' came a sudden call from the back garden.

Belle looked at Pete. 'I'm going to kill Dodgy Del,' she told him.
'They've been doing that most of the night. I've had hardly any
sleep.'

'Was it Ethel or Fred making all the noise?' said Pete, with a
grin.

'Humph,' said Belle. 'And Aunty Angie's going to go mad when
she sees what they've done to her winter heathers.'

'So why do I think that you're about to find them something to
eat for breakfast?' he asked, with a twinkle in his eye.

'I don't know what you're talking about,' she said in a lofty tone
before heading out towards the kitchen to rummage around the
vegetable delivery for a couple of carrots.

* * *

The Christmas fete was a huge success, even busier than the
previous year and the inn had had one of its best ever days, takings
wise.

Both the restaurant and bar were packed from opening right the
way through to the evening.

'What a crush!' said Grandma Tilly, coming through the crowd
with Cathy late in the afternoon.

'Did you sell many of the quilts?' asked Belle, pouring them
both a drink.

'I sold the lot!' said Grandma Tilly, with a proud look on her face.

'Thanks to Belle's help,' added Cathy in a pointed tone.

'Yes, many hands definitely make light work,' said Grandma Tilly.

'How's your eye recovering?' asked Belle.

'Oh, it's unbelievable!' said Grandma Tilly, beaming. 'Everything's so clear and bright. I can see all the colours now, especially that red top, my dear.'

Belle glanced down. It was one of her favourites, a deep scarlet shirt.

'But now that I'm fully recovered from my operation I was thinking about expanding,' carried on Grandma Tilly. 'How do you feel about knitting? I had a great idea about hats and scarves!'

'I think Belle is probably a bit busy at the moment,' said Pete from the other end of the bar as he looked out across the busy room. The customers were still flooding in from the cold air outside.

'Let's go and find a table, if we can,' said Cathy. 'My feet are aching.'

'I can always get you a couple of chairs from upstairs,' said Pete.

Meanwhile, Cassie and Rachel were rushed off their feet serving in the restaurant. There was even a demand in the bar for food so they had begun to serve at the tables in there as well.

Later on, Belle noticed a plate that needed clearing and was shocked to find that the customer sitting alone was none other than the newspaper restaurant critic who had given such an awful review on opening night.

'You're back!' said Belle, staring down at him.

'I came for the Christmas fete and heard rumours of a great new chef,' said the man, before unexpectedly breaking out into a wide smile. 'And I'm so glad I returned. The food has been simply marvellous.'

'That's great!' said Belle, smiling back at him. 'Let me get Pete. He'll be so pleased.'

In fact, Pete was so overjoyed at the man's reaction and subsequent promise of a stellar review in the newspaper that he almost pulled the man's arm out of his socket as he shook the critic's hand enthusiastically.

Halfway through a still busy evening, Belle received a call from her aunt and uncle and moved out into the quiet back garden so that she could hear them properly.

'Oh, I'd forgotten about the Christmas fete,' said Aunty Angie in a wistful tone. 'It was always one of my favourites.'

'And we're missing you too,' said Uncle Mick.

'I miss you both as well,' said Belle. 'But at least you'll be back in Europe soon so we won't have to worry about the time difference too much.'

She was just about to tell them how well the inn had done business-wise that day when there was a hee-haw from either Ethel or Fred who were still in the garden.

Aunty Angie looked up at her alarmed. 'What was that?' she asked.

'Nothing,' said Belle quickly. 'A rooster, I think.'

She hung up with promises to call on Christmas Eve and then on Christmas Day too. This year Pete had invited her to spend the day with the Kennedy family which she was grateful for. But she had spent a few happy daydreams hoping that she might be able to meet him under the mistletoe at some point as well.

57

Christmas morning dawned with yet more snow swirling around in the air.

Belle looked outside and felt a little wistful. She was missing her aunt and uncle terribly. She had even tried to make contact with her parents leading up to Christmas, but, as usual, their responses were half-hearted.

Uncle Mick and Aunty Angie were currently in the Suez Canal and so were planning to call later that morning. Belle was looking forward to catching up on all their news. They certainly seemed more relaxed these days.

And perhaps so was she.

If you didn't count Dodgy Del's donkeys, that was. Ethel and Fred had thankfully been moved on after the church nativity service, where, apparently, they had almost eaten the three wise men from the much cherished ancient crib before Glenda, the vicar, had managed to intervene. Now the donkeys were tucked up in a nearby sanctuary and hopefully keeping nice and warm.

Belle didn't know what her aunt was going to say about the state of the garden when she returned. Actually, she knew exactly what her aunt was going to say and Dodgy Del had better take cover when she discovered that the donkeys had eaten all her winter flowers and the grass would almost certainly need relaying before the summer.

But for now it was all about Christmas. Belle felt a bit nervous about spending Christmas Day with the Kennedy family. It had been very kind of them to offer and Pete wouldn't take no for an answer.

'What are you going to do otherwise?' he had said. 'Spend the day by yourself?'

Christmas morning was normally a bit of a rush and then Uncle Mick would open the inn at midday so she would spend the day with the customers who would sometimes join them. Pete had decided that they would only open the bar in the evening and not the restaurant, to allow the staff to be with their families at Christmas.

But a proper family Christmas lunch was something else entirely, Belle was beginning to realise.

When they arrived upstairs at Josh and Amber's apartment late morning, it was a full-on Christmas atmosphere.

Michael Bublé was crooning from some nearby speakers. What appeared to be a far too large Christmas tree was decorated with every red and gold ornament that could ever be found. Holly and fairy lights were strung up everywhere.

In the kitchen, Grandma Tilly and Cathy were chopping up vegetables with the help of a glass of sherry.

'Happy Christmas!' cried Amber, sweeping Belle into a hug.

'They're here!' Belle heard Cathy shout from somewhere muffled in Amber's bear hug.

And then it was a whirl of champagne, presents and laughter before they finally sat down at the meal at two o'clock in the afternoon.

Belle stared down at the feast in front of them. There was barely room on the table for all the dishes and accompaniments.

'This looks wonderful,' said Belle. 'Thank you so much for inviting me.'

Cathy smiled at her from the head of the table. 'You're family, dear,' she told her. 'There was no way we were going to let you be on your own today. Besides, it's so wonderful to have Pete here on Christmas Day for the first time in years and he would never have come if we hadn't invited you.'

'That's right,' said Grandma Tilly. 'You two are a team now.'

Belle was flushed with embarrassment and spotted Amber giving her a look across the table.

'More than that, I hope,' said Cathy, with an obvious wink to everyone else around the table.

Pete rolled his eyes. 'Belle and I are just friends, Mum.'

'Of course you are, dear,' said Cathy smoothly. 'Now, who's for more gravy?'

It hadn't occurred to Belle that Cathy and Grandma Tilly would assume that her and Pete were an item. She was ready to self-combust with embarrassment. It was almost too much to bear, knowing that he didn't feel that way about her.

'You okay?' murmured Pete, who was sitting next to her. 'You look a bit flushed.'

'I'm fine,' she said, trying to think of anything but Pete's leg pressing up against hers. It was hard to think straight when Cathy asked about her aunt and uncle's cruise.

'They're really enjoying themselves,' Belle told her.

'There's a first time for everything,' said Grandma Tilly, looking surprised. 'It must have been exhausting living with them when they were arguing all the time.'

'Not as much as living with my brother,' said Josh, which earned him a bread roll lobbed across the table. He easily caught it with one hand. 'Thanks,' he said to Pete with a winning smile. 'Not sure we'll sign you up for the village cricket team this summer with that shot.'

'I was always better with one-to-one sports,' said Pete with a wicked grin.

Josh laughed. 'Yeah, I remember the long line of rejected girlfriends that used to go around the block.'

Cathy gave him a stern look. 'That was a long time ago,' she said in a warning voice. 'And besides, I don't suppose Belle wants to hear about that.'

Belle went to answer, but Pete was already getting up. 'Anyone for seconds?' he asked, walking into the kitchen.

Belle fixed a smile on for those remaining at the table, but inside, her heart was breaking. Everyone seemed to think that they were good together except Pete.

* * *

After they had all enjoyed far too much Christmas pudding, Pete offered to do the washing up with his brother whilst the women all sank onto the sofas clutching their full stomachs.

Pete felt happy but somewhat exasperated at the way his mother and grandmother were constantly referring to him and Belle as some kind of couple.

'What's up?' asked Josh.

'Their teasing about Belle,' muttered Pete. 'It's not right.'

'Well, if you can't beat them,' murmured Josh to his brother before laughing at Pete's cross expression. 'You're so uptight today. What's wrong?'

'Nothing,' whispered Pete. 'I just don't need setting up by my own mother, that's all. I'm thirty-two!'

'So?' asked Josh, leaning against the sink. 'Would it be so wrong?'

'With Belle?' said Pete, with a shrug of his shoulders. 'Of course. We've known her forever. Since we were young, you know that.'

'Yeah. And? I don't see a problem, do you?'

Pete turned away. 'I don't want to talk about it, okay?'

His brother laughed again.

When Belle came over to offer a hand, Josh slipped away with the excuse of going to check on Amber.

Pete turned to look at her. 'If my family embarrassed you, I apologise,' he said softly.

She smiled up at him. 'That's okay,' she replied. 'We both know that my own family would win that contest, let's be honest. Yours are lovely, warm, friendly, loving. You're so lucky.'

He caught the wistful tone in her voice and it touched his heart.

'Did you hear from your parents?' he asked, suddenly concerned about her.

Her smile faded. 'I left a message and got a short text from Dad.'

He had a sudden desire to give her a hug, but there was no way he could do that with his mum's laser vision from across the other side of the apartment.

Frustrated, he muttered, 'I just wish mine wouldn't interfere.'

Belle laughed. 'They're just glad to have you here. They worry about you.'

He was perplexed. 'Why?'

She rolled her eyes. 'Because they care and want to see you happy.'

'They don't think I'm happy?' he asked before pausing. 'Do you?'

She put her head to one side studying him. 'I think you are happier these days,' she told him.

'Do you know why?' he asked.

'Because you're home in Cranbridge,' she told him simply.

But when they were interrupted by Grandma Tilly wanting to switch the kettle on, Pete realised that being home wasn't the whole story.

The real reason that he felt more happy and peaceful these days was because of Belle.

58

It had been a lovely Christmas, thought Belle, as she added another log to the roaring fire in the inn that evening.

She'd missed her aunt and uncle of course. They had rung her from the end of the Suez Canal and were now beginning to cross the Mediterranean. She couldn't wait to see them in two weeks' time.

To her surprise, it was actually quite busy in the inn with villagers who had walked from their homes. The sound of laughter and happy conversation filled the air. But they weren't just neighbours and customers that evening. It felt like an extended family and everyone was in good spirits.

Even Ned had come in after enjoying his roast turkey lunch with all the trimmings that Brad had made for some of the villagers.

Everyone was excited about the New Year's Eve party that they were throwing in a week's time.

Belle glanced down at her top. She was wearing her favourite turquoise top for the occasion after a quick shower and change earlier on.

'That's such a lovely colour on you,' said Cathy, suddenly appearing by her side.

'Thank you,' said Belle. 'I just figured it was time to move on from the darker clothes.'

'I agree,' said Cathy. 'I'm sure Pete feels the same way.'

Belle looked at her. 'It's not going to work out like that,' she told Cathy. 'Anyway, we'd be rotten together. Between my stubbornness and his ego, we'd drive each other crazy.'

Cathy shook her head. 'I'm not so sure. I think you make a good team. He drives us crazy too, you know.'

'That's because he always likes to be right,' said Belle, laughing.

Cathy smiled. 'Todd was just the same. But with a good woman by his side, in other words me, it calmed him down. Like I said, it made us a team. As long as you've got love, you can make it work.'

Love? Belle gulped.

Cathy reached out and squeezed her arm. 'He bought the inn for you. If that's not love, I don't know what is.'

Belle was startled. He'd bought the inn for her?

Cathy studied her perplexed look. 'He cares for you and he's always been so protective towards you. It was the same when you first arrived. He was always dragging Josh outside so they could go and play, but Pete was the one making sure you were okay.'

Belle glanced up at the bar where Pete was laughing with Tom and Lucy. Was it true? She didn't think Cathy would lie to her. But she still didn't know where they would move on to from there.

* * *

'We need some music around here,' said Dodgy Del. 'You need a jukebox in here.'

Pete laughed. 'No, we really don't,' he said, with a grimace.

'This place just needs a bit of festive spirit,' carried on Del, frowning.

'That's in your gin,' said Tom, nodding at the double gin and tonic that Del had ordered.

Pete moved along the bar to check on the number of glasses that they had under the counter. When he straightened up, he found Josh standing next to him with a serious look on his face.

'What's up?' asked Pete. 'Is everything okay?'

Josh nodded. But he hesitated before he spoke again. 'I just miss Dad sometimes, especially at Christmas.'

'That stupidly enormous Christmas tree,' said Pete, with a smile.

'The year he bought us all a dinghy and tried to get Grandma Tilly in it on Boxing Day,' said Josh.

Pete laughed. 'I'd forgotten about that,' he said.

'Most of all, I miss him playing his guitar,' said Josh.

Pete took a deep breath. 'Me too.' He looked into his brother's eyes. 'Do you think Mum misses the music as well?'

Josh nodded. 'I know she does,' he replied.

Pete stared at his brother for a long time, wrestling with his decision.

'You could do it,' said Josh. 'If you really wanted to.'

Pete gulped. 'I'm not sure I'll be up to much,' he said. 'It's been so long.'

'Like riding a bike,' Josh told him. 'Besides, it's Christmas. It's a time for miracles, isn't it?'

Pete nodded. 'Let's hope so.'

Before he could talk himself out of it, he turned and headed upstairs to the apartment to pick up his guitar.

Josh was still standing at the end of the bar when he returned and his big brother gave him a nod of encouragement as Pete stepped out holding the guitar.

'Now that's what I'm talking about!' shouted Del.

His loud voice carried across the inn, causing a few heads to look up, including Belle. Pete looked at her as her mouth fell open in shock at seeing the guitar in his hand. After all, he had told her that he couldn't play any more.

But as their eyes met across the room, she too nodded her encouragement for him to play.

With the support of Josh and Belle, Pete sat down next to the fireplace on an empty seat and placed his hands in the right position. Then, with one more glance at Belle, who was smiling softly at him, he began to play.

His emotions were too huge for him to have any kind of voice that night so he just played the chords of 'Silent Night' instead.

The inn fell silent as he carried on, but Pete hardly noticed as he became lost in the music instead.

It was only when he finished the carol that he woke up from his semi-dream and looked around him. Everyone clapped and cheered, including his brother nearby.

He looked over to where Ned too was clapping and nodding his approval. He was even smiling, which was a Christmas miracle in itself.

His mum came up to him, the tears streaming down her face as he stood up to give her a hug.

'It's so wonderful to hear the guitar again,' she told him, clinging onto him tightly.

He looked over her shoulder to where Josh was standing and also looking highly emotional.

Finally, he looked at Belle whose dark eyes were glittering with tears.

'Well, this will never do,' said Pete, before clearing his throat to sound less emotional. 'This is supposed to be a celebration. What shall we have next?'

He played on for the rest of the evening until last orders were finally called at 11 o'clock.

And it was one of the best evenings of his life.

* * *

When last orders were called, Belle smiled at how reluctant everyone was to leave. The Kennedy family in particular were glowing with happiness. And possibly a few too many gin and tonics as well.

'It's been the best Christmas ever!' said Cathy, drawing Pete into yet another bear hug.

Pete rolled his eyes over her shoulder at Belle, but he still let his mum hold him.

It had been an incredible evening, thought Belle. She had had no idea what had caused Pete to have a complete change of heart regarding playing his guitar, but she was glad. He finally seemed happy, whole even.

Josh gave his brother a brief hug before clapping him on the shoulder with his hand. 'That was great,' he said.

Pete nodded. 'Yeah, it was,' he replied.

Finally, when everyone had left, it was just him and Belle as he shut the front door and turned around.

'So?' he said. 'I think that went pretty well, don't you?'

She knew he was asking how she felt about him finally playing the guitar.

For once, the words wouldn't come. But she knew what she had to do. What no power on earth would stop her from doing at that moment.

She walked right up to him, reached up to put her arms around his neck and pulled him down so that their lips met.

She felt his sharp intake of breath before his hands wrapped around her back and held her close to him as the kiss deepened.

After what seemed like an eternity, Belle finally drew back slightly.

'We probably shouldn't have done that,' she said, slightly out of breath.

'Then why does it feel so good?' he said, before pulling her back against him once more.

The kiss continued, spiralling deeper and deeper until Belle began to lose all sense of where she was. There was nothing but Pete. Nothing but his passionate kisses.

If he kissed her like that, then he must feel something for her, she thought.

But, for once, she didn't care about the future, nor the consequences.

All she cared about was being with him that night. Tomorrow would arrive eventually, but, for now, all she wanted was him.

59

It had been the best and worst week of Belle's life, she realised, as she hung up the balloons for the New Year's Eve party in the inn that evening.

She hadn't been able to stop herself from kissing Pete on Christmas night. She just knew that she had had to kiss him one more time or she would have regretted it for the rest of her life. But, rather than being rejected as she had expected to happen, something had changed for them both and he had kissed her back. And he'd kept kissing her each and every night since then.

During the day, she couldn't stop herself from smiling at the many customers that were now frequenting both the inn and the restaurant. Word had got out about the makeover and the inn was now a roaring success. The food in the restaurant was getting rave reviews and they had even had to start a lunchtime service for the inn so that people could have a sandwich and a bite to eat when they couldn't get into the constantly full restaurant.

She felt as if her life was complete. Almost.

Because despite knowing how much Pete cared for her, despite how passionately he continued to kiss her and hold her each and every night when they were alone, there was still that tiny element of worry for Belle. Worry that he would ultimately reject her. That he would walk away from the inn and from her. That he didn't love her and therefore her happy time would come crashing down around her at any moment.

After all, to trust in love was to trust that her heart wouldn't be broken. And she still didn't believe that couldn't happen, especially to her.

He had never said he loved her and that was okay, most of the time. But sometimes, late at night, when he was fast asleep next to her, she lay there and worried that they were living on borrowed time. And she still didn't trust him not to run away from her and from Cranbridge.

Her friends, whilst happy for them both, had tried to reassure her.

'You're crazy,' Lucy had told her, when Belle had confided her worries about their relationship. 'Just give him time.'

'He adores you,' said Molly. 'Everyone can see it.'

Amber had squeezed her hand. 'You know how much he cares for you,' she'd said. 'Just be patient.'

But Belle knew Pete better than anyone else and she knew that he was holding back. She didn't know why, or maybe she didn't want to know why. Maybe it was just lust and friendship as far as he concerned.

All she knew was that her heart was in ever more danger of being broken all over again. And yet she still accepted his kisses and kissed him back every single time.

But each time they kissed, she knew how much harder it was going to be to walk away unscathed. Because he left. He had always left. And she just didn't know how long he was staying for this time.

She knew she just had to enjoy her time with him. So that

evening, as the party began downstairs, she pulled out her favourite long red dress.

She had made a promise a long time ago to her grandmother, who had been right all along. Life was better and all the richer for a touch of colour in it. Who wanted to live a black and white life?

Because whatever happened in the future, it was finally time to stop hiding in the corner, she had decided.

* * *

Pete was feeling almost giddy with happiness, a feeling he was sure that he had never felt before. He kept grinning like some kind of village idiot, but he couldn't help himself. He was completely and utterly crazy about Belle.

Belle who had always been so argumentative and strong. The same Belle who was soft and adorable when she was in his arms and he wanted her there as frequently as possible. Some evenings he found he was clock-watching, willing every passing minute to go by as quickly as possible until he could lock the door and take her in his arms again.

The nights passed too quickly though and suddenly she was gone once more.

They had tried to keep their affair a secret, but somehow everyone seemed to know about it.

'Is it that obvious?' he had said to Josh when he had smiled at his brother with eyebrows raised.

'It is,' Josh had told him. 'Don't worry about it. It was like a bloody great sledgehammer when I fell in love.'

'Love?' Pete had been shocked. 'It's not love.'

'Ha!' laughed Josh. 'I knew you hadn't completely changed. It seems as if you still won't say the l word.'

'I can,' lied Pete.

'Oh yeah,' said Josh. 'You've been like that ever since you fell for Janet Porter in year twelve.'

Pete had rolled his eyes. 'That wasn't love,' he'd told his brother. 'That was teenage lust.'

Josh had still been grinning at him as Pete had walked away.

He wasn't in love with Belle, was he? He couldn't be. Pete Kennedy didn't love anyone in a romantic way. It just wasn't his style.

Thankfully, the party was beginning and the place was already full of villagers eager to celebrate. Belle had yet to come downstairs after her shower and yet he was desperate for her to help him as everyone seemed to want a drink at the same time.

He dashed to the bottom of the stairs in the hallway to call up for her, but she was just coming downstairs and upon seeing her, the words died in his throat. He stared, knowing that he was open-mouthed in shock, but he had no power to move.

Belle was wearing her long hair down, which was unusual enough when she was working. But it was the long red dress that she was wearing that had taken his breath away. It was a deep crimson in a soft, silky material that clung to every curve of her. She looked absolutely incredible.

She stopped on the bottom step and looked at him with raised eyebrows.

But still, he couldn't speak and couldn't move.

She smiled and nodded to herself. 'That was exactly the kind of reaction I was hoping for, to be honest,' she murmured, before moving around him and walking into the bar.

It was the chorus of wolf whistles that finally brought Pete to his senses and got his feet moving.

'You look gorgeous!' Dodgy Del was saying as Pete went to stand next to Belle behind the bar.

'Thank you, Del,' said Pete, smoothly. 'I'm wearing my best shirt just for you. Right, who's for another drink?'

But he ended up serving all the orders in somewhat of a daze, hardly able to stop glancing over at Belle in that red dress.

Later in the evening, after being flat out behind the bar, he finally had a spare moment with Belle when they almost bumped into each other in the hallway.

'What a night!' she said, smiling up at him.

'Unbelievable,' he told her, before running his eyes up and down that red dress again. 'Much like what you're wearing.'

'Do you like it?' she asked.

'I'd show you, but my mother's on the other side of this wall,' he replied.

Belle laughed. 'Well, I figured you were brave enough with the guitar so I ought to be the same.'

He reached out to take her hand. 'I never thanked you,' he told her softly, staring into her brown eyes. 'For encouraging me all through these past few months.'

She squeezed his hand. 'Well, that's what friends are for,' she told him, before letting go and walking back into the bar.

Pete should have been relieved. But he wasn't. He just felt sad and upset. He didn't want to be just friends any more. If the past week and months had shown him, friends wasn't enough for how he felt about Belle. How many women had he kissed over the years, but none had affected him like Belle. This was different. Deeper. Stronger. This was love.

He held his breath. He loved her? Since when? But he knew deep down that it had been forever.

60

Halfway through the evening, Belle heard a commotion by the door. She looked across the crowd, where, to her amazement, she saw her aunt and uncle.

She quickly left the bar and weaved her way through the mass of people to get to the front.

'There she is!' cried Aunty Angie, sweeping her into a massive hug before stepping back to stare at her niece in wonder. 'What are you wearing? You look wonderful, darling! Doesn't she, Mick?'

'She sure does,' said Uncle Mick, pulling her into yet another huge bear hug.

'What are you both doing here?' asked Belle when they finally released her.

'We got off at Malta,' said Uncle Mick.

'We missed you too much,' said Aunty Angie.

'And I needed to have my feet on the old terra firma again,' said Uncle Mick.

'Christmas wasn't the same away from Cranbridge,' said Aunty Angie.

Belle stepped back so that they could see both the renovated bar and the new restaurant.

'This place looks incredible,' said Uncle Mick, nodding his approval.

'And so does our niece,' said Aunty Angie, giving Belle another once over. 'Is that your grandmother's dress?'

Belle nodded. 'Come on,' she said. 'I'll tell you all about it over a drink.'

For the next hour, Mick and Angie were surrounded by their friends, all desperate to hear the news of their epic voyage.

'What will you both do now that you're no longer landlord and landlady?' asked Dodgy Del.

'Divorce mediators?' murmured Tom innocently, gaining him a nudge from Lucy's elbow.

'We've got big plans,' said Mick with a nod.

The conversation and drinks flowed, but finally Belle found a moment to speak alone to her aunt.

'You and Uncle Mick seem...' her voice trailed off as she wondered how to find the words.

'Happy?' prompted Aunty Angie, with a wide smile. 'We truly are. I think that without the stress of the business failing, it gave us time to look at each other differently. We enjoy each other's company now. And we've remembered what made us fall in love all those years ago.'

'I'm so pleased for you both,' said Belle, thinking that if her aunt and uncle could find their very own happy ever after, perhaps there was still hope for her as well.

Just before midnight, as Belle was bringing out the bottles of champagne up from the cellar in preparation for the celebrations, she found Pete at the top of the stairs.

'I need to talk to you,' he told her.

'Is everything okay?' she asked, placing the bottles down on the floor.

He went to open his mouth to speak but instead gave a groan and pulled her towards him.

'You look incredible tonight,' he said, as he leant down to kiss her.

If her aunt and uncle could rediscover love, perhaps there was hope for her and Pete as well, she thought. But as his kiss deepened, she lost reasoned thought once more and gave herself up to the inevitable feelings for him.

'Ahem,' said a nearby male voice, clearing their throat.

Belle and Pete broke apart to find Brad standing in the doorway. 'Sorry to interrupt,' he said, with a grin. 'But I need you to check tomorrow's dessert menu.'

'On my way,' said Pete. But he didn't relinquish his hold on Belle.

After Brad had disappeared, he drew her close once more.

'Talking of dessert,' he said, before stealing another kiss.

Eventually, with a moan, Belle pushed him away. 'Go,' she said softly.

'You're such a hard taskmaster,' he told her, before giving her one last brief kiss and then disappearing out of the hallway.

Belle sighed in contentment.

As she began to fill up the champagne glasses, she was smiling to herself, feeling full of hope for the future.

So when she went to retrieve the last two bottles of champagne, she couldn't help but smile as she heard Pete chatting with someone in the corridor leading into the inn garden.

But she crashed to a halt when she heard Pete ask, 'So how much would you pay for the inn?'

Belle stood, holding her breath as her heart thumped in her chest.

The stranger gave an amount of money so large that she nearly fell over.

The silence stretched out as she waited for Pete's answer.

'That's very interesting,' she heard him finally say.

Belle gasped and dropped both the bottles that she had been holding onto the floor and rushed out of the side door into the darkness beyond.

She found herself standing by the river, trying to keep calm, but all around her everything was breaking. Her trust. Her love. Her heart.

She heard footsteps behind her and knew that they were Pete's so she swung around, the tears streaming down her face.

'I can't believe you,' she told him.

'Whatever's the matter?' he asked, aghast. 'I heard you rush out and there's broken bottles of champagne in the hallway.'

He stepped forward to take her into his arms, but she glared at him.

'Don't you dare touch me,' she hissed.

He stopped short and stared at her, aghast. 'Belle? What is it? What's happened?'

'I heard you.'

He looked puzzled. 'Heard what?'

'Your little jig is up!' she carried on. 'Hoping to make a secret deal, were you? I'm such an idiot!'

She was so angry. Angry with Pete and angry with herself too for believing that he cared for her and the inn.

'Secret deal?' he said. 'What are you talking about?'

'I thought you'd discovered something about yourself here,' she said. 'I thought you liked it here.' Her voice caught as she tried to control her emotions. 'With me.'

He took a step forward. 'I do,' he said urgently.

But she wasn't listening to him. 'I thought you'd changed, but it was all about the bottom line, wasn't it? That's all it's ever been. About the bloody profit!'

'You need to listen to me,' he told her.

But she shook her head. 'You lied to me! You led me to believe in something. In you. In us. And now this! I knew it. I knew I couldn't trust you.'

She couldn't speak any more, her throat was too full of tears and she sank down onto a nearby bench and sobbed.

'Don't cry,' he told her, rushing over to sit next to her. 'I hate it when you cry.'

She tried to shuffle away from him, but there was nowhere to go. He put his arms around her and wouldn't let her move away.

'Yes, I received an offer on the inn,' he told her. 'Somebody has just offered me very good money to buy it, in fact.'

'I heard,' she muttered.

'But I said no.'

She sniffed, wiping the tears away with the back of her hand. 'I don't believe you.'

'I told him that it was a family business and I intend to make sure it remains so,' said Pete.

'Family?' She was confused.

He took her chin gently in his fingers and lifted her face so that she could see into his eyes. 'Well, we haven't exactly got as far as discussing kids yet,' he said with a soft smile. 'But yeah, I was hoping that we could grow old here and have half a dozen children.'

Belle was shocked. 'I don't understand,' she said, staring at him blinking rapidly. 'I thought it was all about business.'

He smiled gently at her and shook his head. 'No. It's love.'

She stared at him, the tears still wet on her eyelashes. 'Love?'

'You asked me once why I never came home,' he said. 'It's because I knew that if I saw you just one more time, I'd fall in love with you all over again.'

She caught her breath. 'All over again?'

'I fell in love with you the first time I saw you,' he told her. 'I had such a crush on you, but you were all hurt and wounded and I couldn't get near you. So I figured being able to see you every day as a friend was the next best thing.'

'And did you?' she asked, needing to know. 'Did you fall in love with me all over again?'

He nodded, looking deeply into her eyes. 'As soon as I came home for Dad's funeral there you were again. And we kissed, but I was in such a wretched state that I didn't want to cause you any more hurt.' He held her hand over his heart. 'You're a part of me, you see? I only bought the inn because of you. This is where I belong. My home is here. Most importantly, so are you.'

And then he kissed her and she knew that everything was going to be all right. That Pete was with her forever.

'I love you,' he murmured.

'I love you too,' she told him. 'It's always been you. From the very first time I saw you too, I think I started to fall in love with you. There's never been anyone else for me.'

He stroked her cheek with his hand. 'I'm never going to sell the inn,' he told her. 'I'm here to stay. If you can put up with me forever, that is.'

She smiled and turned her head to kiss his fingers. 'You're my new dream. You and the inn.' She leaned forward.

'It feels like home again here,' he said. 'You've made me realise what a home really is.'

'By the way, it's *our* inn,' she told him, pulling his head closer to hers. '*Our* home.'

'Yes, it is,' he said, closing the gap between them until they were kissing again.

Hearing the countdown to midnight begin, they took each

other's hand and rushed back indoors to celebrate with their family and friends.

A huge cheer went up inside the inn as the last bell for midnight rang and the new year began.

Everyone was hugging and cheering, but Belle could only think of Pete's hand still in hers. She was safe, she was home and she was loved.

When the noise died down a bit, Josh asked everyone to raise their glasses. 'I'd like to thank our hosts for a wonderful evening,' he said. 'And I now declare this inn The Mucky Duck no longer. Here's to The Black Swan and to Pete and Belle.'

'To Pete and Belle!' chorused everyone.

Pete shot her a wink before putting his arm around Belle and drawing her close for a kiss in front of their family and friends. She barely registered the clapping and whooping from their audience. All she could think was that dreams really could come true if you wished for them hard enough.

61

The bright February sunshine was reflected on the surface of the slow-moving river as Pete stood outside the entrance to the inn and looked across to the other side, whilst he sipped his morning coffee.

Already, the crocus bulbs were pushing up alongside the river and spring was hopefully just around the corner.

He could see Josh and Amber hanging out some heart-shaped bunting across the front of The Cranbridge Stores in time for Valentine's Day that weekend.

Josh looked up from his stepladder and Pete could almost feel his brother rolling his eyes at all the hearts that were decorating the shop.

He grinned to himself, glad that he was growing closer to Josh with each passing day. It felt good to be friends with his brother again.

He was also enjoying talking to all the villagers and not being stuck behind a desk on the phone every day. The fresh air from the village seemed to revitalise him and watching the passing of the seasons gave a rhythm to his life that he hadn't realised he had missed so much.

'Good morning,' said his mum, as she walked towards him, arm in arm with Grandma Tilly. 'Beautiful day.'

'It is,' he told them before giving them both a kiss.

'Aww, look how pretty the shop looks,' said Grandma Tilly, gazing across the river.

'Not just the shop these days,' said his mum, sounding proud.

The three of them turned to look up at the outside of the inn. With its snowy white paint and colourful hanging baskets and flower boxes, it looked cosy and welcoming.

'Angie's done a smashing job with those flowers,' said his mum.

Pete had to agree. Since Mick and Angie had returned from their cruise, they had seemed like a completely different couple as they had settled into a small cottage on the outskirts of the village. Angie had decided that her future lay in a career in gardening and so had begun by decorating the outside of the inn. Mick was enjoying his long-earned retirement but he was happy to help out behind the bar a couple of nights a week to catch up on the gossip. It also meant that Pete could enjoy some time alone with Belle.

'Is it your night off tonight?' asked Grandma Tilly.

Pete nodded. 'We're going to dinner and then to the cinema,' he said.

'Sounds lovely,' said Grandma Tilly, with a nod of approval.

'I'm so pleased for you,' said his mum, giving her son a soft smile. 'Like I've said before, you two have been right for each other since the first time you met. It's just taken you twenty years to get here, that's all.'

He laughed. 'You're absolutely right, Mum.'

'Just give me a couple of grandchildren to cuddle and I'll forgive you,' she said, with a wink.

Pete laughed again. 'Maybe Josh will beat me there,' he told them. 'See you for dinner in the restaurant tomorrow night? I've booked you the best table.'

'Absolutely,' they both told him before heading over to the other side of the river.

Pete smiled to himself as he watched them go. Belle had changed him. She had encouraged him to enjoy his family again and he was so grateful to have them in his life once more.

He turned to look at the inn. The Black Swan had changed him too. He was proud of its heritage and proud of the name. The new letters were bold and could be seen from the other side of the river. And it was no longer the run-down Mucky Duck to the villagers. It was now warm, comfortable and welcoming. A proper English inn for a countryside village.

The restaurant was so busy now that they needed another helper in the kitchen. Brad had suggested another friend from catering college. It had given Pete great pleasure to watch Brad's confidence blossom. His food was getting more adventurous but was still just as tasty. His latest idea was pies. Beef and potato, lamb and mint plus a vegetarian option. All topped with delicious buttery pastry.

The lamb and mint was a particular favourite of Ned's. Each week, Pete would enjoy a pint of beer with Ned in the bar and catch up. Most often, the conversation turned to his father, but Pete found it hurt a little less each time they spoke about Todd. He was remembering his dad again and the happy memories comforted him.

Best of all, he wasn't afraid to love any more. And be loved in return.

Cranbridge felt like home again, but it was Belle that made it special. She was his partner, his best friend and his forever love. Each day, he thanked his lucky stars that he had her by his side and would continue to ensure that he deserved her love.

He opened up the front door to the inn and headed inside to find her.

* * *

Belle looked down at the new menu which Brad had just shown her.

'This looks great,' she told him. 'Mmm, sticky toffee pudding.'

'Uncle Del has been going on about it for long enough,' said Brad with a grin as he headed back into the kitchen.

It wasn't just Dodgy Del who was enjoying Brad's cooking, thought Belle. The restaurant was packed and bookings were almost full each and every day.

News about the revamped inn was slowly getting out. Cyclists were heading in at the weekends after a long ride for a pint and a sandwich. Ramblers were also stopping off. But there were families too and Belle and Pete had big plans to upgrade the beer garden ready for the summer.

But, most importantly, The Black Swan still had heart despite the success. The core villagers who made it their own still came in but were welcoming to anyone new heading over the threshold.

Each night was filled with laughter and conversation in both the bar and restaurant, accompanied by the aroma of delicious food filling the air.

The local butchers and suppliers were all pleased as every ingredient was locally sourced and so business was booming for them. So too were the new drinks on offer in the bar. Wine grown locally was now for sale, as well as cider from Willow Tree Hall and some artisan gin and beer.

The Black Swan was now a place for everyone to meet. More and more villagers were coming in day by day. Different people of different backgrounds, all chatting near the open fire and breathing more life back into the village.

The menu and drinks weren't the only thing that was different these days, she reminded herself, glancing down at her purple top.

She was wearing more colour, each and every day. She found she was happy to stand out a little. There was no need to hide any more, now that she felt loved and supported by Pete.

Aunty Angie had been thrilled about her niece's new fashion choices, but Belle had resisted her aunt's suggestions of fluorescent acid colours for now.

Her aunt and uncle were completely changed too since their return. It turned out that away from the stress of a failing business, their marriage was rock solid and they had become friends again.

Uncle Mick was spending each day helping out in the community with odd jobs and Aunty Angie was loving using her gardening skills, especially now that spring was on the way. In fact, Amber and Josh had asked her to do the flowers for their wedding in the summer.

Belle looked up as Pete came into the bar and felt the same thrill upon seeing him as she always would. Every day he told her that he loved her and she would reply the same. Since getting together, Belle felt more happy, confident and relaxed than she had ever done before. And she knew that it was all because of him and their shared love.

But he too was gaining confidence and a couple of times a week he could be found playing his guitar in the bar. She knew that it was his link to his dad and was pleased that music had returned to Pete's life once more.

'I've had a brilliant idea,' he said, coming to stand next to her in the bar.

'Was it to give me a kiss?' she asked.

'Always,' he told her, taking her in his arms and bending down to kiss her. She would spend the rest of life wanting one more kiss from him.

'Mmm,' she said, when they finally drew apart. 'So what was your great idea?'

'I want to run a weekly lunch club for the most needy in the community,' he told her. 'I thought that it would be a bit more sociable for those that would like to get out a bit more. What do you think?'

Belle was thrilled. She flung her arms around his shoulders. 'I think it's an amazing idea,' she said, giving him a kiss. 'You're wonderful.'

'You're not so bad yourself,' he murmured, drawing her in to kiss her again with a fierce hunger.

'Just think,' said Belle, her mind whirring with ideas. 'We could do a monthly dinner club as well...'

But Pete was nibbling on her neck, kissing along her jaw to her ear and back again and after that it was hard to think straight for a few minutes.

'Hey, it's time to open,' she whispered before allowing herself one more of his sweet kisses.

'Later,' he murmured, looking deep into her eyes.

'Definitely later,' she replied, before giving him a playful shove. 'Go on. Or our customers will be lined up outside.'

'Yes, ma'am,' he told her with a grin.

She too was smiling as she watched him head across the inn floor.

She loved the inn and Cranbridge but felt strong enough now to embrace change and was ready to face whatever life threw at her because it wasn't to be feared. Cranbridge was her home, but Pete was her life. She trusted in love now, with all the wonder and joy that it could bring.

She watched Pete turn the sign over to Open and The Black Swan was ready for another busy day.

ACKNOWLEDGMENTS

A huge thank you to my lovely editor, Caroline Ridding, for being so generous and for supporting me through what has undoubtedly been a particularly difficult year for so many of us. Your encouragement and friendship is, as always, invaluable.

Thank you to everyone at Boldwood Books for all their hard work on this book, especially Jade Craddock for her wonderful work yet again on the copy edits, Nia Beynon for being a marketing superstar and my lovely fellow Boldwood authors for their endless cheer and support.

Thank you to all the readers and bloggers for their enthusiasm and reviews which keep me going on the days when chocolate fails to hit the spot.

Thank you to all my friends, especially to Jo Botelle and the lovely DWLC ladies, Kerry, Claire, Adrienne and Kendra, for their endless support and encouragement of my stories.

Huge thanks to my wonderful family, especially Gill, Simon, Louise, Ross, Lee, Cara and Sian.

Finally, thanks once more to my husband, Dave, for listening and helping bring my imaginary world to life on the pages. As always, I could never have written this book without your love and support.

MORE FROM ALISON SHERLOCK

We hope you enjoyed reading *The Village Inn of Secret Dreams*. If you did, please leave a review.

If you'd like to gift a copy, this book is also available as an ebook, digital audio download and audiobook CD.

Sign up to Alison Sherlock's mailing list for news, competitions and updates on future books.

https://bit.ly/AlisonSherlockNewsletter

Explore more feel-good novels from Alison Sherlock.

ABOUT THE AUTHOR

Alison Sherlock is the author of the bestselling *Willow Tree Hall* books. Alison enjoyed reading and writing stories from an early age and gave up office life to follow her dream.

Follow Alison on social media:

facebook.com/alison.sherlock.73
twitter.com/AlisonSherlock
bookbub.com/authors/alison-sherlock

ABOUT BOLDWOOD BOOKS

Boldwood Books is a fiction publishing company seeking out the best stories from around the world.

Find out more at www.boldwoodbooks.com

Sign up to the Book and Tonic newsletter for news, offers and competitions from Boldwood Books!

http://www.bit.ly/bookandtonic

We'd love to hear from you, follow us on social media:

facebook.com/BookandTonic

twitter.com/BoldwoodBooks

instagram.com/BookandTonic

Printed in Great Britain
by Amazon

37009187R00185